WHISPER

WHISPER

LYNETTE NONI

KCP Loft is an imprint of Kids Can Press

Kids Can Press gratefully acknowledges the financial support of the Government
of Ontario, through the Ontario Media Development Corporation.

Published in Canada and the U.S. by Kids Can Press Ltd.
25 Dockside Drive, Toronto, ON M5A 0B5

Kids Can Press is a Corus Entertainment Inc. company

www.kidscanpress.com
www.kcploft.com

The text is set in Minion Pro and Eurofurence

Edited by Kate Egan
Designed by Emma Dolan

Printed and bound in Altona, Manitoba, Canada in 1/2018 by Friesens Corp.

CM 18 0 9 8 7 6 5 4 3 2 1
CM PA 18 0 9 8 7 6 5 4 3 2 1

Library and Archives Canada Cataloguing in Publication

Noni, Lynette, author
Whisper / written by Lynette Noni.

ISBN 978-1-77138-938-9 (hardcover)
ISBN 978-1-5253-0041-7 (softcover)

I. Title.

PR9614.4.S87W45 2018   j823'.92   C2017-903223-2

To Victoria —
The sand didn't lie

PROLOGUE

They call me "Jane Doe."

They say it's because I won't tell them my real name, that they were forced to allocate me a generic ID. The name is ironic, since there's nothing generic about me.

But they don't know that.

They could have given me any name, but there's a reason they chose "Jane Doe." I hear the whispers. They think of me as little more than an unidentifiable, breathing corpse. That's how they treat me. They prod, they poke, they badger and tweak. All of them want to coax a response from me. But their efforts are in vain.

Two years, six months, fourteen days, eleven hours and sixteen minutes. That's how long I've been locked away from the world. That's how long I've been pried for information, day in, day out. That's how long I've been experimented on, hour after hour, week after week.

They don't tell me much. It's all confidential, highly classified. But they did give me the rundown when I first arrived. They prettied it up and wrapped a bow around their words, selling a dream and not the nightmare I've been living. They said all the right things, lulling me into a false sense of security. But it was all lies.

"Lengard is a secret government facility for extraordinary people," they told me. "It's for people *just like you*."

I believed them. That was my mistake.

I was stupid.

Gullible.

Hopeful.

I know now that there isn't anyone else in the world *just like me*.

I'm different.

I'm an anomaly.

I'm a *monster*.

My name is not "Jane Doe." But that is who I've become. And that is who I'll remain. It's safest this way.

For everyone.

CHAPTER ONE

"Subject Six-Eight-Four, place your hands above your head and turn to face the wall."

The crackling voice comes through the intercom speaker beside the door to my cell. I know I have only ten seconds to do as I'm ordered before the guards come storming in here and force me to obey. My body can't take any more abuse after my session with Vanik today, so I quickly stand and do as I'm told.

"We're entering the room. If you make any sudden movements, we won't hesitate to stop you."

I don't acknowledge their words. There's no need. I know the drill by now. I know that even breathing too loudly could scare them into sending a Tasered bolt of electricity into my body. It's happened before.

The guards take their jobs seriously at Lengard, the secret government facility buried deep underground that constitutes my "home." I'm classified as a Level Five threat. They don't know what that means, and that makes them nervous. All they know is that I'm dangerous. They're wrong.

But they're also right.

The door glides open and a *whoosh* of air hits the back of my bare legs. The regulation clothing I wear is little more than a shapeless pillowcase with holes at the neck and shoulders, falling to just above my knees. It offers no protection, no warmth, no comfort. It is durable; it is versatile. It's a constant reminder that there are no luxuries in life, not anymore. Not for someone like me.

"Subject Six-Eight-Four, you're coming with us. Remain in place until we have you secured."

I'm still facing the wall, so they don't see my forehead crinkle with confusion.

Life at Lengard follows a strict, unchanging routine. Every day is the same. I'm woken first thing in the morning by a bowl of fiber-enriched, protein-infused, tasteless gruel being shoved through the slot at the bottom of my cell door. I have ten minutes to eat before I'm escorted to the bathroom and given five minutes. From there, I'm sent straight to Dr. Manning for my daily psych evaluation. That lasts two hours, and afterward I'm delivered to Enzo, who oversees my physical strength and endurance training for the next three hours. After that, I'm given fifteen minutes to shower and change into a fresh pillowcase uniform before I'm sent back to my cell for an hour, during which time another bland, protein-enhanced meal arrives. Following lunch, I have two hours of hell — officially referred to as "experimental therapy" — with Vanik, and if I make it out of his lab still conscious, I'm then shuffled between visiting practitioners and evaluators until they decree that I'm done for the day. That can take anywhere between two and six hours. I'm then given a nutri-shake — a drink filled with vitamins and nutrients to keep me in optimal health — and have five final minutes in the bathroom before I'm shoved back into my cell for the night.

The routine has never changed. Not once.

Until now.

My day is meant to be over. It's nighttime; I've ingested my nutri-shake and I've visited the bathroom for the final time. I'm supposed to be locked away until morning, when it all repeats again. I have no idea why they're deviating. But I stand still as the guards approach me from behind and reach up to grasp my arms, then yank them down and secure them in metal handcuffs behind my back.

When they turn me around, I see that the two men who stand on either side of me are double my size. The handcuffs are unnecessary. I'm no threat to them physically. And no bindings will keep them safe from the real danger I present. Nothing can keep them safe from that.

"Follow us and remain silent," says the man on my left, reciting the same words the various guards use every time they lead me out.

He wraps his hand around my upper arm, and I almost wince at his painful grip, but I manage to keep my face carefully blank. I don't nod — I don't even blink. I stare straight ahead and place one foot in front of the other as they guide me out of the cell.

It's bright in the corridor. The overhead lights sear my retinas, and I struggle not to flinch. Instead, I tilt my head down and let my hair shield my eyes. I continue to focus on the gleaming black and white tiles underfoot as we proceed. I don't dare ask them where we're going. I heard their orders; I will remain silent. Even if I chose to ignore their warnings, I still wouldn't ask my questions. But they don't know that. And I won't tell them.

The guards lead me along hallways and through doorways, some paths I've traveled before, some of which I haven't. Lengard, I discovered early on, is built like an underground labyrinth. A sterile, ultramodern, high-tech maze. Only those with the highest level of clearance know how to find their way around the facility, while I move about the corridors as good as blind, relying on them to deliver me where I need to go.

Right now we're moving deeper into the facility than I've ever been. The tiles are still black and white, the lights are still blinding, but there's more warmth to this area. I can't explain it — it's more a feeling than anything else — but the sterility doesn't seem as intense.

There are doors spaced out along the corridor, some of them labeled, but I don't read their descriptions. My head remains lowered, my eyes on my bare feet. I only glance up when we come to a halt. We've stopped at a dead end revealing a single doorway. It looks just like all the others we've passed, whitewashed and unassuming. There is no label on this one. I have no idea where it leads.

The guard not squeezing the blood from my arm moves to the panel beside the entrance and inputs his clearance code on the touch screen. My wariness grows when he lowers his face for a retinal scan and pricks his finger for a blood swab. In my whole time at Lengard, I've never been delivered to a location with such stringent security measures.

A quiet *beep* sounds, and the door slides open. I don't keep my head down anymore; my curiosity is piqued. But all I see is another identical corridor, black and white tiles, unassuming doorways.

I want to ask where we are, why clearance was needed to enter this area, what's different about this corridor. It looks the same, but there must be a reason for the added security at the entrance. Lengard has secrets — this much I already know. Other than the guards, I've never seen people walking the hallways. Everyone else — if there even *are* others — is locked up. Just like me.

"Move."

The pincer-grip guard yanks me forward, and I realize that I've been standing motionless for too long. I stumble a little at his rough action but regain my feet and move obediently onward.

We're halfway down the corridor when something unexpected happens.

A doorway only a few feet in front of us bursts open, bringing with it a sound I haven't heard in over two and a half years.

Laughter.

The guards jerk me to a halt when three children surge out of the entryway. Two golden-haired boys are cackling gleefully, one holding a rag doll above his head. A little girl with a head full of dark ringlets is chasing after them, shrieking and near tears.

"Give it back, Ethan! Isaac, make him give it to me! It's *mine!*"

"You'll have to catch us first, Abby!" taunts the boy with the doll, keeping it out of reach when the girl jumps for it.

"Don't hurt her!" Abby cries, attempting to claw her way up the boy's body. When the other boy pulls her away, she screams, loud and clear, "*Mummy!*"

I'm frozen to the spot, mesmerized by the sight in front of me. They're so young. So carefree. It's been a long time since I've seen an interaction so ... normal.

"Abby, what on earth is the matter?"

A woman steps out from the doorway, wiping soapsuds off her fingers with a dishcloth. Her eyes sweep over the scene, and she places her hands on her hips. "Ethan, Isaac, you know better than to steal your sister's toys. Give the doll back and apologize." When the boys hesitate, the woman steps forward and lowers her voice. "*Now.*"

Isaac quickly mumbles an apology, and a grumbling Ethan does the same as he hands over the doll. Little Abby clutches it to her chest and runs to hide behind her mother's legs.

"Back inside, all of you," the woman says. "You know you're not allowed to play in the hallways. I don't know what you were thinking."

She turns to shoo them back through the doorway, and as she does so, they catch sight of me for the first time. The children merely look curious, but the mother's reaction is much stronger. The emotion flooding her features — I've seen it before.

Pure, unadulterated fear.

"Kids, inside. Right now."

She all but shoves the children through the doorway and slams it shut behind them.

I feel as if I've lost a rainbow of color in my otherwise bleak, white-washed world. Seeing people — normal people — sparked something in me. A memory. An emotion. A hint of a life long forgotten. But now it's gone again, hidden behind yet another doorway.

"Let's go," grunts the pincer-grip guard.

And just like that, it's as if that flash of beauty never happened.

We walk for two minutes, three minutes, four minutes and more, until we come to another dead end with a door, but this one is open. My non-gripping escort reaches out to rap his knuckles on the entry, and a commanding "Come in!" beckons us forward.

We step into some kind of office. There are no adornments on the walls, no framed accreditations or photos. There's not even a bookcase. The room is without personality; perfectly functional, nothing more. A large mahogany desk takes center stage, but even that lacks the usual disordered chaos. No loose papers, no wayward pens, not even a coffee mug. The only disturbance on the otherwise-pristine surface is a touch screen tablet, powered up and emitting a soft glow.

A wave of apprehension overcomes me, and I look away from the tablet to meet the gaze of the man seated behind the desk.

"Jane Doe."

His voice is as gravelly as his salt-and-pepper hair. Appraising eyes take me in, from my bedraggled hair to my bare feet. He tilts his head slightly, a muscle tenses in his jaw and he waits.

I don't know if his words are a question or a statement. Either way, I see no point in responding. He's wrong — and he's right.

A silent beat passes as he continues to stare me down. I maintain eye contact even though I want to look away. Something tells me it's important to hold his gaze.

Finally, he nods and turns to my guards. "Release her. And leave us."

I can feel pincer-grip's surprise. And his hesitation.

"But, sir —"

"That's an order."

The guard's grip instantly disappears, while my other escort releases me from the handcuffs.

I move my hands around to my front and rub my wrists, while the two guards step back through the door and close it behind them. Only then does the gravelly man stand and walk slowly toward me.

He's taller than I expected, and, despite his hair color, his face shows only a few wrinkles, suggesting he is younger than I first believed. He's immaculately dressed in business attire — including a sapphire button-up shirt underneath his blazer. He wears no tie, but his lack of regulation Lengard military uniform still puzzles me. I'm not the only person at the facility with clothing restrictions; all the people I've encountered here have been color-coded based on their position. The guards wear gray; the doctors, scientists and other evaluators wear pristine white; and the physical trainers wear a brownish-beige. There are no striking colors, no eye-catching shades of beauty. The inhabitants are nearly as whitewashed as the walls. But this man's blue shirt — it's almost hypnotizing.

I should have been watching his progress across the room rather than noting his clothing. Before I know it, he's standing directly in front of me.

"Jane Doe," he says again.

And again I don't respond.

"I've been looking forward to meeting you for some time."

I want to ask why. And I want to ask why he waited. But I stay silent.

"I don't suppose you'll tell me your real name?"

A stuttered breath is the only response I give him. It's been so long since anyone has asked me, since anyone has tried to find out who I really am.

"No? Nothing?"

He continues to wait, and only a slight tightening of his features reveals his frustration when I remain silent.

"I guess 'Jane' will have to do, then. For now. I'm Rick Falon."

He holds out his hand, and I look at it with trepidation.

Rick Falon. I've heard the guards whispering. I know exactly who he is.

Maverick Falon.

Director Falon.

The man in charge of Lengard.

"I understand that you've been down here for some time, but social courtesies haven't changed much since your arrival," Falon says, wiggling his fingers pointedly.

Feeling unbalanced, I slowly reach forward until my hand is clasped in his grip. He gives me a firm shake before releasing me once more.

"There now. It's good to see you haven't forgotten how to act like a human being. Vanik's reports imply otherwise, but I know he tends toward the dramatic."

I have no idea how I'm supposed to respond to that.

"Have a seat, Jane." Falon gestures toward one of the chairs facing his desk, and he moves to retake his original position. "We've got lots to discuss."

I don't want him to notice my confusion, so I'm quick to follow his instructions. The plum seat is plush, and my tense body sinks deep into its softness.

When I look up, Falon is watching me. He appears pleased by what he sees, like he can tell that the chair has magical properties that are soothing the ragged edges of my tension.

"'Subject Six-Eight-Four,'" Falon recites, picking up his tablet and reading directly from the glowing screen. "'Allocated ID: Jane Doe. Date of birth: unknown. Current age estimation: eighteen. Parents: none listed. Other relations: unknown. Recruitment status —" he lifts his eyes to me "— transfer.'"

He lowers the tablet but holds my gaze. "I'm curious, Jane. Our records show that you were transferred to Lengard after a short stint at a psychiatric institute that you reportedly checked yourself into."

My stomach lurches, and I struggle to beat back the memories his words call forth.

"Our scouts discovered you three weeks into your time at the institute, and after confirming your potential, they delivered you to this facility — a much safer alternative than a psych ward for unstable and dangerous youth. That's why I find myself curious, Jane, because from all I've read, it appears as if you've been wholly uncooperative since your arrival."

His eyes remain fixed on mine as he finishes, "I would very much like to know why."

I keep my mouth shut. No words escape my lips.

"In preliminary testing, your results gave us reason to believe that you would be a distinct asset to our program."

I fight against my brow furrowing, having no idea about any "preliminary" testing or the program he's speaking of.

"Despite that, you've since shown nothing to prove your worth," Falon continues, his eyes skimming over the tablet again. "Dr. Manning says it's easier to draw blood from a stone than it is to evaluate your psychological disposition. I've already alluded to Vanik's opinion of you, and many of your rotating evaluators tend to agree with his assessment. Only Lieutenant Enzo has anything encouraging to report, claiming that you are surprisingly committed to your physical training. He seems impressed by how far you've come in the time you've been here."

A flicker of warmth stirs inside me. Of all the people at Lengard, Enzo is the only one for whom I hold any positive regard. He knows I'm classified as a threat, even if he doesn't know why, but he has no fear of me. And for that I respect him. I do what he says and push my body to its limits daily. It feels good: the running, the sparring, everything else he demands of me. I'm stronger than I've ever been. Faster. Fitter. That knowledge is what keeps me going on the days when all I feel is weakness.

"Enzo's report is the only positive among a slew of negatives," Falon says. "Your apathy and lack of cooperation in every other area should have prompted us to remove you from Lengard long ago. It's true that Vanik believes your brain chemistry is —" he searches for an appropriate word "— *unique,* but we have others who can assist him with his research. So, why are you still here, Jane?"

I assume the question is rhetorical; I don't think he expects me to answer, since I can't possibly know what he wants me to say. I have no idea why they're keeping me here. I have no idea why I was brought here to begin with. I have no idea why, day in, day out, my hours are spent undergoing tests and — in Vanik's case — torture.

Lengard is a secret government facility.

That's all I've ever known.

But *why* it's secret, I'm not sure. Nor do I understand my purpose here. That is something that has never been explained, never made sense.

And I've never asked.

I *couldn't* ask.

So I've waited, hoping one day someone would tell me.

No one ever has.

Falon spoke true when he said they pulled me from a psychiatric institution. But I'm just as much a prisoner here as I was there — perhaps more so.

There, at least, I understood. By placing myself in that hospital, I locked myself away from the world. There, I knew the rules. But here? Two years, six months, fourteen days, and I still don't know what game we're playing, let alone whose rules I should follow. I am nothing more than a glass pawn in a black-and-white chess set: out of place and utterly breakable.

Falon releases a breath and wearily rubs a hand across his face. I'm not sure if it's a genuine display of fatigue or if the gesture is all for show. He could just be trying to make me feel empathy. I have no idea why he would try to manipulate my reaction, though. I have no idea about anything when it comes to this man.

"I've decided that we're going to attempt something different with you, Jane. On a trial basis only. So far you've given us nothing to help further our goals, and I feel it prudent to warn that if you continue to resist the intentions of Lengard, I will have no choice but to eliminate you from the program. Do you understand what that means?"

Despite knowing nothing about this so-called program, I've always understood I would never be released back into the real world as a civilian. The one thing they did tell me, right at the beginning, was that Lengard must be kept secret from the general population … and that the government would do whatever it must to ensure that remains the case.

Since I have no intention of walking free again, the threat has never alarmed me. I understand exactly what Falon is saying — that if I fail whatever this new trial is, that's it. Lengard will get rid of me … and no one will even know that I'm gone.

I can see Falon is waiting for a response, and this time I must give it to him. I nod once, and his eyes light with approval at my gesture. Maybe he really did think I was insane, as Vanik likely suggested in his reports. Perhaps Falon wondered if I was just sitting here, an empty shell of a girl, unaware of his words. He can't possibly know that words are all I'm ever aware of. Every hour, every minute, I weigh them in my mind. Words are everything to me. They are life. They are death. They fill all the spaces in between.

"Good," Falon says. "Then you'll start working with Ward as of tomorrow. Your schedule will remain mostly the same, and your evaluations with Dr. Manning, Lieutenant Enzo and Vanik will continue, but you'll no longer be moved from person to person in the afternoon. Those hours will be allocated solely to Ward. You will do what he says — *whatever* he says — and if he doesn't come to me with any indication of progress after one month, then you'll be evicted from the program. Do you agree to those terms?"

I nod again, because I know that's what he expects. I wonder who Ward is and what he'll do when he discovers for himself how apathetic I am. A month is a long time, but nothing he does can be worse than Vanik's experiments. And at least I now have a time frame. An expiry date.

It's best this way. I know it is. And yet … now that I'm facing my end, I can't ignore the whisper of unease in the back of my mind. Because … what if a month isn't long enough?

"We're done here, then," Falon says, standing.

I follow his cue and rise from my seat, resisting the urge to glance longingly down at it.

"I do hope you make the most out of Ward's training," he adds, then calls for the guards to escort me back to my cell. "Very few people are granted one-on-one time with him. Don't waste this opportunity. It may well be your last."

Message delivered, Director, I think. Then I'm again cuffed like the monster I am and manhandled back to my cell.

CHAPTER TWO

True to Falon's word, the next day starts out normal for me. Or Lengard's version of normal, at least. Dr. Manning analyzes my silence and tries to make me reveal my secrets, Enzo attempts to banish physical weakness from my body and Vanik does his best to strip away my sense of self. None of them succeed, except, perhaps, Enzo. But that's because I find his training therapeutic. He doesn't want me to talk to him like Manning does, to spill the words that flood up from deep within me. He doesn't try to be like Vanik, peeking into my brain and shredding my nerve endings one by one. Enzo only wants a single thing: to train my body into compliance. He expects me to build strength and develop endurance. These I can do. These I *enjoy*.

I revel in my time spent under Enzo's watchful guidance. The burning muscles, the sweat in my eyes, the straining heartbeat ... they make me feel alive.

The only problem is that every day after Enzo, I have to go to Vanik. And if the time with Enzo brings me to life, my hours with Vanik all but kill me over and over.

I have never understood the reasons behind his obtrusive tests. Once I heard him utter the word *incredible* under his breath while examining my brain waves, a word that preceded a particularly painful experiment — agonizing enough that I blacked out and woke in my cell hours later. I have no idea what Vanik is searching for or why he seems convinced that I'm the one in whom he will find it. Falon may say there are others who can take my place, but I don't think Vanik would agree. He needs me. It's the only reason he hasn't risked pushing me to the point of brain damage — or beyond.

Not yet, anyway.

Today's session is no different from all the others. I somehow manage to survive his poking, his prodding, his attempted violation of my mind. I'm now being escorted down yet another black-and-white-tile corridor, on my way to find out who my new evaluator is and what he plans to do with me.

My guards — two again, but not the same ones from last night — stop me in front of a closed door that has no label. One guard uncuffs me while the other presses a hand to the scanner, prompting the door to slide open.

I can't keep my eyes from widening. That is my only outward reaction.

It's some kind of library. Every wall is covered with books. Hundreds of them. No, *thousands* of them. Maybe more. Tome after tome after tome line the shelves spread all around the moderately sized room. I've never seen such a beautiful sight. So many words. So many wonders.

"You can leave us. I'll call for you when she's ready to go."

I'm startled, not only by the words that imply it'll be my decision but also by the speaker. I was so taken by the books that I failed to notice the room's sole occupant.

He sits facing me, casually resting on the only piece of furniture: a couch that looks even more comfortable than the chair in Falon's office. I want to sink into it without delay, but I don't. I don't move at all, in fact, not even when I sense the guards leaving and hear the door slide closed behind me. It takes every ounce of my willpower to remain impassive as I study the person in front of me.

This can't be Ward.

I'd assumed he'd be middle-aged, like Falon, Vanik and Manning. He can't be more than a year or two older than me, about Enzo's age. But Enzo's limited years make sense; his job requires physical fitness and little else. Age doesn't matter. Ward's position, however …

Maybe he doesn't need to have the wisdom, knowledge and experience of years behind him for whatever he plans to do with me.

"Would you like to have a seat?"

He motions to the space on the couch beside him. It's not an order; he's giving me a choice.

I can't remember the last time someone gave me a choice.

It was before I arrived at Lengard, that much I know.

"I don't bite," he adds.

Seeing my hesitation, he even throws in a crooked smile, a single dimple indenting the tanned skin of his left cheek. But as teasing as that dimple is, my gaze is focused on his eyes. I've never seen such a bright green. Falon's sapphire shirt was dull in comparison.

When I continue to remain frozen in place, he rises to his feet, and I struggle not to stare. Golden hair, broad shoulders, narrow hips, long lean legs. Everything about his body is strong, hard, intimidating. But at the same time, his expression is soft, warm, inviting. I have the strange desire to run toward him — *and* away from him.

He's messing with my head, and he's barely spoken two sentences.

Irrationally, I blame the clothing. He's wearing jeans — *jeans* — and a fitted black T-shirt that clings to every inch of his torso. I miss jeans. I miss T-shirts. I miss blues and blacks and colors in general. Like Falon, I have no idea why this guy in front of me doesn't have to wear regulation attire, but his lack of uniformity — and his presence in general — is disarming.

"Seriously." He throws out an arm. "Please sit down. I feel weird with you just standing there."

I blink at that. Not because he feels weird — I'm used to people being nervous around me. No, I'm caught off guard by his manners. I'd forgotten how nice the word *please* sounds, how beautiful its intentions are. I find myself responding unconsciously, and I move to sit on the farthest corner of the couch, where I sink deep into its cushions.

I was right: it *is* more luxurious than Falon's chair. But I don't allow myself to relax. I sit perched on the edge of the lounge, stiff as a concrete slab, waiting to see what will come next.

"Thanks," he says, taking his seat again. "I always feel strange sitting down when other people are standing."

I'm surprised by his admission. I thought he was anxious about my threat-level classification, but apparently that isn't the case.

I wonder what he knows about me. Surely he wouldn't still be smiling that crooked smile if he'd read my file.

"I'm Landon Ward — 'Ward' to most people, but you can call me 'Landon.'"

I will do absolutely no such thing.

"As for you …"

Ward's gaze rakes over me, from head to toe and back again. Something causes his eyes to light up. He presses his lips together, looks away, smiles a secret smile.

"You are definitely *not* a Jane Doe."

Eleven hundred years. That's how long it seems to take before I can manage a breath.

I don't know what to make of Ward's statement. I fight the blood that tries to find its way to my cheeks, and wrestle away my urge to tuck a strand of hair behind my ear. I want to move my hands, to cross and uncross my legs, to bite my lip, but I resist the impulse to fidget. I won't let him see that he's unsettled me. I refuse to give him that kind of power.

"No, definitely not a Jane Doe," he says again, almost pensively. "But I've been told that you won't give us your real name. So, what should I call you?"

If he expects an answer to that question, then he really *hasn't* read my file.

"We could go with something descriptive. Your hair is so dark, but your eyes are so bright — we could do something there." He tilts his head and goes on, "Maybe we could go with something unexpected, something imposing … like 'Butch.' How do you feel about 'Butch'?"

I'm amazed by the words that are pouring from his mouth. For the first time in two and a half years, I'm fighting what feels like a smile.

"You don't look like a Butch, though, do you? No more than you do an average Jane Doe." He appears amused, and I still don't know why. "What about some kind of flower? 'Blossom' could work."

My nose wrinkles before I can suppress the impulse. I quickly wipe my expression clear, but the damage is done.

Ward's dimple reappears. "Not a fan of that one, huh? No flowers, then. Promise." He strums his fingers on his denim-clad thigh. "It looks like you'll have to leave it with me. But don't worry, I'm sure I'll come up with something once I know you better."

Who *is* this guy?

"Right!"

He claps his hands and jumps to his feet. I jerk at his sudden movement and hope he doesn't notice.

"We'd better get started. We only have —" he glances at his watch "— five more hours together. You know what they say: time flies when you're having fun."

Five *hours*? It's not uncommon for me to have longer sessions in the afternoons, but usually the time is split between multiple evaluators. It's been years since I've spent that long in the presence of just one person.

"I'm thinking we'll take it easy today while we get to know each other," Ward says, striding over to the nearest bookshelf. "That work for you?"

No. It doesn't work for me. I don't know what "easy" means to him. I don't know why he wants us to "get to know each other."

"Besides," he adds, perusing the titles, "I'm still wrecked from last night, and I don't have the mental capacity to do anything too strenuous. It was my sister's eighteenth birthday, and when I say she knows how to celebrate, I mean it. I'm only a year older, but sometimes I feel like an old man in comparison."

I don't understand what is happening here. He's talking to me like we've known each other for years. Why isn't he taping electrodes to my scalp, sending Tasered pulses into me and demanding that I follow a strict set of instructions? His behavior makes no sense.

"Heads up."

When he tosses a book my way, I catch it just before it hits me in the face.

"Nice reflexes." He looks impressed. "Enzo's always bragging about how well you've responded to his training."

I shift on the edge of my seat, wondering not only what Enzo has been saying but also why he's been talking to Ward about me at all.

"You should get comfortable. That one's a classic. It'll be ruined if you read it sitting like there's a pole stuck up your ass."

He doesn't catch my stunned expression; instead, he continues to scan the shelves. While he's distracted, I tear my eyes from him and look down, reading the title. It's not one I've heard of before.

"All right, I lied. It's not a classic per se." Ward returns to the couch with his own book. "But it should be. You'll agree by the time you're done, trust me."

I don't trust him. Not even a little bit.

But that doesn't mean I'm not completely stumped when he eases back into the cushions, spreads an arm along the back of the couch — alarmingly close to me — and begins reading his own selection.

One minute. Two minutes. Three minutes pass as I sit there watching and waiting. But all Ward does is read. I see his eyes flicker from line to line, page to page as he absorbs the words only he can see.

When we reach the five-minute mark, he uses a finger to keep his place and glances up to catch my perplexed gaze.

"If you don't relax and start reading, I'll have to begin narrating out loud. And fair warning, I do voices. *And* accents."

He clears his throat dramatically and looks down at his book before reciting in a thick Scottish brogue, "'I don' wan'a cup'a tea,' McNally told the old widow. 'I wan'a see Cormack.' 'I told ye,' she replied. 'Cormack don' wan'a see ye. Ye'll hav'te wait till —'"

Ward stops butchering what should have been an enchanting accent the moment I snap my book open.

"You should see your face right now," he says, grinning. "But come on, I wasn't *that* bad."

I beg to differ. I feel like my ears are bleeding.

"Why don't you put your feet up and get comfortable. We've still got a long afternoon ahead of us."

He's right. And I have nothing to lose at this point. If it turns out that this is an elaborate hoax or some new psychological experiment, then that would be disappointing. But if I really do get to spend the next few hours reading, I might as well get comfortable.

I shrink back into the cushions, once again wedging myself into the farthest corner of the couch. After another moment's hesitation, I tuck my bare feet up underneath me. I don't have to look at Ward to sense his approval. Instead, I ignore him and allow my eyes to take in the beauty of the words spread out before me.

CHAPTER THREE

"Chip? Hey, Chip, wake up. It's almost time to go."

Someone gently shakes me until the muffled words penetrate my sleeping mind. I lurch upright, my head only just missing a painful collision with Ward's face.

"Easy there, Chip. I'd like to keep my nose unbroken, if you don't mind."

I'm sure I must be looking at him like an idiot, but my sleep-addled mind is struggling to figure out why he's so close to me.

It's been almost two weeks since I started "working" with Ward. My time with him has been the same every day. He's friendly — too friendly — and I find myself unconsciously warming to him while at the same time straining to keep up my defenses. Somehow he knew right from the beginning about my love of reading, and that's all we do in our time together. I don't get it. But I love it. Before Ward, I hadn't read anything in over two and a half years. Now, in the last twelve days, I've read five whole books from cover to cover. I've spent over thirty months alone in my own mind, and suddenly I have a cast

of characters clamoring for my attention. It's refreshing. Relaxing.
Amazing.

"I'm flattered that you find my company so stimulating."

Ward's dry comment draws my eyes to his.

"Or is it your reading material that has managed to keep you so
energized?"

I glance down at the paperback still resting on my lap. It's a favorite
of mine, one I read many times in the years before Lengard. So, no, the
book didn't cause me to drift off. But there's no way I'll admit to Ward
the real reason I was unconscious for the last — I peer up at the clock
on the wall — three hours.

Ward is watching me, so I mask my shock at how much time has
passed. I'm not sure why he let me sleep so long. Why he let me sleep
at all is also a valid question. But I don't ask. Because if I did, he'd want
to know why I fell asleep to begin with. And I don't want him to know.
It's none of his business.

The truth is, Vanik's experiments have been worse than usual for
the past two weeks. Today was especially brutal. I feel as if he shredded
my brain in a food processor and put it back together again like a
jigsaw puzzle. Only, he didn't care about joining the pieces in the right
places. Instead, he just shoved them all together and hoped to retain
some semblance of workability.

For whatever end, Vanik needs my *unique* brain to be perfectly
healthy and functioning at optimal capacity for his research. He'd
never do anything to cause me permanent damage, but that doesn't
mean I'm not harmed in his labs. The damage leaves no physical scars.
But his tests still hurt like a son of a —

"Seriously, Chip, what's with you today?"

I press my lips together and look across the room, avoiding his
gaze. I hate that Ward chose the name "Chip" for me. I hate it, because
I love it.

"I've decided to call you 'Chip,'" he told me at the end of our first day together. He flashed me a dimpled grin before explaining, "Every time you hear me say it, it'll be like a chisel is *chip, chip, chipping* away at your icy exterior. One day I'll chip enough away that I'll be able to see the real you. I bet it'll be well worth the wait."

I haven't been able to get his words out of my head. And sure enough, every time he addresses me by the stupid, awful, horrible … *beautiful* nickname, I feel myself melting — *chipping* — little by little.

"You're not going to tell me, are you?" Ward runs a hand through his hair, frustrated. "Fine. But you were shattered yesterday, and today you're even worse. I want you to get a good night's sleep so you don't come back tomorrow looking like death warmed up again. Okay?"

The appropriate response is to nod, so I do that. What Ward doesn't realize is that I *have* been sleeping well at night. It's the days that are killing me.

"We're finished here," Ward says. "I'll take you back to your room before you doze off again."

He stands and, before I can stop him, reaches for my hand and pulls me up beside him. My fingers spasm in reaction to his skin against mine. Startled, I suck in a breath. It's been so long since I've felt the gentle touch of another human being. The closest I've come was my handshake with Falon — though that hardly counts — and my sparring sessions with Enzo, but I always have gloves on for those. I'd forgotten how warm other people are, especially since all I've felt is cold for over two and a half years. No, longer than that. Ever since —

I force the memories away before they can take root, and I focus on the fact that regardless of how long it has been, I'm not cold now. Or my hand isn't, anyway. That's why it takes me more time than it should before I yank it away.

The action seems to startle Ward. He raises his palms in an "easy there" gesture and looks at me with questions in his eyes.

Questions I refuse to answer.

He doesn't press for answers and leads the way to the door. Usually this is when he calls for my guard escorts, but tonight he continues into the hall and heads toward my cell.

I've never been in the hallways without a set of guards, and I've never walked *anywhere* in Lengard without being bound by handcuffs. I revel in the sense of freedom.

We travel the corridors in silence. I wonder if I offended Ward by snatching my hand from his; then I wonder why that possibility bothers me.

"This is you, right?" he asks when we reach my numbered door.

That's me, all right. Subject Six-Eight-Four.

I nod, and Ward presses his hand to the touch screen mounted on the wall. The door slides open, and I wait to see what he'll do next. I am unsure — yet, unsurprised — when he enters before me.

"This is your room?" he asks again, staring around the small space.

I try to see it from his perspective. Four whitewashed walls. A thin foam mattress on a pallet in the corner. A lumpy pillow. A ragged, threadbare blanket. It may not be five-star accommodations, but it provides everything I need to survive.

I don't understand the tension I see lining Ward's features. His green — so green — eyes are blazing, his jaw is clenched impossibly tight and a muscle is pulsing erratically in his cheek. His hands are in fists by his sides as if he's fighting the urge to hit something. Or some*one*.

Nervous, I step back, and the movement returns his hard eyes to me. His gaze sweeps my body, taking in my bare feet, my pillowcase uniform and what I'm sure must be my exhausted features. I realize that probably for the first time, he's seeing me as I really am. He's spent the last twelve days trying to befriend me for unknown reasons; perhaps until now he has never truly understood that I'm not a person here at Lengard — I'm a prisoner.

A million moments pass while he stares at me. I want to look away, but I sense the importance of holding his gaze. He needs to know that I'm aware of his dawning comprehension. And I need to witness the moment when his façade cracks, when he finally morphs into the uncaring evaluator he's supposed to have been all along.

I wait and I wait, but that moment never comes.

"I can't believe this."

His voice is low, and I can tell he's not talking directly to me.

"I don't know what they're playing at here."

He shakes his head and looks in my direction but avoids my eyes for the first time since I met him. His focus is somewhere over my shoulder when he says, "Get some sleep, Chip. I'll see you tomorrow."

With that, he strides straight past me and out the door. It slides closed after him, leaving me with nothing but the company of my exponentially increasing list of questions.

CHAPTER FOUR

After eight hours' sleep, I feel like a whole new person the next morning. There's a spring in my step as I'm escorted through the whitewashed hallways and into Dr. Manning's office. The therapist notices my buoyant spirit and sends a smile my way as he gestures for me to take a seat.

"You're looking upbeat today, Jane," Manning observes.

His beady black eyes are watching me.

"Anything you'd like to share?"

He already knows my answer to that. It's the same one I've given every day for over two and a half years. Nothing but the sound of silence.

No one can say Manning hasn't tried his hardest. But some things are best left unsaid. *All* things, in my case. So while we've spent two hours together each morning since I first arrived at Lengard, it can hardly be considered therapy.

I'm unsure why Manning endures my presence; why Lengard insists that I continue with our sessions when I'm only wasting the doctor's time, when I'm only adding to his premature baldness. I have nothing better to be doing. But Manning? Surely there is someone else who would benefit from his attention.

The one thing I do know is that right from the very beginning, Lengard has always been concerned with my mental health. So, I still sit here, day in, day out, the comfort of silence surrounding us.

Some days Manning asks me questions: What's my favorite color? Do I like the taste of nutri-shakes? Are the guards treating me with respect? How do I feel my time at Lengard is improving my outlook on life?

The last one nearly caused me to scoff aloud when he first asked it. But I managed to hold my tongue, just as I always have.

Today we follow the usual pattern. Manning begins with his questions and waits patiently to see if I'll respond. When I don't, he leans back in his chair and stares.

I found it unnerving at first. Then I realized that was what he hoped for: that I would be provoked into breaking my silence if only to ease my discomfort.

I know the game now, however. He's a master, and so am I.

When our time is over, he doesn't seem disappointed by our lack of progress — he never does, not outwardly. Like any good therapist, he hides his feelings behind a pleasant expression and a tranquil façade.

"We'll pick this up again tomorrow, Jane," Manning says as the guards arrive to escort me away. He utters the same farewell every day, as if we've covered ground and he can't wait to continue in our next session.

Part of me wonders if he's delusional. Another part of me knows he's just stubborn. But so am I. And I know he'll never break through my walls, because they're rock solid.

As I head back through the corridors, my mind drifts to what happened last night when Ward delivered me to my cell. I'm not supposed to see him again until later this afternoon, so I don't know what to think when I arrive for my physical training session and find him there, talking with Enzo.

"Mornin', JD," Enzo greets me after the guards release my handcuffs and leave the gym-like room.

Something I appreciate about Enzo is that he doesn't call me "Subject Six-Eight-Four" or even "Jane Doe." Like Ward, he's given me a nickname, even if it is only the initials from my ID. My traitorous thoughts whisper that it's not as good as "Chip," though.

"You know the drill," Enzo says. "Clothes are in your locker. You've got three minutes to get your ass back out here. Go!"

I don't need his instructions, but he gives them every morning regardless. As usual, I nod once and head for the changeroom, sliding my eyes straight past Ward. I have no idea why he's here. I just hope he'll be gone when I return.

One of the reasons I enjoy my time in physical training is that it's the only part of the day I don't have to wear my uniform. Even Lengard recognizes the impracticality of exercising in a pillowcase. For three hours each day I get to enjoy the comfort of gray shorts and a white tank top that cling to my skin, allowing me to move freely. I still don't get to wear shoes — and I have no idea why that is — but I've learned to make do without footwear.

Other than Enzo, who has watched me grow from a scrawny adolescent into a strong young woman, no one else has seen me in my tight-fitting training clothes. With Ward waiting in the next room, I wonder what others see when they look at me. I wonder what *he* sees.

I haven't looked upon my own reflection since before I first arrived at Lengard. There are no mirrors in the facility; at least, none that I've seen. So all I can do is take a deep breath, school my features into nonchalance and head back into the training rooms.

"Cutting it close today, JD." Enzo stands with his bulging arms crossed over his chest, his dark skin gleaming under the halogen lights. Jerking his head toward Ward, he adds, "You know Landon, of course."

It's unnatural to hear Ward called by his first name. It makes him sound more … relatable.

"You're looking much better today, Chip."

It takes a supreme effort of will not to read into Ward's comment. I'm sure he's just referring to the fact that I'm not about to drop to the ground anymore, but I'm aware of how fitted my workout clothes are. I can't even meet his gaze.

"Chip?" Enzo repeats.

Ward shrugs. "Potato chips, Enz. She loves them."

His lie doesn't make sense, but Enzo doesn't seem to notice.

"I didn't realize you were allocated additional carbs." Enzo frowns at me. "I would've factored the extra calories into your training schedule."

Ward claps him on the shoulder. "Too late now, Enz. And besides, it doesn't look like she has anything to worry about."

I feel his gaze leaving a burning trail along my skin like a tangible force.

I will not react. I will not react. I will not —

"Right, let's get to work."

Thank you, Enzo.

"I'll meet up with you for lunch, Lando. You need to get out of here before JD spontaneously combusts. If her face turns any redder, she'll melt the polar ice caps."

I want the ground to open beneath me and accept my burning body as a sacrificial offering. But, like most things I want, that doesn't happen. Instead, Ward's dimpled smile causes my capricious heart to stutter in my chest.

"I mean it, Lando," Enzo adds. "If JD's been sneaking extra carbs, it's my job to work them off her. I'll drag your ass out of here myself if I have to."

"I'd like to see you try. Remember what happened the last time you took me on?"

"Just *go*." Enzo pushes Ward's shoulder — hard.

"All right, all right, I'm going," Ward says, his voice ringing with amusement. He turns toward me and adds, "See you in a few hours, Chip. Feel free to come dressed just like that."

I have to put an end to this before it spirals out of control.

I may not have any power at Lengard, but I *have* managed to retain some semblance of self-respect.

Enzo reads the intent in my eyes, his own lighting in response.

"I've changed my mind, Lando," Enzo says, reaching an arm out to stop Ward from leaving. "Why don't you hang around for a few minutes. See for yourself what JD can do 'dressed just like that.'"

Pointing to me, Enzo orders, "You, stretch." His finger moves to Ward. "You, give us some space."

Ward silently obeys Enzo's command, watching me the whole time. His look is spine-tinglingly uncomfortable, but I switch off my awareness of him and focus on Enzo, who has stepped away to retrieve our boxing gloves.

I stretch my muscles in preparation for what is ahead. By the time Enzo returns to my side with his gloves already strapped on, I'm feeling confident about my decision to prove myself to Ward. I won't let him mess with me. At least not outwardly.

Enzo passes my gloves over, and I look down at the garish hot-pink leather, resisting the urge to smile. I never see anyone at Lengard aside from the guards and the various evaluators during my scheduled sessions. That has always been the case, except for once. A few weeks after I first arrived, I began to feel trapped by the walls of Lengard and the realization that this place would be my prison for the rest of my life — however long or short that might be.

After a horrific day where Enzo knocked me unconscious in our sparring session and Vanik introduced me to one of his more ... *extreme* experiments, I was curled up on my pallet, my body aching, my mind screaming, when the door to my cell slid open and Enzo hurried in. He held a finger to his lips as he approached my side, handing me a bag.

"It'll get better, JD. You can survive this," he whispered, glancing nervously back toward the door. "Every time you put these on, I want you to remember that, okay? Just don't give up."

I opened the bag to find the hot-pink gloves inside — the only hint of color I'd seen in weeks. A token of hope, perhaps, for a brighter future.

Apart from that one time, I've never seen Enzo outside of training. But his kind gesture made its mark, even if he had to take the gloves with him when he left that night so they wouldn't be confiscated. Now he hands them over every day when we train, and his words are forever burned into my brain.

Don't.

Give.

Up.

Those three words have helped me more times than I can count. They've helped me through the long hours of silence and isolation; they've helped me fight the memories and the nightmares; they've helped me survive the tests and the torture. No one could take them from me — not Vanik, not Manning ... not even myself.

"You ready for this?" Enzo asks, pulling me back to the present.

I tighten the straps around my wrists, raise my hands and bounce on the balls of my feet.

Enzo grins at Ward. "I suggest you take some notes, Lando. You might think you can kick my ass, but it's been a while since we last sparred. You're about to see how wrong you are."

Instead of listening for Ward's comeback, I lunge forward and land a solid double punch to Enzo's torso, then follow up with a round-house kick that has enough power to push him back a few steps.

I'm surprised by his lack of defense. Normally, he's much more guarded. But he recovers quickly and begins his own attack in earnest.

Other than strength and endurance training — those being muscle-burning, high-intensity workouts — my physical sessions with Enzo cover all forms of martial arts, from Taekwondo to Aikido to Jiu-Jitsu, as well as boxing, wrestling and kickboxing techniques. I could train for a hundred thousand years and still have more to learn, but after the time I've spent with Enzo, I can hold my own against him — at least for a few minutes.

I've never fully understood why sparring is a part of my daily routine. When I first began training with Enzo, he started to explain about the importance of having control, before cutting himself off and instead sharing that physical health and mental health are intercon-nected. "Healthy body, healthy mind" is what he told me. I understood the implication. Lengard wants my body in peak condition so that my mind can handle whatever tests, whatever *program,* they're running with me.

Regardless of the reasons, I'm never going to object to the physically demanding sessions. Not when they make me feel so much better than anything else at Lengard.

As we circle the room, striking out with dummy shots to test each other's defenses, I catch the look in Enzo's eyes. He's enjoying this. Enjoying having Ward as a witness. I don't know why. I don't *care* why. All I know is that I have a point to make. I want Ward to know I'm not some delicate wallflower wearing form-fitting clothes. I'm more than that. More than he could ever imagine.

Aware of my own limitations, I'm surprised Enzo keeps allowing me to make contact. An uppercut here, a leg swipe there, a few well-timed punches in between. True, he lands his own hits as we continue circling, but I know — I *know* — I'm not as good as he's letting me appear to be. A glance at Ward reveals his open wonder. But I don't want to impress him simply because Enzo is holding back.

We're a few minutes into our match, when I've had enough messing around.

Ducking under Enzo's next strike, I throw a left-right-left combination into the belt of his stomach, directly underneath his rib cage. His tense abdominal muscles protect his internal organs, but there's still enough power behind my blows for his body to contract in response. I don't give him time to hit back at me. Instead, I use my swinging momentum to propel my right fist upward and clip him across the jaw — hard. Normally, we have an unspoken rule to avoid aiming above the neck, but right now I want this half-assed match to be over. I'm not above taking cheap shots, and if the approving smile I see on Enzo's lips is any indication, he doesn't seem to care.

Knowing for certain now that he's not even *trying*, I decide to finish it. I lunge in close, hook my leg around the back of his knee and yank it out from under him, shoving his chest with my hands. I don't bother jumping on him as he topples to the ground. It's clear our match is over.

Enzo has the nerve to grin as he hauls himself back up to his feet. Slinging an arm around my shoulders in an uncharacteristic display of affection, he guides me over to where Ward is standing.

"How exactly do you think you can kick my ass if you've just had your own handed to you by GI Jane?" Ward asks Enzo, amusement lighting his eyes.

"Consider me a regular Mr. Miyagi," Enzo responds. "I've taught this young grasshopper everything she knows. And, hey, if GI JD can take me down, imagine what she can do to you, Lando."

All right, enough's enough.

I shove Enzo's arm off and stalk away from them both, toward the treadmill. No one won this round — not me, not Enzo, not Ward. All I can hope is that I've made some kind of point: I can defend myself. I do have some dignity.

I run flat out for five miles before I gather the courage to slow down and glance around the room. Ward is nowhere in sight.

I step off the treadmill and approach Enzo.

"Don't look at me like that," he says, amusement threading his tone. "I didn't plan that match. But you can thank me later."

Thanking him is the last thing I want to do, and he knows it.

Annoyed, I blow out a breath and shake off my irritation. What I need is a proper workout to release my frustration. Fortunately, that's exactly what Enzo has planned, and by the time my session is finished, I'm a panting, sweaty mess, buzzing with endorphins.

Too bad that only lasts for my shower and lunch break, because the moment I step into Vanik's lab, I feel the usual crushing weight of gloom settle upon me.

"Sit down, Six-Eight-Four," he says when my escorts depart. "We have much to cover today."

I move woodenly toward the reclining vinyl chair. Dread wells up inside me when I lean back into the stiff material, but my face remains perfectly blank. I realized early on that Vanik gets a sick sense of enjoyment from seeing me squirm; I no longer give him the satisfaction.

He tugs my hair back and tapes monitoring wires to my skin, starting at my head and working his way down the rest of my body. As he does so, I consider the incongruity of his appearance. His white lab coat and polished shoes are immaculate, the picture of perfect hygiene and personal care. The same can't be said for the rest of him. His face is covered with a perpetual sheen of oil, his sunken eyes have dark shadows underneath them and his hollow cheeks make him look more skeleton than human. But it's his hair that repulses me the most, greasy as it is and permanently parted in an unflattering line down the middle of his flaky scalp. For someone who's supposed to be a genius, I fail to understand why he can't remember to buy some shampoo.

"We're trying something different today, Six-Eight-Four," Vanik tells me when he finishes hooking me up to the various machines positioned around the room. They used to scare me when I didn't know what their purposes were. I've long since realized my fears were justified.

"It's come to my attention that you may not be with us much longer, so I've decided to move up my schedule."

Vanik doesn't look pleased by the altered timeline.

"Over our last few sessions, I've been pushing the boundaries of what I believe to be acceptable risks, but today we'll be going even further. I need you to remain as still as possible. We don't want to cause any … irreversible damage. But don't worry, Six-Eight-Four. It'll all be over soon."

He says this like it's meant to offer me some kind of comfort.

Remaining motionless is nearly impossible as Vanik begins his tests, prodding and poking, shocking and jabbing me over and over. I'm screaming on the inside, screaming so loud yet knowing no one will hear me, no one will help me, because no sound escapes my lips. It hurts — God, it *hurts* — and not just physically. Vanik tears away every part of who I am — any dignity that I regained with Enzo is now but a passing memory. I am a whisper of the girl who was sparring just minutes ago. If Enzo or Ward could see me now … if *anyone* could see me now … all they would see is a shell of a human being waiting — *praying* — for the pain to stop.

But Vanik doesn't stop, not until our time is up.

"That's enough for today," he finally says, releasing me from the manacles he used to strap me down when my body began jerking uncontrollably. "We'll pick up from here tomorrow."

I want to scream at him, but before I can decide whether it'd be worth opening my mouth, a pair of guards walk through the door.

They won't hesitate to punish me if they see me as a threat, and I can't take any more today. I demurely place my trembling hands behind my back and wait while they bind my wrists. I can't hide a wince when the cold, unyielding metal presses against my tender flesh.

It takes all my energy to keep upright as my escorts lead me to my session with Ward. My skin feels tight and clammy, and while my nerves are on fire, my teeth are chattering with cold. My head is splitting with an ache so deep that it makes me wonder if Vanik performed intrusive neurosurgery without me realizing. But I don't think he's that desperate — not yet.

When my guards bring me to a halt outside the library room, they undo my handcuffs and wait for me to step through the doorway. It took only two days for Ward to make it clear that my escorts are not welcome inside his evaluation area. All the guards have strict orders to release me outside and send me in alone. Only, today is the first time I could actually use their support. Because when they walk away and I take a step forward, I stumble — literally stumble — into the room, and I don't have the strength to catch myself before my body falls like a sack of grain onto the carpet.

Ward calls out to me in alarm, but I'm unable to respond. He's saying my name, I think, repeating it with increasing volume as he approaches my unmoving body. Questions pour from his mouth, and he turns me onto my back, brushing hair off my skin and moving it behind my ears. My eyes are closed, but I find the will to open them, and I discover his concerned face hovering just inches above my own.

"Talk to me, Chip."

He rests his hand against my cheek and sucks in a breath. "You're freezing. What the hell happened to you?"

I can't do anything but look up at him, shaking violently. Then my eyes roll to the back of my head as I'm overcome by the sweet silence of oblivion.

CHAPTER FIVE

I'm not sure how long I'm unconscious, but when I eventually wake up, I'm not in my cell. I'm also not in Lengard's medical facility, a place I've visited a handful of times. The sterile hospital smell doesn't linger in the air here, nor do the bleached walls assail my vision. That in itself causes me alarm, since during my time at Lengard I've never seen any other kind of walls. The ones around me, however, are dark gray, and I bolt upright in my comfortable bed to peer around the rest of the room.

Shades of gray and white meet my eyes, coloring everything from the blankets to the bedside table to the abstract painting mounted on the wall. I have absolutely no idea where I am. But I can guess. And that guess makes my mouth turn dry and my heart start to race.

I draw back the covers and drag my legs out until I'm seated on the edge of the bed, where I look down at my body in confusion. Magical elves must have changed me — or so I try to convince myself — because my pillowcase uniform is gone and I'm wearing an oversized, fleece-lined hoodie with an equally warm pair of track pants. Woolen socks cover my feet — a luxury that I haven't experienced in what feels like forever — and I wiggle my toes in awe. I feel warm all over for the first time in years, and I try to appreciate this fact rather than fear it. But when the door opens, I know I can no longer maintain any illusions.

"Good, you're awake."

Ward steps into the room, and I rise to my feet. I wobble unsteadily, and he rushes forward to keep me from collapsing.

"Hold up there, Chip. I don't think you should be standing just yet."

His grip on my arm is gentle but firm as he moves me into a seated position again and kneels in front of me.

"How are you feeling? Any better?"

I don't understand his concern. He shouldn't care about me — he's my evaluator. I have no idea what, exactly, he's been evaluating during our library sessions, but I do know he has a job to do. To him, I'm supposed to only be a test subject. Six-Eight-Four. Jane Doe. Not —

"Chip?"

No.

I'm not supposed to be "Chip" to him. I'm not supposed to be *anything* to him. And I don't understand how he can kneel in front of me thinking otherwise, while his gentle — too gentle — fingers cup my chin, and his green — too green — eyes probe mine for answers. I want to pull my hair in frustration, because even after two weeks, I still have no idea why I have sessions with him, let alone for so many hours each day.

It.

Doesn't.

Make.

Sense.

All my other evaluators have clear purposes: Enzo disciplines my body, Vanik pokes at my brain and Manning assesses my psyche — or attempts to — while everyone else tries to break me and put me back together again. That's their script, and they act out their roles, even if I may never know why.

I've managed to shut them all out for so long. To just let them do their jobs and be done with it. I haven't cooperated, but I haven't resisted. Like the gruel I eat every morning for breakfast, I do what I'm supposed to do but nothing more. I'm functional but bland. I survive, but I don't thrive. That's the life I've chosen to live. It's how I stay safe — and how I keep others safe *from me.*

Or at least, it *was,* until Ward came along with his prophetic nickname. Without me being able to stop it, I've been thawing. Two weeks is all it took for him to chip away at me, just as he said he would.

"Give me something here, Chip."

Ward reaches for my cheek, his fingers skimming my skin. My eyelids flutter at his touch, and I don't pull away despite everything inside me warning that I should.

"At least tell me you're okay."

I inhale deeply and meet his gaze, offering a barely there nod that says everything I can't: Yes, I'm okay. No, I won't tell you what happened. Please don't ask, because I won't answer.

He releases a sigh of relief, and I wonder if his performance is even real. As an evaluator, he would know better than to form any meaningful attachment. He must be aware of the clock ticking down to my last day. He is the noose tied around my neck, after all, just as much as Falon is the hangman.

"You've been out of it for almost nine hours," he tells me. "It's nearly midnight."

That causes my eyes to widen. I've never been away from my cell so late.

"We're in my personal quarters right now," Ward continues, rising to his feet again. "I didn't know what to do with you, just that you needed to get warm, so I brought you here."

He clasps his hands behind his back, and I fight to keep my eyes on his face when his T-shirt tightens.

"My aunt is Lengard's head medic, and I convinced her to come and check you over — off the record. She said that as far as she could tell, you were mostly suffering from shock."

His eyes sweep down my body and back up again.

"In case you're wondering, she's the one who changed you into my clothes."

Not as good as magical elves, but better than the alternative.

"You must be hungry. I'll get you something to eat, but then you're going back to sleep. Esther — my aunt — says that's the best thing for you right now. You're normally pale, but this is ridiculous."

He almost sounds angry, and for the second time in twenty-four hours, I wish I could see my reflection.

As if bracing for a battle, Ward says, "You're staying here for the rest of the night, no objections. You wouldn't be able to walk back to your …" He trails off, seemingly unable to find the word he's after, then he clenches his jaw and continues, "… *accommodations* on your own anyway, and I'm not carrying you around again, when you can sleep in a perfectly good bed here."

I can't think about anything — not the emotion I see in his eyes at the memory of my cell, not the idea of him carrying me *anywhere*. All I can focus on is one thing: I don't want to sleep in his room — again. No way. It's much too personal, crossing too many boundaries even without him in here with me. He is my *evaluator*. And he can never — *will never* — be anything else.

"Don't try to fight me on this, Chip. You won't win. So don't waste the energy."

With those words, he turns and walks from the room.

I'm thrown by his abrupt exit, my thoughts reeling. I want to object, to escape his company and the unbalanced feeling he ignites in me.

But he's right — I'm light-headed just sitting here. Regardless, I try to take advantage of his absence by standing again. Or attempting to. But once more my legs give out, and I collapse onto the bed just seconds before Ward strides back into the room.

"Here," he says.

He hands me a steaming bowl filled with some kind of aromatic soup. Despite my churning stomach, my mouth waters. I can't remember the last time I ate anything other than bland, regulated meals. The offering before me is like something from a dream.

"Go on. You need to get your strength back."

As much as I want to refuse any help from Ward, I'm not prideful enough to turn my nose up at a good meal. Especially when it might be one of my last.

I ladle a spoonful of soup and blow on it before placing it in my mouth. I can't keep my eyes from closing — it's either that, or have them light up with pleasure.

The soup is divine. Thick chunks of chicken, creamy stock and lashings of vegetables — real vegetables. Nothing can compare, certainly not my gruel and nutri-shakes.

"Nice, huh?" Ward says.

I force my eyes back open and find him watching me.

"Esther is a real whiz in the kitchen. She's tried teaching me, and I'm not too bad, but she's a cooking ninja. Luckily for me — and you, today — she keeps my fridge well stocked. There's plenty more where that came from, so eat as much as you want."

I wish he would leave again, but he doesn't. Instead, he remains standing and waits while I eat. I force myself to act indifferent, even if his continued presence is ruining the nicest meal I've had in years.

When I'm finished, Ward asks if I'd like any more. I feel so content, being both full *and* warm, so while I'm tempted by his offer,

I know better than to push it. The last thing I need is to bring it all back up over his shaggy white throw rug.

When I don't respond, he sighs again — irritated this time — and leaves the room with my empty bowl in hand, promising he'll be right back.

Upon his return, I watch apprehensively as he walks over to me. When he stretches his arms out, I recoil. It's an automatic response, honed by years of self-preservation. Ward's eyes narrow a fraction, and a muscle tenses in his cheek, but his anger isn't directed at me.

"I won't hurt you, Chip. You know that, right?"

My only response is to turn my face away. He can read from that whatever he wants.

"Look," he says, "I'm guessing you need to use the bathroom, and I'm pretty sure you won't be able to walk there on your own. Prove me wrong if you can, but otherwise you're going to have to let me help you. Either that or I call my aunt. It's up to you."

Unfortunately, he's right. I *do* need to use a bathroom. And Ward's medic aunt is right about me needing to rest. I only wish I wasn't being forced to sleep *here,* use the bathroom *here,* get help *here.* Much as I'd prefer to be cared for by his unknown aunt, I don't want to take up any more of her time or attention.

I grit my teeth and reach out a shaky hand, wordlessly giving him my answer.

He laces our fingers together without a word and pulls me to my feet. When I sway, he unlocks our hands and circles his arm around my waist, drawing me flush against his body. I have enough energy to feel mortified by my new position, but there's little I can do about it. It's a struggle to keep my legs from buckling, and I end up having to lean most of my weight against him.

"I've got you," he says.

As if I'm not acutely aware of this fact.

"Let's do this quickly and get you back into bed."

Quickly isn't fast enough, but I nod anyway and let him guide me down a short hallway and into a tastefully decorated bathroom.

"Do you need me to stay?"

My eyes snap up to his face. He looks one hundred percent serious and not uncomfortable at all. My skin is on fire at the very idea of him remaining in the room while I go about my … business.

With jabs of my head I make it clear that I want to be left alone. He has the audacity to let out a quiet chuckle.

"Fine," he says.

He swivels me until I'm leaning against the wall.

"Knock when you're ready for me to come back in. If I think you're taking too long, I'll check on you regardless."

The moment he exits the room, I use the wall for support and hurry over to the toilet. When I'm done, I move to the basin and rest my weight against the bench. I'm halfway through washing my hands, when I look up and see something that causes me to jerk with shock.

There's a girl staring straight at me.

Her blue eyes are big — too big — and her dark hair is messy — too messy. There's a rosy flush in her cheeks, but she looks exhausted otherwise, with deep shadows marring her pale skin.

I reach out a trembling hand and press it against the mirror. I can't believe what I'm seeing, that it's really my reflection staring back at me. I look the same but different — so different. When I look at myself now, all I can see is my parents. Their faces flash across my mind until stars burst in my vision. I realize that I'm holding my breath, but I can't seem to force oxygen down my clogged throat. I'm suffocating on the knowledge of what was, what is … and what will never be again.

"Time's up, Chip. I'm coming in."

Ward's warning is all it takes for me to rip my hand from the glass, but I can't yet remember how to draw air into my lungs. I watch through the mirror as he opens the door and catches sight of my shell-shocked face. He hisses out a quiet curse and strides quickly across the room, then turns me from my reflection until I'm facing him.

"I'm sorry. I forgot about the mirrors."

The stars in my vision are blurring now, with flashes of light and dark. All I can see is *them*.

And *me*.

Them and me and me and them and them and me and —

"Hey, listen to me, okay? I need you to take a breath. We'll do it together. In and out. Come on, Chip. Listen to me breathing. In —"

Something about his urgent tone penetrates through the fog of memories. I focus on his commanding voice and shove the images away, sucking in a ragged gasp of air.

"That's it," he encourages. "And let it out again."

I do as he says.

"Good, Chip. Again. In … and out. And in … and out. Just like that."

My vision is beginning to clear, and with visual clarity comes the stark realization that once again I'm pressed up against Ward's body, but this time his arms are around me, supporting almost my entire weight. It's been a long time since I've had a panic attack, and I've never had one as severe as this. I'm not sure what would have happened if —

"You're doing great."

Ward squeezes me reassuringly.

"Let's get you back to bed, yeah?"

He doesn't wait for me to agree before he reaches for a better hold on me and swings me straight up into his arms.

I let out an audible squeak of surprise, and his arms tense around me. His startled eyes meet mine, but I press my lips together, bite the inside of my cheek and look away from his wondering gaze.

A lifetime passes before he turns and carries me back to the bedroom. There, he lowers me gently onto the bed, then tucks the covers around me.

I'm holding my breath again, but not from panic this time. Or at least, it's a different kind of panic. It's the *I'm-so-stupid, What-was-I-thinking, Does-he-realize-what-almost-happened* kind of panic.

I know he heard me squeak.

And he must be wondering: If I have a voice, why won't I use it?

A thousand scenarios flash across my mind, ones where Ward sits, ones where he remains standing, ones where he calls Director Falon or even Vanik. In every scene, the questions come pouring out. I can't envision a way for me to get out of answering, not after what Ward heard.

What I don't expect is for him to raise a hand to rub the back of his neck, releasing a breath that relaxes his visibly tense body.

Nor do I expect to hear what comes out of his mouth next, spoken in a soft, almost warm voice.

"Get some sleep, Chip. The director is away now, but I contacted him earlier, and he's agreed to give you tomorrow off. Rest as long as you want, and I'll see you in the morning."

Just like that, he's gone, leaving me gaping after him.

What happened to the interrogation? To the unending questions? To the demand for answers I will never be able to give?

Perhaps he's coming back with Vanik after all. Or the guards. Or — no. I don't believe he is. Because I saw the look on his face, and I heard the warmth in his voice. There will be no answers asked of me tonight, despite the questions I saw in his eyes. For some inexplicable reason, he's giving me a reprieve.

I'm confused. But I'm also grateful. And I'm going to take advantage of his silence for as long as he'll let me. Or at least for however long I have left.

Sixteen days and counting.

After that, I won't have to worry about questions ever again.

I won't have to worry about *anything* ever again.

The thought leaves a tangy taste in my mouth, the dread almost overwhelming.

I've never been suicidal. There was a reason I locked myself away from the world rather than eliminating myself from it — I don't *want* to die.

Sometimes it's hard to remember that, especially when I'm alone in my cold, hard cell late at night. But here, tucked safe into the warmth and comfort of Ward's bed, it's easier to recall the dreams I once had, the future I once envisioned …

… the life I once lived.

Everything changed in a split second. And nothing will ever be the same again. I know that. Every single day, I remember. And tonight, Ward had a front-row seat to what happens when I take a trip down memory lane.

He was there through it all. He held me close and carried me to safety. And then he didn't ask the questions I know he's desperate to have answered.

I can't help thinking that maybe he's not really my evaluator at all.

But if that's the case, then I don't know what he is. Who he is. *To me.*

All I know is, right now, I'm in his room and I'm not going anywhere. I might as well enjoy this luxury, even if it is only for one night.

Because tomorrow, I'm back in my cell. And all the silence that comes with it.

CHAPTER SIX

When I wake the next day, I'm feeling almost completely better. It's amazing what a comfortable bed and a ridiculous amount of sleep can do for the human body. Even my head no longer aches.

I roll my neck and shoulders, and it feels so good that I flex my other muscles, moving downward until even my toes are limber. Part of me knows I'm putting off the inevitable — once I get out of bed I'll have to face the day, and that means seeing Ward. But there's no point in hiding, so I throw aside the blankets and push myself out of bed.

I'm pleased to discover that I'm only slightly wobbly, but I take my time heading to the door. Each step seems to bolster my strength, and by the time I reach the hallway I'm walking with confidence, ready to meet Ward and deal with whatever may come next.

The only thing is, it's not Ward I find in the kitchen.

My steps falter at the sight of the girl rifling through the fridge. I wonder if I should retreat before she sees me, but I don't decide fast enough, and she turns around, catching a glimpse of me.

"Oh!" She places a hand to her chest, startled. "I didn't know you were awake. I wanted to have breakfast ready for when you got up."

My brow furrows. She looks too young to be Ward's aunt.

"I'm Landon's sister, Cami," she says, moving toward me. "He told me I can call you 'Chip,' but you don't look like a Chip to me." She tilts her head and waves of golden hair pour down her shoulders. "I know Jane's not your real name, but for now, I think I'll stick with that — if it's okay with you?"

I don't know why she's asking me. I don't even know why she's *here*.

Ward is nowhere to be seen, so I wonder if he's tasked her with watching me, to make sure I don't take off — not that I'd even know how to get back to my cell from here. In any case, Cami doesn't look like she'd make a very good guard. She's all angelic smiles and sunshine, glowing from the inside with all the color that the rest of Lengard lacks.

"I hope you like pancakes," Cami says, motioning for me to follow as she moves back to the fridge. "I don't know how to make much else, but my pancakes are amazing."

She pulls out milk, eggs, butter and a pint of strawberries. After she dumps them on the bench, she opens the cupboard and retrieves some flour, syrup, vanilla extract and — are those chocolate chips? I haven't seen chocolate, let alone tasted it, in years.

Cami laughs suddenly. "You should see your face. Here." She hands the chocolate packet to me. "Have at it." When I hesitate, she nudges me and says, "Go on. From what I've heard, you haven't exactly been spoiled during your time here. You deserve a little indulgence."

Needing no further encouragement, I tear open the bag and pour a handful out onto my palm. One by one I place the chips on my tongue, closing my eyes in ecstasy when the taste hits me.

Cami snickers. I know I must look ridiculous, but I can't help it. Chocolate is considered a girl's best friend for good reason. Nothing can compare.

I tip out another large handful and force myself to place the bag back on the bench before I'm tempted to finish it off.

Cami shoves a bowl into my arms. "Whisk this for me, will you? Stop when it's light and fluffy."

I haven't baked anything since I was a child, but I'm relieved she's given me a task. It means I'm not standing around awkwardly, wondering what to do. Wondering why I'm not coming up with a plan to escape before Ward returns. It also means Cami trusts me to complete her instructions with limited supervision, and I feel a trickle of anxiety when I realize that I don't want to disappoint her. It's been a long time since I've cared what another person thinks.

I can't handle where my mind is leading me, so I focus, instead, on following Cami's instructions while she bustles around the small kitchen, turning on the stove and melting butter in the pan.

I'm not sure what "light and fluffy" means, but when I think I've whisked enough, I tilt the bowl for her inspection and watch her eyes light up. Cami's eyes are green like Ward's, but hers are darker, richer. Less … *knowing*.

"Perfect!"

She takes the batter from me and stirs in the choc chips before moving to the stove.

As she begins cooking, I wash and slice the strawberries. I finish just in time for her first batch of pancakes to be ready. We grab plates, cutlery and the bottle of syrup and move to the table to take our seats.

"You have to try it like this," Cami says, sliding a perfectly golden pancake onto my plate, dousing it with syrup and piling on the strawberries.

It looks like a mouthful of cavities waiting to happen, but I'm willing to risk a trip to the dentist if it means I get to enjoy what's resting in front of me.

"Dig in," Cami says, constructing an identical mountain of sweetness for herself.

A single bite is all it takes for me to realize that my life will never be the same again. And it's not because of the incredible taste; it's because I stupidly — *stupidly* — moan out loud …

… Just as Ward walks into the room.

He stops dead at the sound and stares at me in astonishment. It's all the proof he needs that my squeak last night wasn't a figment of his imagination.

The pancake turns to ash in my mouth.

Cami giggles. "I think she likes my cooking. Don't you agree, Landon?"

Ward's eyes are locked on mine. "It certainly sounds that way."

I think I may throw up.

"Have a seat, big brother. This is one of my best batches yet. But Jane did all the whisking, so half the praise goes to her."

Ward moves slowly toward us and lowers himself into a chair. Cami passes him a plate, and he finally flicks his eyes away from mine when the door opens.

"I hope you've saved some for me," Enzo says, sauntering into the room and dropping casually into the seat beside me as if we've breakfasted together every morning of our lives.

Cami creates a pancake mountain for him and dances back to the kitchen to cook up more batter. I'm left sitting at the table with Ward opposite me, Enzo beside me and gaping silence surrounding me.

At last, Enzo speaks. "Nice outfit, JD," he says between mouthfuls. "Looks comfy."

"Enz," Ward says, his voice carrying a warning.

"What? It does! She should wear your clothes more often is all I'm saying."

I'm grateful when Cami returns with another steaming pile of food.

She flips a second pancake onto my plate and places the remainder in the middle of the table. Ward and Enzo devour the offering so fast that I'm left staring. When I catch Cami's amused eyes, I can't stop my lips from curling up at the corners, a secret smile I share only with her.

Or, that's what I think, until I see Ward staring at my mouth, just before Enzo says, "I've never seen you smile."

His words have the same effect on me as a bucket of icy water.

"Over two and a half years," he continues. "I've been missing out."

I drop my fork with a clatter and push my plate away, unable to stomach any more. I wonder if that was Enzo's intention, since he surely can't be pleased about the calorie intake.

No one says anything. But then —

"I asked you not to come over this morning, Enz," Ward says.

He reaches for my discarded plate and claims my leftovers as his own. I force myself not to react even though I'm surprised by his overly familiar action.

"Did you really think I'd miss a chance to have Cami's pancakes?" Enzo asks through a mouthful of food. "Besides, with JD here, I knew it was bound to be an interesting meal. A laugh a minute, this one. Can't get her to shut up."

Cami snorts, presumably at my less-than-impressed expression. Enzo grins right along with her, and even Ward's dimple makes an appearance.

"You're right, Enz," Cami says. "It *is* interesting having Jane here."

"'Jane,' huh?" Enzo says. "You're not going with 'JD'?" He flicks his gaze over to Ward. "Fake or not, it still makes more sense than 'Chip.'"

I will not look at Ward. I will not look at Ward. *I will not look at —* Damn it, I'm looking at him. Worse, he's looking back at me. Between us, we hold a secret, and despite everything, despite knowing better, I still love — and hate — the reason he chose his name for me.

I suddenly realize I need to get out of here. These people are too normal. They're too real. They're too … *colorful*. I'm used to bland. I'm used to whitewashed. I'm used to pillowcase uniforms, regulated meals and unchanging schedules. I don't know what to do with fluffy beds, warm clothes, steaming soup, reflective mirrors, chocolate chips and laughing angels. That's not my life — not anymore. And it never will be again.

I feel warm — too warm — so I draw the sleeves of Ward's hoodie up to my elbows. I'm trying to figure out how to escape back to my safe, quiet, *uncolored* cell, when Cami lets out a gasp. She reaches across for my hands and latches on to them before I can pull them away.

"What the hell is this?"

I look down and see the skin around my wrists streaked with black and blue. Before I can do anything — like yank my hands back — Ward and Enzo both lean in for a closer look.

"Handcuffs are uncomfortable, but they don't leave bruises," Enzo says.

That's not always true. But in this case, Enzo is correct.

"You didn't have those yesterday," Ward says, his voice tight. He turns to Enzo. "She didn't, right?"

Enzo shakes his head. "Definitely not. It must have happened some-time after our session."

I see the moment when realization hits them both, and Enzo spits out the name, "*Vanik*."

"Vanik?" Cami is alarmed. "You didn't mention anything about her working with Vanik."

"We're not allowed to tell you details. You know that," Ward says, his voice soft, gentle … careful. "There are rules, Cami. Even for me."

"We know how you feel about him, Cam," Enzo states, also using a gentle tone. "And you have reason — you *both* have reason — to feel that way."

His inclusion of Ward piques my curiosity, but no further details are offered.

Cami's grip on my hands is unyielding. "You have no idea how I feel about him," she snaps.

"You don't like him," Enzo says. "We get it. Trust me, we do."

"I don't *like* him?" Cami lets out a laugh so bitter that it gives me goose bumps. "I don't just *not like him,* Enzo. I *hate* him. I wish he was *dead.*"

Five words. That's all it takes for my world to stop. They take half a breath for Cami to say, but they play on repeat in my mind for an eternity.

I wish he was dead.

I wish you were dead.

"Jane?"

I hate you. Both of you. I wish you were dead.

"Chip?"

I'm never talking to you again.

"JD, you cool?"

You're dead to me.

A rough shake interrupts the screaming in my mind, enough for me to I realize I'm trembling and taking unnaturally large gulps of air.

"What the hell, JD?"

Enzo gives me another shake, though not as forcefully this time. I see Cami and Ward both half raised out of their seats and staring at me in concern. I quickly turn aside, only to find Enzo's eyes scanning my face as if he's trying to judge my sanity.

I jerk away and jump out of my chair. I stumble backward a few steps, needing a moment before I can get my legs working properly. Then I tear off down the hallway without looking back at any of them. When I reach the bathroom, I slam the door shut and move straight over to the counter, where I brace my hands against it. It takes a few tries before I can summon Ward's voice from last night, but when I manage it, he gives me exactly what I need.

"In ... and out. And in ... and out. Just like that."

I'm not sure how long I stare down at my hands and focus on my breathing, but eventually I get myself under control and am able to look up at my reflection. My skin is so white it's almost blue. My pupils are dilated, and my lips are quivering. Every muscle in my body is lined with tension. I can't look anymore. Because the more I do, the more I see *them*.

I move to the far side of the bathroom until the mirror is out of sight, and I slide down the wall, drawing my knees up and wrapping my arms around my legs. It's in this position that Cami finds me when she slowly pushes open the door.

"Jane?"

My eyes remain closed, my head cocooned by arms that protect me from the world.

I can feel her hesitation like it's a tangible thing. Then something changes, and she moves until she's sliding down the wall beside me, wrapping an arm around my shoulders.

I stiffen and try to pull away, but her grip only tightens.

"It's okay," she whispers. "You're going to be okay."

She's wrong. Nothing is okay. I *know* this. But there's something about her tone that soothes my anguish, filling me with peace.

Other than Ward, no one has held me like this in years. We might be on the cold, hard floor of a bathroom, and I might be beating back images that want to destroy me, but with Cami's arm around me, I feel an illusion of safety. She can't possibly know how much I need this. *I* didn't know. But there's no denying the comfort of her embrace.

She hums a quiet melody and combs her fingers through my hair. My heartbeat begins to settle, my breathing begins to stabilize, my trembling begins to ease and my thoughts begin to quiet.

I'm not sure how long she cradles me, but eventually she stops humming and softly asks, "Better?"

I nod into her shoulder, knowing I owe her that much.

"Think you're ready to get up?"

This time I don't respond, since I dread facing Ward and Enzo after my meltdown.

"The boys are gone," Cami says, as if reading my thoughts. "You've been given the day off, but they haven't. It's just us girls now."

She must feel the remaining tension leak out of me, because she pulls her arm away and stands, holding out a hand for me. I look up at her open, caring face, and I make a decision. I don't understand — or trust — her brother's motives, but Cami's not my evaluator. She doesn't have to be nice to me. She just *is*. Even if it turns out that she's in on Ward's plans, I don't have it in me to distrust her, not when my defenses are at an all-time low. So, better judgment or not, I place my hand in hers and let her guide me to my feet and out of the bathroom.

CHAPTER SEVEN

I can't remember a better day, certainly not since long before I arrived at Lengard.

Cami doesn't leave my side for more than a few minutes at a time. Maybe Ward put her up to it, maybe she's just bored, but either way, I don't mind her presence. She's talkative — so talkative — and she has a vibrancy about her that, rather than making me feel exhausted, fills me with energy. With her, I smile more in a few hours than I have for years. Unlike Ward and Enzo, she doesn't gape at me when it happens.

I don't know what the time is now, just that the day is almost over. Cami and I had a late lunch, and she let me help her in the kitchen again, even if it was just to make sandwiches this time. But sandwiches were perfect for me because, again, they were different — and I'm being reminded more and more today of how wonderful "different" can be.

After lunch, we settled in on Ward's couch, and we haven't moved since, mostly because Cami pulled a pile of movies from her bag and we've been watching them on the flat screen for hours. It's been so long since I've seen any kind of movie, and I'm enjoying every thrilling second. Especially since Cami cooked up a massive bowl of buttery popcorn — an indulgence I'm sure Enzo will make me work off over my next few sessions.

The credits are rolling at the end of our third movie, when the door to the suite opens. I'm relaxed in Cami's easy presence, with my feet tucked underneath me and my face cushioned in the armrest. But when Ward walks in with a large paper bag and finds us lounging on the couch together, I stiffen automatically.

"Hey, Lando," Cami greets.

Her head is resting on the crook of my bent knee. She refuses to budge even when I shift my leg pointedly under her.

Ward has frozen just inside the doorway and is staring at the two of us like he can't comprehend what he's seeing. I don't blame him. I doubt he's ever seen me so off guard.

Clearing his throat, he says, "Aunt Esther invited us over for dinner." His eyes shift to me. "She wants to make sure you're okay, Chip." He moves closer and hands me the bag he's carrying. "This is for you."

His offering causes Cami to sit up — finally — and she peers into the bag with me as I open it.

"Oooh, pretty," Cami coos, reaching for the material inside and holding it up against my rigid body. "Good pick, Landon. It's the perfect color for her. But where did it come from? If you were going topside today, you should've taken us with you — especially to go shopping."

Ward ignores her. "Esther wants us there in ten, so do what you need to get ready. Enzo is meeting us there."

I think he says the last as a warning to me. Not that it's necessary. I'm already panicking, mostly because of the dress. I don't need to put it on to know it's the most beautiful thing I'll have worn in years. And sure enough, after a quick trip to the bathroom to change out of Ward's borrowed clothes, I'm left staring once again in the mirror, startled anew by the person I see staring back at me.

"Jane, you ready?"

Cami knocks once on the door and lets herself in. She sees me and whistles through her teeth.

"Look at you."

I am looking at me. I can't seem to draw my gaze from my reflection. The summer dress fits perfectly, and try as I might, when I look at myself, I have a hard time seeing any traces of *them*. I'm not sure if that upsets me or fills me with relief.

"Here, let's do something with your hair."

I stand perfectly still and let Cami pull my wayward locks up into a messy bun.

"Perfect." She smiles at me through the mirror and grabs my hand, pulling me out of the room. "Time to go."

I'm examining my woolen-covered feet as we enter the main area of Ward's quarters and wondering whether I should take the socks off, when Cami gives my hand a squeeze. I glance up in question — and halt at the expression on Ward's face.

My face is burning again; I can feel it. I wish they would both stop looking at me. I didn't choose to wear the pretty — too pretty — dress. As much as I hate my uniform, I would wear the same pillowcase for the next thousand years if it meant I'd never have to feel this uncomfortable again.

"Don't we have somewhere to be?" Cami asks when the silence lingers, and I'm grateful for her intervention.

Ward shakes his head as if to clear it. "Yes. We do."

Without another word, he leads the way from the room, and a grinning Cami drags me after him. She stops us at the door to hand me a pair of flip-flops. I exchange them for my woolly socks, and they fit perfectly.

"I thought we looked around the same size," Cami says, nodding to my feet. "I'd let you keep them, but the wacked-out rules here say you can't have any footwear until you've committed yourself to the program. What's with that?"

Her mention of the increasingly mysterious "program" piques my interest more than Lengard's footwear rules. I consider how I might press her for more details, but Ward calls to us loudly from farther down the corridor, closing my window of opportunity.

"Are you two coming?"

"He's so uptight tonight." Cami laughs quietly and drags me after him again. "I'm loving this. You're seriously good entertainment, Jane."

I don't think anyone has called me "good entertainment" — ever. Not even back when I made an effort to be someone people wanted to spend time with.

I try to get my bearings as Ward leads us down a hallway, but I have no idea what area of the facility we're in. The doors on either side of us all look the same, and the unending, colorless walls offer no clarity. When we come to a stop in front of a door, I frown, because something about this area seems familiar. I don't have time to figure out why before Ward knocks twice, opens the door and motions for us to enter. Cami is still tugging on my hand, so I follow as she pulls me past her brother and into the room beyond.

What I see causes me to stop dead.

"Mum! They're here!"

Cami releases me and opens her arms for two golden-haired boys, who run directly toward her. She has to bend to embrace them, and she squeezes them in a hug until the boys are laughingly begging for her to let them go.

A high-pitched squeal rings out, followed by an excited, "Landy! Landy! Mummy, Landy's here!"

I watch with wide eyes as Ward kneels just in time to catch a blurring missile of dark ringlets.

"Beautiful Abigale, gorgeous as ever." He rises to his feet with the little girl still in his arms, her legs wrapped tight around his torso.

He throws her up in the air, and she cries out, "Again! Again!"

"Anything for my favorite girl," he says, his smile almost as bright as hers.

I'm sure my mouth must be hanging open, but I can't help it.

He's my evaluator. He's my evaluator. *He's my evaluator.*

I can't pull my eyes away from them. Not until —

"Hey! I've seen you before!"

I turn to look at the boy who spoke. He's the older of the two, though not by much.

"Ethan, this is Jane," Cami says, her hand resting on his shoulder. She turns to me. "Jane, meet Ethan and Isaac."

The older one — Ethan — gives me a curious look, while his younger brother, Isaac, offers me a grin and a shy wave.

"I'm Abby!" cries the little girl, still clinging to Ward.

She pushes against him until he sets her back on the ground, then she takes a running leap that leaves me with no choice but to catch her. I automatically draw her up into my arms, and she doesn't hesitate to circle her hands around my neck.

"We have the same hair! Look!" She pulls on a strand that has escaped my bun and holds it up against one of her own ringlets. "We could be twins!"

I can't fight my smile. She's simply too adorable. But of course that's the moment Enzo walks in from another room, accompanied by a blond-haired woman I've seen once before. Unlike the last time — when she found me with the guards in the hallway — she's not staring at me in fear. Still, she appears wary.

"Well, I'll be damned. There's that smile again." Enzo crosses his arms and grins at me. "Who the hell are you, and what have you done with JD?"

I don't have it in me to wipe my face clear, not when Abby is now plaiting our hair together. It's becoming one big, tangled mess, but that doesn't seem to stop her.

"Enzo! Watch your mouth," says the woman, whom I presume is Esther.

Enzo winces. "Sorry, Es. My bad."

"We're not allowed to use the D-word," Abby informs me, her little fingers still weaving through my hair. "Or the H-word."

"Ethan used the H-word in front of Dad last week, and he was told to sit in the corner for ten whole minutes," Isaac says, timidly taking one step closer, then another, until he's right beside me. He curls his little hand around the hem of my dress and tugs gently, so I lower myself into a closed-knees squat, balancing carefully with Abby still in my arms. He leans in farther, like he has some great secret only I can hear, and whispers in my ear, "You're really pretty."

With three words, this small child does the impossible.

He causes me to laugh.

I don't know who's more shocked — me or everyone else. It's one thing to smile. But to laugh? Unheard of. For so — *so* — many reasons.

Enzo is gaping at me. Ward's head is tilted, and his dimple is out. Cami looks like she's about to burst into joyous tears. Esther still appears wary, but her eyes have warmed toward me. The only people in the room who don't seem to understand the significance of what just happened are the three small humans now asking their mother how long until dinner is ready.

Esther clears her throat and orders her children to go and wash up. I let go of Abby and watch as she runs off after her brothers.

"I'm Esther — Landon and Cami's aunt," the woman finally greets me. She holds out a hand, and I hesitate only a beat before reaching to meet it with my own. "You're looking much better tonight. A day of rest seems to be exactly what you needed." She turns to Ward. "No problems?"

He glances at me, and I wonder if he's going to mention my panic attack. But when Ward turns back to his aunt, he just shakes his head. "All good. But do you have something to help her wrists?"

I'd forgotten all about the marks left from Vanik's manacles. I don't resist when Esther reaches for my hands and gently turns them over.

"I didn't notice these yesterday. The bruising must have come out overnight." She frowns before giving me a searching look.

Enzo explains with only one word. "Vanik."

Esther's smoky eyes darken. "I should have something among my medical supplies. We'll be right back."

I give Cami a pleading look as Esther pulls me away, but Ward's sister just sends me an encouraging smile and waves me from the room.

"There's no need to worry — this won't take long," Esther says, opening the door to a bathroom much larger than Ward's. She sits me down on the edge of a tub filled with colorful toys and tells me to wait a moment while she rifles through the medicine cabinet.

She returns to my side with a tube of ointment and kneels in front of me, then carefully applies the balm to first my left and then my right wrist.

"I remember seeing you that night with the guards," she says as she massages the gel into my skin. "I knew who you were the moment I laid eyes on you."

Since she is the head medic, someone must have warned her about my threat level, prompting her fear of me. I feel my body bracing for a blow.

"But you should know I wouldn't be allowing you into my home and around my children if I thought you might harm any of us."

I jerk in surprise. It's only a slight movement, but she catches it all the same and sends me a reassuring smile.

"I was afraid of you then, for many reasons," she says. "And when Landon called me last night to come and help you … To be honest, I almost didn't respond."

Esther continues to rub soothing circles on my wrists, and as I watch, the bruising begins to fade. My eyes widen, having never seen such swift healing. I didn't realize such an effective ointment existed.

"I became a medic years ago after I was greatly in need but there was no one around who knew enough to help me," she says. "I almost died, taking my newborn baby — Ethan — with me. When we managed to survive, I made a promise to myself that I would never allow another to suffer if it was within my power to do something." Her eyes meet mine. "So I'm glad Landon called me to see to you last night. Not just because I can tell today that it made a difference, but also because watching you tonight, especially with my children ..." She trails off, smiling again.

Her words spread through my body like liquid sunshine. But then, in the space of a heartbeat, the warmth is replaced by a cold so deep I have to fight a shiver. I don't deserve her acceptance, her children's affection, not even the kindness Cami, Ward and Enzo continue to bestow upon me. Esther was wrong in what she said before — I *could* cause them harm. All of them. I slipped up with Isaac earlier; it was just fortunate that all I did was laugh. But if my defenses keep shattering at the rate they are, it's only a matter of time before something disastrous happens. And I can't afford to make another mistake like —

"I have to admit, I'm not sure what to call you." Esther's pensive voice breaks into my troublesome thoughts. "It's clear to everyone that 'Jane Doe' is not who you are. But I also have a feeling you're only 'Chip' to one person." Her eyes light up like silver moons among the stars. "So that one's out. Which brings us back to 'Jane' — unless we pick something else. You'll end up with a multiple personality disorder if we're not careful."

She says it jokingly, but I'm inclined to agree with her.

"Okay, you're all done."

Esther screws the lid onto the tube of ointment and places it back in the cabinet. I look down at my hands and see that the bruising is almost completely gone. I wonder again about the balm and how it worked so quickly.

Noticing my look, Esther grins and says, "Secret recipe. It's great for the rapid healing of smaller injuries — and comes in handy when you have three troublemaker children, believe me."

It's a shame it only works on small injuries. I'm guessing there's no medication in the world that can help with the longer-term damage Vanik has done.

"I hope you like lasagna," Esther says, leading the way back to the others. "I know you're not used to eating anything too rich, but hopefully you'll be all right."

Lasagna? My mouth waters at the prospect. I used to love Italian food. When I was younger, we had Italian every Friday night. Pizza, pasta, garlic bread; even gelato for dessert. My dad would cook and —

No.

Stop.

StopStopStopStopStop.

"Jane? You okay?"

Busy focusing on my flip-flopped feet and trying to keep my memories in check, I glance up to see that Esther has led me to the dining room. Suddenly I'm the center of attention, with Cami's concern drawing everyone's eyes to me.

"You look like you have a sore tummy," Abby says, entwining her fingers with mine and leading me to a chair at the table. She pulls me down and crawls up into my lap. "When I have a sore tummy, Mummy sings to me. Do you want us all to sing to you?"

"Abby, sweetheart, maybe we should give Chip some space," Ward says, watching me carefully and missing nothing.

Abby appears adorably confused. "Who's Chip?"

"That's what he calls Jane," Cami tells her.

The little girl scrunches up her nose. "That's a silly name."

"It sure is," Enzo murmurs.

As I listen to them, the knots in my stomach begin to unravel and the memories drift away. I give Abby a grateful squeeze.

"You don't look like your tummy is sore anymore," she observes. "But we haven't sung to you yet. Do you still need space, like Landy says?"

"All right, baby girl. Come here."

Ward swoops Abby right out of my arms and tickles her sides until she giggles with glee. He settles her into a chair with a booster seat, and Ethan and Isaac jump up into the seats on either side of her, opposite Enzo and Cami. Ward spares me another lingering glance, almost like he's asking if I'm okay. I tilt my chin up slightly in affirmation. His eyes warm — damn it, I responded instinctively *again* — and he takes off toward the kitchen. Only a few seconds pass before he returns with Esther, both carrying what looks like an incredible meal.

When I take my first bite of lasagna, all I want to do is moan with delight. But I don't slip up again; instead, I just fork more into my mouth, then chase it with Esther's perfectly roasted vegetables.

So many wonderful tastes, so many delectable flavors … I keep being reminded that the real world isn't segmented into different shades of bland. After all I've experienced today, how will I return to my everyday monotony? I had been … well, not *happy,* but resigned, at least, to my life circumstances.

"How's your work with the program going, Cami?"

Esther's question ignites my interest.

All day Cami chatted on about this and blabbered on about that, but nothing she told me was of much consequence — and certainly none of it gave me any idea what she does with her time, beyond babysitting her brother's charity case. Her only mention of the mysterious "program" was just before we left for Esther's.

"Oh, you know." Cami waves her fork in the air. Her eyes flick to me for a split second before she focuses back on her aunt. "It's going well."

"How are you handling your training? Are you growing stronger? All of you?" Esther asks.

I fight the urge to frown as I struggle to understand. Is Cami training with Enzo, too? I need more details — I need their words to stop being so … vague.

Cami's eyes jump to me again. For some unfathomable reason, she looks nervous.

"It's slow," she hedges. "But we're seeing … improvement."

"Do you think now that Jane is —"

Ward clears his throat loudly, cutting Esther off, and she sends him a curious glance. She presses her lips together and turns back to her plate.

"Next time, I'll add more garlic," she says. "Give it more of a kick."

I'm not sure whether I want to laugh again or to growl with frustration. Or perhaps to throw what remains of my lasagna at Ward's head.

I do none of the above. Instead, I spear a roasted potato with my fork and raise it to my mouth. I never end up taking a bite, because at that moment the door to the suite opens and in walks a man — a very familiar man. The whole room grows silent.

I stare at Director Falon, stunned by his presence. His eyes move around the table until they lock onto my own. It feels as if the world has stopped. And then my life is turned on its axis by a single word shouted with immeasurable glee.

"*Daddy!*"

Abby flies from her seat and runs across the room to throw herself at Director Falon. Ethan and Isaac follow, with Esther right behind them.

"Rick, honey, I thought you weren't going to be back until the end of the week?"

"My plans changed," Falon says in his deep, gravelly voice. He bends to give Esther a kiss on the cheek. He then ruffles his fingers through Isaac's hair, squeezes Ethan's shoulder and pulls Abby up into his arms.

Meanwhile, I'm taking deep breaths and trying desperately not to bring my lasagna back up, all over Esther's pristine tablecloth.

Falon is the father of Abby, Ethan and Isaac. He's Esther's husband. That makes him —

"Hey, Uncle Rick," Cami greets him, somewhat timidly.

The reason for her hesitant tone is clear when, yet again, she glances nervously in my direction. But my eyes move quickly away from her. To Ward.

Ward, my *evaluator*.

Ward, who happens to be Director Falon's *nephew*.

CHAPTER EIGHT

"So, Landon, it looks like you and Jane are making progress."

The words fall smoothly from Falon's lips, and I try to keep my fork from trembling in my hand. I wonder what he is referring to, unless he considers me passing out, spending the night in Ward's bed and whiling away a day on the couch "progress."

"You're two weeks down," he continues after swallowing a mouthful of lasagna.

I'm not sure if he's speaking to me or Ward this time — or both of us — when he asks, "Other than what I can see with my own eyes, do you have anything else to give me yet?"

I have no idea why he's bringing up this topic over a family meal, especially given its likely ending. *My* likely ending. His wife and children are present, for goodness' sake.

"You've read my reports?" Ward says, and he waits for his uncle to nod. "Then you know everything I have to say."

I find it hard to believe Ward has anything to report on me. All I do with him is read.

Falon's reaction is almost invisible, but I see the rigidity in his frame. His gaze roams around the table and he asks, "Would anyone like to tell me why Jane is with us tonight?" His eyes settle on me. "Don't get me wrong — it's a pleasure to have you join us. I'm just … surprised."

My forehead crinkles with confusion. His words actually sound genuine.

"You told Landon she could have the day off," Cami says. "When Aunt Esther invited us to dinner, we brought Jane along."

Falon looks skeptical, and I can't say I blame him. "Well, it's always nice to have someone new to talk with at dinner. It keeps the conversation stimulating."

Enzo chokes on his sip of water.

"Silly Daddy," Abby says around a mouthful of giggles. "Jane doesn't talk. Landy told us all about her. We're not supposed to ask her questions, because she can't answer and we don't want her to be uncomforble."

"Uncomfor*t*able, Abby," Esther quietly corrects.

I hear the young girl repeat the word as if from far away, my thoughts spiraling on what she just revealed. Ward told them to make me comfortable? Why would he do that? Why would he *care*?

I glance up to find him watching me. I wish I had the ability to freeze time, just to decipher all that's hidden in his gaze.

"Why *doesn't* Jane talk?" Ethan asks. "You never told us, Landy."

"Ethan —" Esther starts to say, but Falon cuts her off.

"I'm curious about that myself." The director leans back in his seat, his mouth curling with false amusement.

"I like that she doesn't talk," Abby says, bouncing in her seat. "She's like one of my dollies. She and Princess Sparkles would be best friends — I just know it."

No one seems to know what to say to that, but Abby's intervention manages to keep anyone from returning to the previous line of questioning. Instead, normal dinner conversation springs up around the table. Ethan and Isaac tell Falon about a video game they played that day, Esther and Ward talk quietly about his shopping trip aboveground, Cami and Enzo fight over the last of the lasagna and Abby mushes her food into shapes on her plate.

I'm amazed to be witnessing something so normal. Something I haven't experienced in so long. My heart hurts as memories try to flood my mind, but I stay in the moment and enjoy the beauty of what is unfolding around me.

"It's getting late," Falon says once the table has been cleared.

Taking the hint, I rise from my seat along with Cami, Enzo and Ward. The director is a living reminder of my limited time, but I am still reluctant to leave. Something has shifted within me tonight — a reminder of all that I once had, of all that I stand to lose.

I'm not *ready*. Not yet.

But ...

Fifteen days.

That's all I have left.

I can't allow myself to forget.

I *won't* allow myself to forget.

"Daddy, I want to read a story to Jane before she goes," Abby says, her lower lip trembling. "I'm getting really good."

"I know you are, sweetheart," Falon says with undisguised affection. "But maybe another time."

Her eyes brim with tears. "Please? It won't take long. I p-promise."

I think it's the hiccup that does it, because the next thing I know, I'm being led into Abby's glaringly pink room and pushed onto her bed as she settles snugly at my side.

Barely seconds pass before Ethan and Isaac creep through the door and climb up beside us.

These three children know nothing about me, yet they're cuddled against me, just wanting to be held close. They seem to actually *like* me, as unfathomable as that is.

Abby has almost finished the story, when her words trail off, claimed by sleep. With the boys having dozed off earlier, I find myself trapped in a tangle of limbs.

As I consider how to extricate myself, I sense movement and see Ward step into the room. He takes in my predicament with soft eyes and an expression that causes my breath to catch.

"You look like you could use a hand," he observes, his dimple showing.

He wades around a mess of toys until he's beside the bed and moves first Isaac, then Ethan, resting them in positions that no longer have them clinging to me. He reaches for Abby, gliding his hands between the two of us — and causing my stomach to dip — as he gently shifts her away. She whimpers but quickly settles again.

Free now, I slide carefully off the bed, glancing at the children. My eyes well with tears as I feel the phantom touch of their affection still wrapped around me.

"It's late, Chip," Ward whispers. "Time for us to go."

I quickly swipe at my eyes and turn away, hoping he doesn't notice.

He takes my hand and gives it a squeeze, telling me that I didn't turn fast enough. I don't pull away from his touch, even knowing I should. Instead, I let him lead me from the room, our hands still linked.

"Let's get you back to your suite," he says.

I find it interesting that he says "suite" to describe my cell. Then I realize he's not taking me toward my room — but instead, toward *his*.

My feet feel like lead, and I grind to a halt, yanking him to a stop beside me.

He turns to me and opens his mouth, then snaps it shut and studies my expression. His eyes light for a fraction of a second before he looks down at his feet.

"It's not what you think."

I can't tell if he's amused or embarrassed.

"I'm not taking you back to my room. Don't look so worried."

I press my lips together as I realize his amusement won.

"Trust me."

He's said that to me before. And just like last time, I don't — I *won't*. I *can't*.

But I do let him pull me forward again. I don't really have a choice.

Ward stops in front of a doorway in another corridor I've never seen. He opens our joined hands, gently presses my palm against the touch screen bio-sensor mounted into the wall and waits until the door slides open. He then draws his arm behind my back and uses it to guide me into the room.

"Welcome to your new home, Chip."

Six words.

Six words, and I'm left gaping at him.

Surely I must have heard wrong.

"I thought you'd never get here!"

My head jerks to the side, and I see Cami skipping up a short hallway toward us.

She's wearing a pair of drawstring pajama pants with a tank top, her face scrubbed clean of makeup.

I can't mask my confusion, and it grows even more when she spreads her arms out, twirls on the spot and gleefully cries, "This is going to be so much fun! I've always wanted a roomie!"

I dare not breathe. This can't be true. I must have fallen asleep with Abby, Ethan and Isaac, because surely I am dreaming.

"Don't look so happy, Jane," Cami says with a dry laugh. "If you're not careful, I'll think you're actually excited about staying here."

I blink once, twice, three times, and then I reach across to pinch the sensitive skin of my inner elbow. I do it hard enough that I flinch at the pain — pain that makes me realize I'm not, in fact, dreaming.

"This is real, you know," Cami says, grinning. "But if you want to pinch yourself again, go for it."

"Cam," Ward says. "Give us a moment."

Cami looks at her brother for a beat before she turns back to me, her smile wider and brighter than before. "I'll just go and, um … clean my teeth. Don't mind me."

She prances back down the hallway, leaving me alone with Ward. He turns me until I'm facing him.

"You should never have been in that cell — not when you first arrived, and definitely not for any amount of time after that."

Anger flashes in his eyes before he takes a deep breath and changes the subject.

"Cami can be … *enthusiastic* … so if you find her too difficult to get along with, let me know somehow, and I'll see if I can get you a new room allocation. It might take a while, but I'll make it happen."

My world is spinning. Every word out of his mouth is like a gift I never imagined I'd receive. I can't — I don't — I'm so —

Ward steps into my space, so close that I have to tilt my head up to look him in the eyes. His hand moves out, and his fingers trail whisper-soft against my cheekbone. I'm certain my eyes are as wide as oceans, but before I can decide whether to lean into his touch or jump away from it, he steps back again. He removes his hand and runs it restlessly through his hair, causing it to stick out like golden straw piled into a haystack.

"Someone should have moved you into a place like this ages ago. But we can't change the past, only the future."

His voice is rougher than normal, as if he's speaking more to himself than to me.

"Cami will show you around," he continues. "Your schedule hasn't changed, but the guards will pick you up and drop you off here from now on." He pauses, seems to debate saying more, lets out a breath and goes on. "I'm still working on getting them to leave off the handcuffs."

The ground is dissolving under my feet. Surely I must be sinking into an alternate dimension. One where silent girls are befriended by armored knights and bouncing children and swallowed up in dreams so real they bleed life into the very walls, turning the blandness of whites, grays and beiges into rainbows so dazzling that the air itself comes alive with their colors.

I open my mouth, close it, open it again and then snap it shut. More than anything, I want to say something. I want to give voice to my gratitude. I'm nowhere near willing to trust him, but he's given me something precious, and I want him to know just how much it means to me. So, tentatively — very, *very* tentatively — I stretch my hand forward and wrap my fingers around his forearm, squeezing gently for a fraction of a second.

From a normal person, an arm touch isn't anything special. But from me, the simple gesture is like a shout. And Ward's expression tells me he understands all the words I'm not saying.

"Chip —"

Cami interrupts us, gliding down the hallway again. "Time to say goodnight, Landon."

Ward looks like he's swallowing words as he pulls in a sharp breath and turns away, nodding.

"'Night, Cam." He kisses her forehead. "Call me if you need anything."

"Yeah, yeah." She waves him toward the door with a smile. "Don't worry, we'll be fine."

"See you tomorrow, Chip," Ward says to me. After one last glance, he disappears through the door, and it seals shut behind him.

I'm in a daze as Cami grabs my hand and shows me around. The suite is a more colorful version of Ward's quarters but with an extra bedroom. She's talking excitedly, but my mind is stuck replaying the moment I just shared with her brother. It's only when we reach my bedroom that my attention returns to the present.

I stand in the doorway, fighting back tears for the second time tonight. The room — *my* room — is like something from a daydream. Since we're underground, there are no windows, but an oil painting on the pale-yellow wall shows a beach leading into an endless blue ocean. It's better than any view a window could offer, but as wonderful as it is, it's nothing compared to the bed — which is just as luxurious as Ward's.

With a skip in her step, Cami leads me over to a wardrobe and opens it to reveal a plethora of clothes — all for me. I don't know whether to laugh or cry. I run my fingers along the materials, overwhelmed.

"No more uniforms for you," she says happily. Reading my expression, she quietly adds, "It's a lot to take in, isn't it?"

When I nod, she curls an arm around me and pulls me into a side hug.

"Don't worry, Jane. We'll have you feeling like a human again in no time. Then all this will seem normal to you, just like it should."

Perhaps she's right, but how long will those feelings last?

I only have fifteen days left to offer a convincing reason for why I should be allowed to remain at Lengard. And no matter how much my circumstances may have changed, I will not — I absolutely will not — answer any of their questions. I *can't*. Which means the clock is still counting down, becoming louder with every pass of the minute hand.

Cami doesn't know. Ward wouldn't have told her, I'm sure. That pleases me, because it means she won't treat me like I'm a ticking time bomb. I just might be able to enjoy the days I have left, a final gift I could never have allowed myself to imagine.

The room, the bed, the clothes, the company — they're perfect. For the first time in over two and a half years, I don't feel alone, cold, scared or uncomfortable. I'm determined to hold on to this feeling of freedom for as long as I can …

For as long as I have left.

CHAPTER NINE

Twelve more days pass without Ward mentioning the countdown.

When I see him every afternoon, he hands me a book as usual, and I read. Sometimes he speaks, saying words that have little or no consequence. Other times he writes, reads or just sits there, staring at nothing — or staring at me. It's the latter that makes me uncomfortable. I always keep my eyes averted when I sense him watching me, but it still makes me feel like my skin is simultaneously freezing and burning.

It's been twenty-six days since our first session together, and I still know very little about Landon Ward. What I do know is that things changed after I spent the night in his room, and not just with Ward — Enzo has been different, too. Both have been uncharacteristically protective, to the point that, the day following our dinner with the Falon family, Enzo insisted on walking me back to my suite after our training session rather than sending me off with the guards. He waited while I showered — and since it was in my own private bathroom, there was no time limit, which was absolute bliss; he ate lunch with me

— and it wasn't my usual bland, protein-enhanced meal but, instead, the leftover lasagna and vegetables that Esther had dropped off for Cami and me that morning; and then he hung out on our couch until it was time for my session with Vanik. Enzo then personally escorted me to the laboratory — which meant no guards again, as well as no handcuffs — and he proceeded to blow my mind by leaning against the wall, crossing his arms over his chest and glaring so intently at the scientist that I felt chills break out on my skin from the frosty look on his face.

"Ward spoke with you?" Enzo had said to Vanik, who nodded tightly in response. "If you think he wasn't serious, you'd be wrong. I'm here to make sure you know that."

Vanik had audibly gulped at that, and I'd been left staring at the two of them, tossing Enzo's words around in my mind and wondering what Ward had said to my greasy-haired tormentor. It sounded as if Ward had threatened Vanik. But why would he do that — and for *me*?

Whatever words Ward had used — or whatever threat Enzo's presence provided — they were enough that, for the first time ever, I left Vanik's session that day without even the slightest headache. He'd treated me like cotton wool and spent most of his time glancing nervously at Enzo, who stood flexing his muscles and scowling for the entire two hours.

I hadn't been able to contain my smile when we exited the laboratory. The grin was still on my face when Enzo escorted me directly to Ward and left me with him. I didn't care that I wasn't filtering my reaction; I was simply too happy that my brain was still intact. And I felt that I owed it to both Enzo and Ward to let them know how grateful I was, in the only way I could. My smile said all the words I couldn't. And they'd known as much.

Since that first day, Enzo has continued with the new schedule, joining me for lunch, hanging out in the suite and supervising all my sessions with Vanik. The scientist has been barely able to control his frustration. Over the last couple of days, he's looked almost ready to crack, but he still manages to keep up the cotton-wool charade, being overly gentle with me. I can't remember a time when I've felt so good, physically *and* mentally — not at Lengard, anyway. I have both Ward and Enzo to thank for that.

Cami and I don't get to see each other much — only during breakfast and after I finish my readathon sessions with her brother at the end of the day — but our moments together have been highlights of my past twelve days. Never before have I met anyone so full of life and so willing to share it. I have no idea how I can feel so connected to her after such a short time, but I do. And I know that's dangerous.

"Time for a change of plans," Ward says, jolting me from my thoughts and bringing me back into the library room. "We're doing something different for the rest of our time today."

I close my book and look up at him in question. We've never done anything new during our sessions, not even in the days that have passed since things changed. I'm curious — and apprehensive — about what he'll say next.

"It's a good thing you wear normal clothes now, Chip, because otherwise you'd look really out of place where we're going."

I blink at him and mentally replay his words: *Where* we're going?

"Come on, Esther's waiting for us."

Ward opens the door and motions for me to follow him into the corridor. I'm hesitant, uncertain and not just a little bit wary. I've seen Esther only once since our lasagna dinner, and I haven't seen her children since they fell asleep on me. I'm not thrilled about the possibility of running into her husband today, not when I only have three days left until my time runs out. But it seems I don't really have a choice. Some things haven't changed.

"Tick tock, Chip."

Ward's words mirror my thoughts perfectly, even if he's just trying to motivate me out of the room. He jerks his head in a "hurry up" gesture, so I let out a quiet breath and move past him into the hallway.

When we reach Esther's door, she greets us both warmly. The kids come running, full of smiles, their bright faces easing the tension within me. There is no sign of Falon.

"Are you guys ready?" Ward asks. "Got your shoes? Coats?"

Esther catches my wondering gaze and aims a raised eyebrow at Ward. "You didn't tell her?"

He shrugs, smiling. "I thought she might appreciate the surprise."

"You're terrible," Esther says. "Put the poor girl out of her misery while I get the kids organized."

She follows her children, calling out instructions as she goes. I'm still waiting for someone to explain why we're here — why *I'm* here — and I tap my foot on the ground, an indication to Ward that my patience is waning. His smile only grows. But he does take the hint.

"My position here at Lengard allows me to come and go at will," Ward tells me. "You've been down here for a long time — too long — so I thought you might like to take a trip topside. A change from our normal routine."

He looks uncomfortable, as if his thoughtfulness is something to be embarrassed about. Or perhaps he's just reacting to the shock I can feel plastered all over my face. I can't help it. He might as well have just announced that the Easter Bunny is real.

Topside.

As in *outside*.

I haven't been outside for nine hundred and fifty-one days, eight hours and fifty-four minutes. I haven't seen the sky in that time, breathed fresh air in that time, felt the sun's warmth on my skin in that time. My heart is beating rapidly; my breath is shallow. I'm not sure if I'm excited or terrified at the thought of leaving the safety of these walls. Of leaving my prison.

"The kids don't get out that much, so I told Esther we'd take them with us," Ward continues, scratching the back of his neck. "I — I hope that's okay."

Okay? Nothing about this is okay. Everything about this is terrifying.

And yet … everything about this is also perfect.

Three days. That's all I have left. And in taking me outside, Ward is giving me the greatest gift of all.

He's allowing me to say goodbye.

That must be the reason he won't meet my eyes. He knows as well as I do what is coming.

"Here, Jane, you can borrow this," Esther says, returning to us and handing me a black jacket. "You have a few hours of sunshine left, but it's still quite chilly out there. Autumn winds and all that."

I take the coat numbly from her and slide my arms through the sleeves, glad that I decided on jeans and a plain T-shirt after my session with Enzo. Last time I was aboveground, this would have been a passable outfit.

Esther tilts her head and studies me. "You know what? When you're back, you can keep it. It looks good on you."

My eyes widen, and I shake my head firmly — for a lot of reasons, the main one being that I won't have long to enjoy it — but she just reaches out and brushes some lint from my shoulder.

"I insist. Think of it as payment for looking after my children this afternoon."

I wish I could tell her it's been so long since I've been outside that they'll probably be the ones looking after me.

"You'll need these, as well." Esther hands me a pair of dark boots, and I send her a grateful look. Despite my new wardrobe, shoes are still not permitted.

"We're ready, Landy! We're ready!" Abby squeals, running full speed toward us. Ethan and Isaac follow her more slowly, but I can still see the excitement in their eyes.

"Make sure you stay close to Landon and Jane, and do everything you're told," Esther says to her children, straightening their coats and kissing their foreheads. "Best behavior, understood?"

A chorus of "Yes, Mummy" (Abby) and "Okay, Mum" (the boys) meets our ears, and Esther nods approvingly.

"Take care of them, Landon," she says quietly to him. Her eyes then settle on me and she adds, "*All* of them."

I'm warmed by her words, since her emphasis can't be misinter-preted. I send her a soft smile of gratitude, and in return she leans forward and kisses my forehead, just like she did with her children.

I blink once, twice, three times, fast, and swallow back the tears clogging my throat as I recall the last time such affection was bestowed upon me. Some memories are buried for a reason, but it's still hard to keep them at bay. A mother's loving touch has the power to break through even the most fortified mental defenses.

One breath, two breaths, three breaths, and I am almost in control.

"Are we going?" Ethan asks, impatient.

"We're going, buddy," Ward responds, but his watchful eyes are on me. "Why don't you wait in the corridor. Chip and I will be out in a moment."

The three children scurry through the door as Esther bids us a quiet farewell and disappears into another room. Once we're alone, I glance at Ward, wondering why he sent the kids on ahead of us. He appears torn, almost apologetic, and I look at him in question.

"I'm sorry, Chip, but the only reason my uncle agreed to me taking you topside is because I promised I'd get you to wear these."

He holds out a pair of handcuffs, and I sigh. It would have been nice to be allowed outside with complete freedom, but I understand why

Falon would object to that, especially considering, well, *everything*. I'll still be seeing the sun. Handcuffs can't take that away from me.

I press my wrists together and hold them out, nodding at Ward in a gesture for him to go ahead. He reaches for my left wrist and secures the cuff around it but takes me off guard by cuffing the other half of the pair to *his* right wrist, effectively binding me to him.

"I didn't want you wearing these," Ward continues as if he never stopped speaking, "so this was my compromise."

He jiggles our hands, and I stare mutely, wondering what he's thinking. I never imagined us having this sort of connection. I never *wanted* this sort of connection. But now …

"We're in this together, Chip. Imprisoned or free."

I have to close my eyes as his words wash over me. I can't handle the weight of them. Can't he see that he's just making this harder for me? Every kind gesture, every soft touch, every caring word just makes me more aware of what I'm going to be leaving behind.

Who I'm going to be leaving behind.

My eyes flutter back open when the fingers of his cuffed hand entwine with my own, causing my breath to hitch. He tugs me after him with a quiet warning to keep our coat sleeves covering the cuffs so as not to draw unwanted attention.

I feel another jab of heartbreaking pain when Abby skips over and laces her fingers with my free hand.

"We're going on an aventure!" she cries happily, about three hundred decibels louder than necessary.

"Adventure, Ab," Ethan corrects. "A*d*venture."

"That's what I said!" She swings our hands merrily as Ward leads us down the hallway. "Aventure!"

Before they can argue more, Ward cuts in. "You guys remember the three rules for going topside?"

"Don't talk to strangers," Abby recites.

"Stay in sight at all times," Isaac adds.

"And the last one?" Ward prompts.

"If something happens and we get split up, head straight back to the tower and wait for someone to come get us," Ethan dutifully answers.

I push aside the painful torrent of emotion and look down at the eldest boy with curiosity, wondering about his tower mention.

"Good," Ward says, bringing us to a halt in front of yet another generic-looking door.

I feel a sense of anticipation at the idea of leaving the facility, not just because of what I'll get to experience on the outside but also because, when they first brought me here, I was drugged to the point where all I can remember is the endless bland walls and then nothing until I woke up in my cell. That's it. But now ... well, now I'll get to see *beyond* the walls.

One last time.

"Sorry about this, Chip." Ward pulls a long piece of black material from his jeans pocket and turns toward me. "Director's order."

I don't have the chance to process his words before he spins me so my back is facing him, lifts his hands — bringing my bound one with him — and rests the makeshift blindfold over my eyes, binding it behind my head. This move is executed so smoothly that I'm left stunned, wondering how I didn't see it coming. Of *course* I'm not allowed to see how we're going to leave the facility. I'm a security risk. I should have known. But that doesn't mean I'm not still burning with resentment.

"Are we playing hide-and-seek, Landy?" Abby asks. "I thought we were going outside."

"Not hide-and-seek, baby girl," Ward answers, before blatantly lying. "But Chip is playing a different game. She thinks it's lots of fun."

"She doesn't look very happy," Abby observes. "We should get her an ice cream when we're outside. Ice cream makes everything better."

"That sounds like a good idea, gorgeous," says Ward. "We can all get ice creams — how about that?"

I sigh, choosing to let my irritation go, since holding on to it will only ruin what I'm about to experience.

"Are we ready?" Ward asks, and the children all respond loudly in the affirmative. "Then let's get out of here."

A soft beeping is what I hear next, along with the *whoosh* of the door sliding open. I'm then shuffled blindly forward. But I'm pulled to a halt after just a few steps. I wonder why we've stopped, until the floor underneath me moves and I realize that we must be in an elevator. We travel upward at a rate fast enough that my stomach lurches and my ears pop from the pressure.

I try to count the seconds, but it's difficult with the kids' constant chatter. I think it takes almost a whole minute before the elevator comes to a stop and Ward and Abby pull me forward.

"I was wondering when you'd get here," says a rumbling male voice. "The director said you'd put in a request for this afternoon, but it's getting so late that I figured you'd changed your mind."

I try to place the voice but have to settle on assuming the man is one of the many guards.

"Falon cleared Six-Eight-Four to go with you, too. That's weird, right? I'm not sure what he's thinking. Gotta say, though, she sure looks different in street clothes."

The guard lets out a low whistle, and I stiffen at the implication.

"Another word and I'll end your employment here at Lengard." Ward's threat comes out sharp and pointed, leaving a loaded silence — and no room for misunderstanding.

"I meant no disrespect, sir," the other man says, his words careful now.

Sir? When I first met Falon, he said something about few people getting to spend one-on-one time with Ward. But for this guard to defer to him so readily ... Just what kind of position does Ward hold here at Lengard? Why doesn't he have to wear a regulation uniform? Why does he spend so many hours with me, just reading? Why did Falon tell me to make the most of this opportunity?

I still have so few answers, to my unending frustration.

"See that it doesn't happen again," Ward tells the guard firmly.

"Yes, sir. Of course."

"Good," Ward says, and he moves on. "We're scheduled to be back by nineteen-hundred. I'll check in if that plan changes."

"But, uh, sir —"

"We won't be requiring an escort today. The director should have made that clear."

"Well, yes, but —"

"Then you have your orders. Now, let us pass."

There's a moment of silence — of hesitation? — before I hear a shuffling noise and the *whoosh* of another door sliding open.

"Thank you," Ward says, his words still terse. "That'll be all."

"But —"

"You're dismissed."

"I don't like that guy," Ethan mutters as the footsteps move away.

"Me, neither," Isaac quickly agrees.

I want to hug them both.

Abby, meanwhile, is too busy humming to herself to add her opinion, and I marvel at her little-girl ability to remain locked in a happy land despite whatever tension might be circling around her.

"This way," Ward says, leading me forward again.

Not being able to see where we're going is disorienting. I don't like that I have to trust Ward to tell me if there's a step I need to take or an obstacle in my path I should avoid. I'm on edge, and all I want to do is rip the blindfold from my eyes. But Abby's small hand still grips mine, as does Ward's. So I can do nothing but grit my teeth and hope that our journey won't end with a missed step and a broken ankle.

It's not long until I'm tugged to a halt in yet another elevator. This one has a voice prompt asking for security clearance, password included. Ward doesn't respond verbally, so I assume he's inputting the specified information by hand.

When the elevator comes to life and moves us farther upward, I marvel at just how deep underground Lengard must be. Anticipation prickles my skin. We must be very near the surface by now.

A quiet *ding* is the only indication I have that the doors are sliding open, that and the lively noises greeting my ears. It sounds like people — lots and lots of people.

Abby gives an excited squeal, squeezing my hand tightly. She tugs me forward with so much force that the tip of my booted foot catches in the gap between the elevator and the landing, causing me to trip. I know I'm about to go down, so I yank my hand from Abby's to keep her from tumbling with me, but there's nothing I can do about being shackled to Ward.

Before I can dread the coming impact, his arms snake around me, hauling me upright and into his strong body.

"I've got you," Ward whispers into my ear.

He does. He very much does have me. And he's not letting me go, though I *very much* want him to.

Or ... so I try to convince myself.

I squirm in his arms — which are still tightly wrapped around me — and the microseconds it takes for him to release me feel like years. Once free, I quickly step away, only to stumble again, because judging by the "Ow!" I hear, I've just walked into Ethan. Yet again, Ward's arms are all that save me from falling for the second time in less than a minute.

"If I didn't know any better, Chip, I'd say you just wanted to cuddle."

I don't have a chance to melt into a puddle of embarrassment, because he lets me go and almost immediately the blindfold is whipped off my head.

I blink, blink, blink and try to comprehend what I'm seeing.

The number of people makes perfect sense considering where we are. But I have no clue how we can be here. It doesn't seem possible.

I spin around and see the elevator behind us, then I whirl back to take in the sight before me again. I'm overwhelmed by unanswered questions, and I turn incredulous eyes to Ward.

All he does is send me a knowing — and dimpled — grin.

My gaze narrows, and for some unfathomable reason, he bursts out laughing.

Not one to be left out, Abby joins in with her own giggles. Ethan and Isaac just look confused — which makes three of us. Of all the questions brimming in my mind, one takes precedence: How can Lengard — a *secret government facility* — be located deep beneath Centrepoint Tower, right in the heart of Sydney?

Another important question is, how did I *get* to Sydney? The psychiatric institution I checked myself into was located on the other side of the country. Just how drugged *was* I when they delivered me to Lengard?

I'm itching to know the answers, but I release a breath and decide to let my curiosity go. With so few days left, there's little point in adding to my list of unresolved questions.

When I turn back to Ward, his humor has passed, but he still has a smile on his face as he gives our cuffed hands a tug and starts leading the way forward. Abby skips ahead with Ethan and Isaac, and Ward calls out a reminder for them to stay close. They slow down, but it's clear they're struggling to rein in their excitement.

"They don't get to come out very often," Ward tells me again as we head toward the exit of the shopping center located underneath the tower. "It's hard to keep the facility a secret if we have people coming and going all the time."

"Ice cream! Ice cream! *Ice cream*!" Abby chants, skipping around us.

I smile at her exuberance, but when we step out of the shadow of the tower and onto Market Street, it's all I can do to remain standing as I take in my surroundings.

The *noises* — the crowds, the traffic. The *colors* — the blue sky, the sunshine, the clothes. Everything is so overwhelming. There are no whitewashed walls here, no silence of forgotten dreams, no nightmares of unending futures. Instead, here there is *life.*

I move a trembling hand out in front of me, marveling at the way the sunlight whispers across my pale skin. I can't remember the last time I felt such beautiful warmth. I can't remember the last time the wind teased my hair and tickled my flesh. I can't remember the last time I felt so completely, *gloriously,* alive.

This is likely the last time I will feel any of this.

Three days isn't long enough.

But that's all I have, so I'm going to make the most of it.

"Okay, kids, do we want the park, or do we want the water?"

At Ward's question, I tear my gaze from the fluffy white clouds overhead and come back down to earth.

"Park!"

"Water!"

"*Park!*"

"*Water!*"

And thus begins the rather heated debate, until Ward reminds them that they'll have to wait longer for ice cream if we walk to Darling Harbour, whereas Hyde Park is only a few minutes away.

No one argues after that.

*

It's the perfect afternoon.

After strolling casually along Market Street — and purchasing ice creams along the way — we arrive at the park and sit around the

Archibald Fountain to enjoy our treats. By my calculations, there's only a month left until winter hits, so it's not ideal weather for ice cream. But as Abby reminds us all, any time is ice-cream time. So, enduring the wind and the spray of the fountain, I enjoy the food, and the company, as well.

The kids are delighted to be outside — almost as much as I am. They run, they jump, they squeal with joy. And when they've had enough of the park, we end up walking to the harbor after all, crossing the Pyrmont Bridge over Cockle Bay and then meandering our way back along the waterfront. A troupe of street performers doing acrobatics holds our attention for some time, and later a group of traveling magicians amazes the children so much that Ward and I eventually have to drag them away. But that's also partly because Abby starts telling anyone who will listen that "my mummy makes magical pictures when she doesn't know I'm looking."

I'm not the only person in the audience who smiles at her indulgently as she makes her claim, though it does grow old rather quickly, which is why we don't linger after the magicians finish their performance.

When the sun falls across the horizon and the light of the day begins to dim, I know the end of our outing is fast approaching. I don't want to go back, not after the explosion of wonder I've experienced this afternoon. It hasn't mattered that I've been cuffed to Ward — the children have kept me so entertained that I've barely noticed. But they're beginning to droop now as their energy wanes, and I know it's time we returned them home.

As if sensing my thoughts, Ward says, "We'd better start heading back to Lengard."

I nod in agreement and he sends me a compassionate smile, almost as if he understands that I'm trying not to think about this being my last chance to experience the outside world. There are still three days left; maybe he'll bring me out again. I hold on to that thought — it's the only thing keeping me together as we begin the journey back to the tower.

The children are unwilling to end the day, regardless of their exhaustion. But after a few words from Ward — and the promise of food back at their suite — their grumbles turn into resigned acceptance. They trudge along, knowing that they'll get to come out again at some stage in the future. I, however, have no such guarantees.

Especially given what happens next.

CHAPTER TEN

We're halfway along Market Street and nearly back to the tower when it happens. One minute the kids are three steps in front of us and chittering about the magician show, and the next Abby is screaming, "HORSIE!"

Startled, I look up just in time to see the mounted police officer on the other side of the road, and then the world shatters around me as Abby leaps into a sprint — and hurtles right out onto the street and into peak-hour traffic.

"ABBY, *NO!*" Ward yells, surging forward, yanking me with him, heedless of the oncoming vehicles.

Suddenly, Abby stutters to a halt in the middle of the street. She takes her eyes off the horse and sees the city bus headed straight at her, screeching on its brakes.

I react without thinking.

I throw out my free arm, I open my mouth and, in a voice hoarse from lack of use, I scream a word that wells up from an anguished place deep within me.

"STOP!"

At my command, the world freezes.

People halt mid-walk; they pause speaking mid-talk. Birds heading to their nests for the night rest suspended in the air. All noises cease. It is eerily quiet, eerily still. As for the bus that is now a hairbreadth away from Abby, it's immobile, trapped in place by stoppered time.

My heart is pounding, my breath trapped somewhere between my lungs and my throat. I force myself to release a strangled gasp of air, but it brings me no relief. There's nothing that can help me now; I am consumed by the terror of what I have done.

I reacted on instinct, and while I may have saved Abby's life, it was stupid. So very, very stupid. Because in saving one life, I may have just frozen the entire world — *forever*.

"It's true."

I jump nearly out of my skin and whip around to find Ward staring at me. And *blinking*.

My mouth opens in shock, and I don't have the capacity to close it. How is he not frozen when everyone else — and every*thing* else — around us is? I want to ask, but the words are stuck in my throat. It's been so long since I've said anything. And for good reason. Because when I speak, the world listens. When I speak, things happen. Like when I call out "Stop" — and the world simply *stops*.

"You're a Speaker," Ward says. He takes his eyes off me and glances around at the silent, still landscape. "And not just a Speaker. You're a Creator, aren't you? Vanik was right."

I have no idea what he's talking about, but my pulse skyrockets even more at the mention of Vanik.

"We need to get out of here," he states, still looking around the paused world. "We need to get you back underground."

He returns his gaze to me then, and whatever he must see in my expression causes his tense features to soften — if only slightly.

"Thank you for saving Abby. I mean that — really. But you should have said something about what you can do sooner. I would have been able to help you."

A choking noise is all I manage. He's wrong. No one can help me.

When it becomes clear that I have no intention of responding, his lips form a firm line and he shakes his head, stepping onto the street. Still bound to him, I follow as he strides over to Abby's motionless body and swiftly plucks her out of harm's way. She is as stiff as a mannequin in his arms, her limbs rigid and inflexible.

Once we're back on the sidewalk, Ward places her on the ground in front of us and turns to me.

I wait for him to say something, do something, *explain* something, but all I can wonder is why, why, *why* is he moving freely when no one else is?

As with everything else when it comes to Ward, it makes no sense that he is somehow able to withstand the impossible power within me.

"Whenever you're ready," he tells me.

I have no idea what he's waiting for. No idea what he expects me to do.

He takes in my expression and raises his eyebrows. "You don't know how to undo it?"

I shake my head, hoping he can read the gesture as helpless. I don't just not know how to undo it — I don't even know if it *can* be undone. I have no idea how it happened in the first place. All I know is that it's not the first time my words have changed the world — or *my* world, at least.

Ward looks astounded. "No one's told you how Speaking works? What about —"

He cuts off mid-sentence, choosing not to finish his question. If I were willing to risk causing more damage, I would beg him to continue, to help me understand. Clearly, he knows much more than he's saying. Instead, I just shake my head again.

"Wow." He blows out a breath. "Okay. Um. Wow."

He releases a burst of laughter — but it's not filled with humor. It's almost like he's having trouble believing me.

"That explains a lot."

He looks stunned, like he's not sure what to say or do. That makes two of us.

"I always wondered why my uncle asked me to take on your case," he says, rallying his thoughts. "I just had no idea that *you* had no idea. I presumed you kept silent just to be stubborn. This, though … complicates things."

What kind of a person doesn't speak for over two and a half years simply because she's *stubborn*? Then I blink when I realize that technically, he's right. It *was* stubbornness that kept me silent — because I alone understood what the consequences could be.

"There's a lot to tell you, especially if you don't know anything. But I need to talk to Falon and find out what the hell is going on before we have that conversation, so that means you need to fix up this —" he waves an arm, indicating the motionless world "— so we can get back to Lengard."

I'm pretty sure we already decided that a few minutes ago. Ward must be in shock or something.

"I need you to concentrate," Ward tells me, looking deep into my eyes. "You're a Creator, which means your words are filled with creative potential. *Literal* creative potential. As a Speaker, what you say, happens —" this much I already know, unfortunately "— so you need to use your imagination and focus on what you want to happen. In this case, I want you to think about unstopping the world. Think about life carrying on as normal. People moving, talking, going about their usual business. Close your eyes and see that picture in your mind."

I send him a skeptical look, but he returns it with a "just try it" gesture. So I follow his instructions, closing my eyes and visualizing the world doing what it's supposed to be doing.

"Now, I want you to Speak."

Ward's voice is soft enough not to disrupt my mental image.

"Say whatever comes naturally. The words don't matter as much as their intent. Just … let go and *feel* it."

Let go and feel *it?* Is he for real?

Despite my fear that I can't undo the damage I've caused, I at least try to do what he's asking. With my mental image well in hand, I open my mouth and speak for the second time in over two and a half years. The sound I make is barely a whisper, but the power behind it knows no bounds.

"Go."

I'm not sure why I used that word. Maybe because, while Ward claimed that the actual word wouldn't matter, in my head "go" is the opposite of "stop." I would have felt strange saying something like "burrito" in an attempt to make the world move again.

Especially since it *worked.*

Sounds inundate us once more, the most invasive of which is the blaring horn from the bus driver. Through the windshield, I can see his face is as white as the seagulls again soaring overhead. But there's no need for the driver to look so ashen, not anymore. While the bus is still screeching on its brakes, Abby is back on the pavement beside us.

My head is whirling. Somehow Ward coached me into undoing what I'd done — a miracle in and of itself — but there are consequences. Not the least of which is a relieved bus driver, baffled onlookers, and a terrified and confused little girl.

"Landy?" Abby looks up at him, visibly trembling.

He scoops her into his arms. "You're okay, sweetheart." He looks at me and says, "Make them forget."

My eyes widen with disbelief.

"Preferably before that cop gets over here."

Ward has no free hands, so he nods toward the mounted police officer making his way to us from across the street. Even if the spectators are shaking their heads and trying to convince themselves that what they saw must not have happened — in their eyes, one second Abby was in the middle of the road and the next she wasn't — there's no way the police officer won't ask questions. He would have heard Abby's excited squeal of "HORSIE!" and watched every heart-stopping moment of her bolting toward the animal. There is no explanation for what happened after that.

But … I still don't understand what Ward is asking me to do. Or how, exactly, I'm supposed to do it.

"Seriously — you have maybe a minute before we're all detained for questioning. I'd prefer not to spend the next few hours in a holding cell."

He has a point.

"Do it just like before," Ward tells me quickly. "Focus on what you want. Focus on the people around us — the police officer, the bus driver, all the witnesses. You don't have to picture them individually. Just center your thoughts on Abby, and imagine the people who watched that happen forgetting what they saw. Then Speak."

He's asking the impossible. But I already know the impossible is possible when it comes to me. And yet, if I do what he's asking, I could cause even more damage. What if in trying to make people forget one single event, I make them forget everything they've ever experienced? There is no undoing *that*, surely.

Ward must see the fear on my face, because his eyes capture mine, his gaze intent and steady.

"This won't mean anything to you yet, but I protect others from the words powered by Speakers like you. I can help control what happens when you open your mouth."

I suck in a breath and hear his words repeat in my mind:

Speakers like you.

Speakers like you.

Speakers like you.

Does that mean there are more people who can do what I can do? Other ... *Speakers?*

I want to demand answers, but the mounted police officer is almost upon us, so I try to stay focused on him.

"Trust me," Ward says. "I will protect them. I will protect you."

It's a whisper of promise, and God help me, I believe him. So I close my eyes and concentrate harder than I ever have before, hoping that I'm not making another mistake as I breathe out a single word.

"Forget."

I open my eyes as the second syllable falls from my lips, and I hear Ward whisper something too quiet for me to hear. Then something astonishing happens. A soft light bursts out of me and a corresponding one from Ward. The two lights merge into one, touching Abby first, lighting her eyes for less than a microsecond, then moving outward toward Isaac, Ethan, the police officer and everyone else nearby. Their eyes light up when the glow reaches them, like the flash of a camera going off in their retinas. Then, after a quick shake of their heads, they continue as if nothing strange just occurred.

"Landy, I'm hungry. How long until we're home?" Isaac asks, effectively breaking into my stunned disbelief.

It worked — it *actually* worked.

"Me, too," Abby says, squirming in Ward's arms. "I hope Mummy — HORSIE!"

I jump again at Abby's squeal, this one more excited than the last, since the horse — and its uniformed rider — is only a few feet away from us now.

"Good evening, Officer," Ward says to the policeman, who looks baffled, clearly wondering how, why and when he crossed the street.

"Can you please tell us how to get to the nearest train station?"

The police officer furrows his brow but gives a slight shrug and rattles off directions that Ward has no need for. The distraction works, however, and when the officer finishes speaking, bids us goodnight and nudges his horse away from us, I heave a sigh of relief.

"That was a little too close for comfort," Ward mutters, lowering Abby to the ground.

"I'm hungry," Isaac says again. "Is it dinnertime yet?"

Ward smiles at his cousin. There are no signs of a dimple this time, though. His entire expression seems strained, especially when his eyes flick to me and away again. It's almost like — almost like he can't stand to look at me. Now that he knows the truth.

Now that he knows I'm a monster.

"Sure, buddy. We'll be home in a few minutes and you can eat then."

Abby cries, "Hurrah! Can I read to Jane after dinner?"

She starts to move toward me, but Ward pulls her back to his side. He captures her hand in his free one, and I try not to let that small action affect me, but it does. He doesn't want her near me. And I don't blame him.

"Not tonight, sweetheart. There's somewhere else she needs to go after we drop you back to your mum."

I feel the blood drain from my face, wondering what horrors lie ahead for me.

I was supposed to have three days. But now I don't know anymore. What does it mean, now that Ward has heard me Speak? How much does it change things?

Do I even *want* it to change things?

I'm overwhelmed by fear and uncertainty as we walk in silence to the shopping center beneath Centrepoint and come to a stop beside the elevator.

"Rules are rules," Ward says, not meeting my eyes.

I don't realize what he's talking about until he lets go of Abby and draws the blindfold from his pocket. My troubled heart plummets deeper into despair as he ties it into place, a sense of entrapment pressing in on me as we step into the elevator and begin our descent.

Ward knows I am a monster now. And soon enough, Falon and the rest of Lengard will, too. I have no idea what they're going to do with me. *To* me. But if what I've suffered so far while remaining silent is any indication, my outlook is grim indeed.

I never wanted any of them to know. I tried — *so* hard — to keep it a secret. To take it to my grave with me. But … I also can't bring myself to regret what just happened, not when it means Abby is humming quietly at my side right now.

But if Ward hadn't been there, hadn't been able to guide me through it — I don't even want to think about what might have happened.

Lost in my anxiety, I'm caught by surprise when we step out of the second elevator and Ward unties the blindfold. Unending walls assail my vision, and something inside me shrivels up to hibernate once more.

Too soon, we arrive at the Falons' suite, where Esther takes one look at her nearly comatose children and has to hide a smile behind her hand. But then she glances up at Ward and me, and any trace of her amusement flees. I don't know what my face shows, and I don't dare look at him, so I wonder what she can read from our expressions.

I don't have long to wonder, because Ward is quick to make our excuses — quick to get me away from his family.

I swallow the lump that lodges in my throat as we leave their quarters and head down the whitewashed corridors again, a heavy silence between us. All the things we've left unsaid.

I'm trembling from head to toe, something Ward must feel since I'm still cuffed to him. It's the first time we've walked the hallways together when I haven't been free at his side, and that, more than anything else, tells me everything I need to know about what is coming next.

CHAPTER ELEVEN

Tick. Tick. Tick. Tick. Tick.

Swallowed by the too-comfortable chair in Director Falon's office, I feel just like the orbiting second hand of the clock on the wall. No matter how many times it moves forward, ultimately it will end up back where it started. Sixty seconds, and all that work was for nothing.

Two years, seven months and eleven days, wasted by a single word. I'm right back where I began, and it only took four letters:

S

   T

      O

        P

I don't know where Ward is. All I know is that he brought me straight to Falon's office and didn't so much as knock on the door before entering and pulling me through with him. The director was on the phone when we barged in. After one look at Ward's face, he muttered a swift, "I'll call you back," and promptly ended the call.

He rose to his feet, ordered me to take a seat and left the room with Ward in tow.

Tick. Tick. Tick. Tick. Tick.

Whole hours could be passing — days, months, years, perhaps — but all I see is that second hand going around and around. Always moving but never finding any end to its journey.

The door slides open, interrupting my thoughts, and Falon steps back into the room.

Ward isn't with him.

The director doesn't take a seat. Instead, he cocks his head to the side, assessing me. My palms begin to sweat and my nerves are zinging, telling me to do something. Flight. Fight. They don't care which — just *something*. But I do nothing except remain seated, hold his gaze and listen to the clock tick toward its unreachable destination.

It feels like an eternity before Falon's appraisal ends and he abruptly says, "Come with me, Jane. There's something I want you to see."

I blink once. Twice. Then force myself from the chair and move to leave the room. Falon shakes his head, though, and presses his hand against the touch screen mounted next to the door. Following that, he leans forward for a retinal scan. A moment passes before a *hiss* sounds and part of the wall on the left side of the office slides away, revealing a hidden exit.

"This way, please."

With a turn of his wrist, he politely gestures for me to go first.

I'm intrigued. And not just a little terrified. For all I know, he's taking me to some kind of execution chamber. But all I can see as I step forward is another long hallway.

Falon moves through after me, and the secret wall closes behind us, sealing us out of his office.

I ball my hands into fists behind my back to keep him from seeing the visible manifestation of my anxiety. Falon's eyes miss nothing, though, and I'm floored when he sends me a hint of a comforting smile. He dips his head forward, indicating that we're to move, and he starts off down the corridor.

Unlike all the other hallways I've encountered at Lengard, this one isn't on even ground. It slants downward. And soon the walls change colors — something else I've never seen. The change is gradual at first, slowly darkening from sterile white to pastel gray, smoky gray, dark gray. We've reached charcoal by the time we hit an elevator, almost like the walls themselves are saying there's something different about this hidden hallway. Warning. Danger. Take Caution.

We step into the enclosed space, and after another handprint and retinal scan from Falon, the doors seal us inside and the metal box plummets at an incredible speed. I'm not prepared for it since I hadn't imagined there was much farther down we *could* go. But we're dropping like lead, deep into the bowels of the earth.

By the time we come to a stop, my ears are blocked and I feel uncomfortably nauseous.

"It takes some getting used to," Falon says, seeing my pallid expression. "We've reinforced the walls to compensate for the biometric pressure this far below sea level, but you'll need a moment to acclimatize. Even with the air filtration system in place."

I'm already beginning to feel better, at least physically. Psychologically, I'm a wreck.

"We're almost there," Falon says.

He leads the way down a now completely black-walled hallway. The overhead fluorescent lights cast eerie shadows on our path, and while I'm no fan of the unrelenting whitewashed misery up on the higher levels, this strange blackness is disconcerting.

We soon reach the end of the hallway, and Falon raises a palm to rest it against the wall. An unseen sensor scans his hand again, and the wall slides open to reveal yet another secret doorway. He moves into the room beyond and beckons me to follow. I step forward and …

And I gape. It's all I can do not to gasp out loud.

We're standing at the entrance to a room so huge that thick stone pillars are in place to keep the tons of rock above us from caving in. The space is easily the size of a football field, but that's not what has caused my stunned reaction.

It's the people.

They're everywhere. Clustered in twos, threes, fours and more. It's clear this is some kind of training room, like a giant underground gymnasium. The space is bright and well lit, with a combination of luminous white and blue lights bouncing off the walls and pillars. It's like something out of a science fiction movie. But that might also be because of the specific kind of training these people are doing.

They're … *Speaking.*

They're saying things, and things are *happening.*

Their words are creating *responses.*

And just like when Ward guided me into making the people on Market Street forget the incident, I can see light flowing from people all around the room.

A girl to my left yells out, "Hover!" and light bursts out of her, hitting the chest of a man twice her age, three times her size. I recognize him — he was one of my rotating evaluators before Ward, poking and prodding me for a response I never yielded. Despite his bulk, the moment her word … *touches* him, his body rises from the ground and he begins to levitate.

The man barks out a laugh and crosses his legs and arms, assuming the comical pose of a genie. His eyes glint with amusement, and he calls back, "Hiccups!"

The girl makes a groaning sound, but it's cut off when his light reaches her, swallowed by the hiccups she can't stop from bubbling up from inside her.

I don't know what I feel as I watch this play out before me. Wonder, mostly, and disbelief. Hope, too, at my sudden knowledge: I am not *alone*.

I also feel the sting of resentment. For over two and a half years I've been locked away, with no idea there were other Speakers in the hidden depths of Lengard. These people ... *my* people ...

How did I not know they were here?

... Why didn't anyone *tell* me?

Heart pounding, I turn to look at the next group demanding my attention, a set of six people around my age, each person holding what appears to be an imaginary gun. Three of them wear green armbands, three wear blue and all of them are running, ducking, hiding from what I understand to be the opposing teams. They use the pillars, they use other people, but mostly they use the invisible weapons in their hands.

"Bang!" one of the green-banded girls cries out, aiming around a pillar at one of the blue-banded boys.

The boy is caught by surprise, and he lets out a grunt as the light that poured from the invisible gun touches his stomach. I rock backward in amazement when a bright splatter of green paint appears across the front of his T-shirt.

In response, he raises his hands — or, rather, his "weapon" — and takes aim back at her, calling out, "Bang, bang!"

Two wisps of light burst forth, and the green-banded girl ducks behind the pillar just in time for them to soar right into the path of a blue-banded Asian girl. The new girl jerks her shoulder at the impact of the light and stumbles backward as splashes of blue paint burst across her collarbone and her upper thigh. Two shots, two points of contact.

"Hey! I'm on your team, you ass!" she cries out.

The guy raises his hands in the air, one still gripping what looks like nothing. "My bad, Keeda! I didn't see you!"

"Yeah, yeah, because I'm invisible, right?" The girl — Keeda — rolls her eyes and swipes at her paint-splattered clothes, only smearing the color further. Meanwhile, the green-banded girl has already taken off and is now engaged in an imaginary-gun battle with another blue-banded opponent farther into the room.

"I just used the last of my ammo on you," the boy says, shaking the empty air between his hands as if listening for something. "I need to go get another infusion if I want to stay in the game. Cover me?"

Keeda nods and runs off with him, shooting green-banded opponents as they go along, disappearing deeper into the training room.

I don't know what I'm more surprised about: people using intangible weapons for a paintball skirmish match and discharging them with *words,* or Keeda and the other blue-banded boy saying normal sentences to each other among the rest and those words having no consequences. If I had repeated just two of Keeda's words — "I'm invisible" — no one would have ever seen me again. And I don't even want to think about the result that "you ass" could have produced. So how ...

"*Jane?*"

I whip my neck to the side and feel my pulse skitter erratically at the sight of Cami jogging over to me, looking as stunned to see me as I am to see her.

Cami is here. In this place. The betrayal I feel — it's like fire burning in my blood.

Why.

    Didn't.

        She.

            Tell.

                Me?

Her eyes flick from me to Falon. "What — um, what are you doing here, Uncle Rick?"

She looks nervous, agitated, uncertain. I'm feeling the same way.

"According to Landon, Jane had a breakthrough today and, in doing so, saved Abby's life," Falon says.

It's his only indication of gratitude for my earlier actions. But my heart still twists with alarm, especially with his next words.

"It would appear that she's finally ready to commit herself to the program here at Lengard."

The program. The program everyone keeps mentioning but no one has ever explained. I'm beginning to understand now. But — *God* — I have so many questions.

I was given a month to show Lengard that I was worth keeping alive. I guess the only proof they ever needed was for me to open my mouth.

Maybe that was what they were waiting for all along. For me to "commit" myself. For me to prove that … that I am one of them.

But now that they know, where does that leave me?

"What kind of breakthrough?" Cami asks. "Is Abby okay?"

"Go find your brother if you want the details, Camelot." Falon waves a hand in the air dismissively. "Jane and I have much to discuss, so you'll have to excuse us."

He starts walking forward, gesturing for me to keep up. I stumble after him, unable to bring myself to look back at Cami for fear of what I will see in her expression. For fear of what I will feel, wondering how long she has known about me, why she has concealed the truth.

"In here, Jane," Falon directs me. He has stopped outside a door lodged in the side of the massive training room.

I step through to discover a classroom-sized rectangular room with walls made of glossy black material. The floor and ceiling are black, too, though both have veins of pearlescent stone spiderwebbing along the surfaces. Blue and white lights just like those in the larger training area illuminate this new, smaller space, showing me that there is absolutely nothing in the room. No furniture, no books, nothing.

Other than the door we used to enter, there are no exits.

That door slides closed and seals with a *hiss*. Now Falon and I are trapped together in this glossy room. Less than a month ago he was ready to write me off. Now I have no idea what his intentions are.

"I was never entirely certain about you," Falon says.

He looks relaxed, but his eyes are assessing me.

"Vanik was always sure, right from the very beginning. The moment you checked yourself into that institute and your file hit the system, he saw your scans, read your readings and told us we simply had to retrieve you. But when so much time passed and you didn't so much as make a sound ..."

He shrugs, almost as if he's apologizing for his doubt, and continues, "Vanik was adamant about you being a Speaker — and a powerful one, at that. But Landon tells me you're not *just* a powerful Speaker. Do you know how rare Creators are, Jane?" Falon shakes his head, smiles a small smile. "You have no idea, do you?"

Thump. Thump. Thump. My heartbeat is loud in my ears, speeding up with every word that falls from his mouth. I want him to hurry up and tell me. And I want to run away before he can. I'm not sure which I want most, but since I'm frozen to the spot, the choice is taken from me.

"How much do you know about a medication called 'Xanaphan'?"

I stare blankly at him, trying to calm my heart enough to not miss anything.

Falon cocks his head to the side. "Forgive me. Perhaps I should rephrase my question. Have you heard of a medication called 'Xanaphan'? Judging by your lack of knowledge when it comes to Speakers, I'm presuming you haven't."

He'd be correct in such a presumption.

"Xanaphan was created by a team of Australian biochemists and pharmacologists who began testing on human volunteers around forty years ago. Fortunately — or unfortunately, depending on how you look at it — there weren't a huge number of willing test subjects. It was an experimental drug at best, and since its target consumer group was women struggling with infertility, only a small number of those were desperate enough to accept the potential side effects of the medication."

He looks deep into my eyes and continues, "Those complications ended up being more severe than anticipated, and while ninety percent of the women taking the drug succeeded in falling pregnant, almost all of those mothers ended up dying during labor. Around half the children survived, but the loss of life was catastrophic enough for the drug to be recalled from any further human trials.

"After a redesign of the medication, twenty-five or so years ago, it was cleared for human testing again. It was much more successful this time, even if it took longer for women to conceive — sometimes up to ten years after they were first injected with the drug. But this time very few of them suffered complications during childbirth. By all accounts, the medication had enabled them to fall pregnant and carry their children full-term, just like any other naturally occurring conception.

"Now," Falon goes on, "during the time the second round of women were given the drug and slowly began to fall pregnant, the original group of surviving children entered their pubescent years. That's when strange things began to occur."

Goose bumps rise on my skin as I hang on to his every word.

"Things started … happening. Unexpected things. Unnatural things. Tests showed that there was something neurologically abnormal about the children whose mothers had been medicated pre-pregnancy. During puberty, that abnormality in those children … *blossomed,* so to speak. Usually out of the blue, with no warning whatsoever."

An echo of my own voice tries to float across my mind, a whisper of a memory, a vile scream of unforgettable words. But I refuse to acknowledge it, and I shove it away.

"It was as if a switch flicked in their minds, and suddenly they were able to Speak things into existence. Words to make, words to break."

Falon's eyes are glazed; he's looking at me, but I don't think he's really seeing me right now. Wherever he is, it's far away. At least until he shakes his head.

"As soon as the scientists began to realize what was happening with the first-round teenagers, they canceled the drug testing — forever this time. But it was too late to un-medicate the women participating in the second round of trials. There was nothing the scientists could do but wait and watch and see if the changes to the drug would make any difference with the next group of children. Meanwhile, the first teenagers were rounded up by a secret branch of the government and sequestered into highly classified military-run laboratories for testing. And so Lengard was born."

Finally, some answers. But now I have even more questions. Was my mother a part of this drug trial? Is that why I am ... what I am? Did anyone tell her what the medication would eventually do to me? Did she know what I would become?

I wish I could ask her.

Falon's features tighten, and he turns from me toward the far side of the room, unseeing again.

"The tests those original teenagers underwent were ... unpleasant. The government was dealing with a branch of science still not understood today, power that could only be described as supernatural. Because of that, some of the tests were unconventional. Unethical, even. But those teenagers were seen as a threat to the rest of the world, and the government needed to make sure they wouldn't become terrorists who could call forth violence or hatred by throwing a scant number of syllables into the wind."

If I didn't know that what he said was possible, I'd scoff and think he was exaggerating. But I could easily be one of those terrorists. All I would have to do is open my mouth.

"The tests they used were perhaps too severe at times, since not all of the teenagers made it out unscathed," Falon continues. "Some of them died. Some killed themselves. A handful escaped, only to be taken down on the outside. But those who remained and made it through the testing were eventually seen as warriors, not terrorists. Warriors capable of wielding words as weapons."

Is *that* what the program is? The government's mission to train some kind of … super soldier? Someone who would only need to open his or her mouth to stop a war? Or to *start* one?

Is *that* what they expect me to "commit" to?

"The testing changed then," Falon says. "It became less about evaluating the adolescents and more about nurturing them. They were encouraged to find their limits, to discover the scope of their strengths and weaknesses. The kids were put through what was termed the 'Genesis Project' and trained to become the government's secret weapons. Their unique abilities would be used for the greater good."

Falon shakes his head again, as if he struggles to believe his own words. I have no such trouble, since I know what I just saw. Those others — the Speakers in the next room — they've all been through the same as me. And despite my trepidation, despite my resentment at being kept in the dark, I'm also filled with relief. I've kept myself isolated for years, but now … now I am one of many.

"Time passed," Falon says, drawing my eyes back to him. "The teenagers continued their Genesis training and grew into adulthood. Most of their time was spent learning how to control their abilities — and to this day they continue to stretch their self-discipline and fine-tune their talents, as you saw for yourself just a few minutes ago." He nods toward the training room.

"As the years progressed, it became clear that the effects of Xanaphan were the same in the second round of children as the first,"

Falon goes on, telling me something I now already know. "But since the records were destroyed when the experiment failed, it's impossible to keep tabs on all the families. We can only wait and watch for any supernatural events to unfold. When that happens, we send out Genesis agents to collect the new Speakers and bring them here to train in what we have termed the 'Exodus Project.' It's the Genesis do-over — the way it *should* have been done the first time. The Exodus teens are protected from the extreme tests the Genesis Speakers had to suffer through. They just have to train, to develop control and refine their skills. And we're finding that they're much stronger, much more resilient than their senior counterparts. It's fascinating."

There are many words to describe what I have been through thanks to this Xanaphan drug. *Fascinating* is not one of them.

I'm desperate to ask Falon all the questions he's yet to answer. But I can't. I can't open my mouth, because ...

Because I can't control what will happen if I do.

Even though there are now others like me, I'm still a monster.

I always will be. And no one — *no one* — can convince me otherwise.

"You're a part of the Exodus Project now, Jane," Falon says, his voice quiet but heavy with meaning. "In saving Abby's life today, you showed us what you can do. You proved your worth to the program. And now it's time for you to begin your real training."

CHAPTER TWELVE

I don't have a chance to process his last words, because the door hisses open and Ward walks into the room. He nods once to the director, but his eyes skip over me as if I'm not here. There's not a hint of warmth on his face, and I wonder about his icy reception. If anything, *I* should be giving *him* the cold shoulder, especially after everything I've just learned. Everything he could have — *should* have — told me in the past month.

"Perfect timing, Landon. We've just finished our history lesson." Falon turns to me and says, "Landon was a stroke of genius on my part. I knew you weren't being receptive to any of the other evaluators, and after so much testing, as I said earlier, I'd all but given up hope. But then I thought, why not try something different? After all, you'd been isolated for so long — perhaps what you really needed was a companion. A friend, even. Someone you could learn to trust, someone who could … *chip* through those walls you've built around yourself."

I can't help flinching violently at his word choice, one that alludes to far more than all the rest put together. Ward makes a sudden, jerking movement, but he then freezes in place, stopping himself from what, I don't know. I don't turn my searching gaze to him, because Falon isn't done yet.

The director continues mercilessly, "Someone who could take you out of your comfort zone enough that you would eventually … slip up. And I must say, Jane, Landon played his part perfectly, don't you think?"

He might as well have punched me in the stomach, so gut-wrenching is my understanding of his words. Was it all an act? Everything that happened during our month together? Is that what Falon is saying?

"In defense of his character, Landon wasn't eager to play along, especially after he first met you. But one day he will be the next director of Lengard, and he understands what that requires more than most," Falon says. "He listened dutifully to my suspicions about you, and he was aware that I wanted him to get close enough to see what you would reveal. He had to make you like him, Jane. His job was to make you trust him, and he performed better than I could have hoped."

I stare at the wall. *No, no, no.* He's wrong. I never trusted Ward. I wouldn't let myself. All along, I was careful.

But … somehow along the way I must have slipped, I realize. I wouldn't be hurting so much right now if it wasn't true. I wouldn't be feeling so completely and utterly betrayed.

"I can see this upsets you, but you must understand, Landon was just doing what was required of him, Jane. We all have a part to play. The Exodus Project is too important to let a talent like yours be ignored. You'll eventually realize it was for the best, that the end justifies the means."

The end justifies the means. I can't believe what he's telling me. But I know it's true, because when I force myself to look up at Ward, there is not one drop of warmth in his expression. He might as well be a different person.

He was Falon's puppet all along.

"The good news — and there *is* good news, Jane — is that you already have a rapport with Landon. Once you accept that his actions were necessary, you'll find it easier to acclimatize to your new training. He'll be in charge of teaching you everything you need to know about Speaking. The sooner you realize that he can help you, the better off you'll be."

My stomach roils at the thought of having to spend more time with Ward now that I know the truth.

Oblivious to my inner turmoil, Falon sounds almost affectionate as he says, "I'm very much looking forward to seeing what you can do with that enormous talent of yours, Jane, especially now that you'll be staying with us indefinitely."

Maybe I would have been better off leaving this world in three days, if this is the alternative. But while I now understand that I was manipulated into this situation, part of me can't help feeling a trickle of hope at the possibilities my new future might bring.

Assessing me one last time, Falon gives a satisfied curl of his mouth and turns to Ward. "She's all yours, Landon. Are the others on their way?"

I still can't bring myself to look at Ward, but from the corner of my eye I see him nod as he answers, "They're just finishing their training for the day. They won't be long."

Falon makes a sound of approval. "I'll leave you to it, then. Report back to me when you're done."

He doesn't wait for Ward to agree before he strides purposefully from the room.

The moment the door seals behind him, silence descends between the two of us. I sneak a glance at Ward, noting that every line in his body is rigid, like he's waiting to see what I'll do now that we're alone. But I can barely think straight, since I keep replaying Falon's words in my head. As much as I don't want to believe him, I know he was telling the truth. Ward was just playing me; trying to get me to open up, to trust him enough that I would lower my defenses and let him in. Every soft look, every dimpled grin, every gentle touch, every hand squeeze was a part of some grand manipulation.

Despite how dangerous I am, perhaps I'm not the only monster in the room.

Ward sighs loudly. His eyes lock on mine, his once-warm gaze cutting through me like frozen daggers. When he opens his mouth, there is nothing familiar in the way he speaks to me.

"There are a few things you need to know before the others arrive," he says.

His tone is crisp and to the point. I realize that's how he's going to play this. He's not going to defend Falon's accusations, because they were true. From here on out, he's going to keep everything clinical, factual. No room for anything else. He doesn't have to fake a friend-ship with me — not anymore.

"I presume Falon told you about Xanaphan, but I'm guessing he didn't explain much more than that."

I nod, even though it's not a question. I'm just pleased I've managed to swallow back my emotions. I won't let him see how upset I am. I'll take my lead from him and never let him know how much he hurt me. From now on, he's back to being just my evaluator. My *trainer*.

His eyes narrow slightly as he takes in my nod. "You can talk freely in here. This room is soundproof. More than that, the black rock surrounding us —" he waves a hand, indicating the glossy material "— is called 'Karoel.' It's a rare mineral that acts as a buffer and blocks the power behind Speakers' words. No words you Speak will be able to pass outside this room, nor will any unintentional consequences. And the words you *do* Speak in here will be harder to summon than elsewhere, making it less easy for you to lose control."

I want to believe him — I really do. The idea of being able to talk freely, even in this small, dark room, is something I desperately wish for. But I've been so careful for so long, and I'm not willing to make any more mistakes. Mistakes like trusting this new, cold Ward. I cross my arms over my chest and raise my chin. He reads my meaning clearly, if the muscle ticking in his jaw is any indication.

"You'll have to talk eventually. You need to train, and to train you need to Speak. If you don't, you'll be kicked out of the program. You've bought yourself some time, having shown your raw abilities earlier today, but make no mistake, Six-Eight-Four: Lengard has no place for unwilling, untrainable soldiers."

I feel as if he's slapped me. Not because of his threat, though that doesn't sit well. But because of what he called me.

Six-Eight-Four.

Not "Chip."

Not even "Jane Doe," the unidentifiable, breathing corpse.

I am nothing. No one.

I am a test subject, not even worthy of a name.

I bite the inside of my cheek to keep the crushing weight of emotion from revealing itself through my expression.

Ward's face hardens further at what he must assume is my indifference.

"From now on, your days will be spent down here to keep you fully immersed in the Exodus Project," he tells me. "Your psych evaluations with Dr. Manning and your physical training with Enzo have been suspended indefinitely, and your sessions with Vanik will also be put on hold."

I can't keep the hopeful look off my face, until he adds, "Unless you fail to cooperate with us and we need a way to … motivate you."

I'm calling him every dirty name I can think of in my mind right now. What happened to the Ward who took care of me? The one who embraced me in a bathroom while I clung to him for dear life? The one who teased me, held my hand, moved me out of a miserable cell and into an actual home? Who is this stranger in front of me, threatening me with *Vanik* of all people?

If I were braver, I would ask him if any of it was real. But I'm still too afraid to open my mouth, even with his promises about the sound-proofed, protected room.

His promises mean nothing to me now. Just as they never will again.

The door hisses open before Ward can say anything else, and four people walk in. Two of them I already know.

"What's up, JD?" Enzo sends me a wink and a knowing grin. "It's about time you joined the fold. I thought you were never gonna Speak."

I feel as if the ground is falling out from underneath me. Did *everyone* keep this secret from me?

"You okay, Jane?" Cami asks quietly, walking over and placing her hand on my arm.

I step back, breaking her contact and avoiding her gaze. But not before I see a flash of hurt flicker across her face.

I can't deal with the fact that Cami is here right now. Or Enzo. I can't handle the idea that they were a part of the performance, too. Playing a role, just like Ward.

Instead, I look at the two new faces. One of them I recognize as the paintball girl, Keeda, who still has blue smears across the front of her clothes and in her dark, over-the-shoulder braid.

The other boy at her side is unknown to me. His black hair is buzzed short at the sides but styled with a bright-red Mohawk on the top of his head. He also has an eyebrow ring and a lip ring, with ears so pierced that I can barely see the skin through the metal.

"Guys, this is JD," Enzo says. "JD, meet Keeda —" he points to the girl, and she waves a paint-covered hand in my direction "— and Crew —" he motions to the metal-pierced Mohawk guy, who stares unflinchingly at me. "Sneak is around here somewhere, as well, but he's shy, especially near girls. He'll show himself when he's ready."

I … have no idea what he means by that.

"She goes by 'Jane,'" Cami says.

Her words are soft, and I can hear in them that she's still upset about my earlier brush-off.

Enzo gives a one-shouldered shrug. "'JD,' 'Jane' — whatever."

"Neither," Ward interjects, his tone hard. "She goes by her real name. If she refuses to tell us what that is, then you'll address her as 'Six-Eight-Four.'"

All eyes look to me, and saliva pools in my mouth. I swallow it down and keep my lips sealed. I don't care if I can talk safely in this room. They can't have who I am. I even convince myself that I don't care if they call me "Six-Eight-Four." It's just a name — I won't let it upset me. Because my real name, my *identity,* is the only thing left in the world that truly belongs to me. I won't give them that.

"Let's, uh, let's just go with 'Jane' for now," Enzo says when it becomes clear that Ward and I are at a standoff. "I'm sure JD will update us when she's gotten to know us all better."

Fat chance, Enzo. But I still send him a grateful look. I don't know where he fits in all this, but at least it seems like he's on my side.

Keeda jumps in before Ward can argue. "Why are we here, Landon?" Her arms are crossed defiantly over her chest. "You said you wanted to use us as examples?"

"*Jane* —" Ward's biting inflection speaks volumes "— is naive to the world of Speakers. She knows nothing about us, about what we can do, about how we do it. You're some of the strongest Exodus recruits down here. The director thinks a demonstration might help her understand better than a lecture."

Crew raises his pierced eyebrow. "She doesn't know what she can do? How's that possible? Has she lived under a rock?"

"Something like that," Ward says.

I wonder if he's recalling my prison cell as clearly as I am.

"It seems she's aware of what *she* can do," he adds, "but she's ignorant to the abilities — and limitations — of other Speakers."

"What *can* she do?" Keeda asks, looking at me with curiosity.

"That doesn't matter," Ward says, his tone firm, "since you're here to show her what *you* can do."

"Why don't you try explaining it to her first," Cami says.

Her voice is stronger now, and the hurt has been replaced by something fiercer. It takes me a moment to realize that she sounds angry — at Ward.

"Like someone should have done, oh, I don't know, maybe when she first arrived at Lengard?" she continues. "It might have been a better idea than locking her up in a prison cell for *years*. Did anyone think of that?"

"Cami, enough," Ward warns.

She throws her hands out. "No, Landon. It's not enough. If even half of what I've heard she's been through is true, it will never be enough."

He regards her through narrowed eyes. "Are you done?"

She returns his gaze, and we all wait to see what will happen next — me most of all. But when Ward doesn't waver, Cami makes an aggravated sound, spins on her heel and storms from the room.

CHAPTER THIRTEEN

Silence descends after Cami's abrupt exit. Then Enzo clears his throat and says, "Right. Well. To play the mediator, here are the basics, JD — er, Jane. The real quick version."

He ignores the glowering Ward and hurries on with his explanation.

"For whatever reason, Speakers don't all have the same ability with words. But we fit under three main categories — physical, mental and emotional — even if our actual abilities differ within those labels. Take Crew, for example." He jerks his chin toward the pierced guy. "His gift is a physical one, and while we don't usually label Speakers with specific names because there are so many different kinds of abilities, we still like to affectionately call him a 'Slayer.'"

Ignoring my puzzled look, Enzo turns to the Mohawked guy. "Sock it to me, Crew. I'll hit Cami up later. Just do me a favor and keep it shallow."

I don't understand their interaction until Crew sends a smirk in my direction and strikes a finger through the air. "Slash," he says, and light surges out of him.

I gasp when the light collides with Enzo, causing a deep cut to open on his upper arm. He's wearing a sleeveless tank, so I know my eyes haven't imagined the magical injury on his dark skin that appeared from nothing.

Enzo hisses out a curse and tears a strip off the bottom of his shirt, using it to stem the flow of blood. "What the hell, man! You call that shallow?"

Crew shrugs. "Like you said, Cami will fix you when you find her. Don't be such a baby."

Enzo grumbles some very unflattering words and ties the cloth tightly around his arm. Even with the pressure, blood quickly soaks through the makeshift bandage, and my insides churn unpleasantly. Not just from the sight of all that red but also from the power Crew just displayed and the delight he seemed to take in doing so.

"Some Speakers have very little respect for others." Enzo throws a glare at Crew and turns to me again. "People like Crew can use words to damage others physically, mentally or emotionally, depending on which of the three categories they fit under."

I can see how the government might have a reason to fear people like Crew. And why they'd want to use people like him, too. He'd be the perfect foot soldier, wounding the enemy before a single gun was fired.

"There are plenty of other physical gifts, ones that *don't* involve hurting people — both Cami and Sneak have them, along with a stack of other Speakers here — so I'm sure you'll see some other examples over the coming days."

I'm intrigued and want to know more right away, just as I'm curious about this Sneak person who has been mentioned twice already, but Ward clears his throat, his patience clearly waning.

With more courage than I would ever be able to summon, Enzo frowns at him and says, "Bro, you said yourself that we're here because

Falon wants us to demonstrate our abilities. It won't take long, so mellow out and quit acting like such a dick about it."

I suck in a breath, not sure if I want to laugh or cower.

Enzo chuckles at the nonverbal response Ward offers and turns his dark eyes back to me. "Next up we have your mentals," he says, with a quirk of his lips at his own wording. "Take Landon, for instance. He's what we call a 'Protector,' since he has an extremely rare protective ability that he uses to help control the power and intent behind the words Speakers use. It's almost like he can *see* the words that are Spoken and can help shape them, guide them, make them safe. Basically, he protects anyone or anything that might be affected by Spoken words — and in some cases, he protects the Speakers from themselves, too."

Remembering how Ward helped me reawaken the world and then make everyone on Market Street forget Abby's near disaster, I have at least a vague understanding of what Enzo is saying. Curious, I throw a glance Ward's way, wondering if he'll give another demonstration, but his glowering expression is enough for me to swiftly turn back to Enzo.

"There are other mental abilities, like being able to create illusions or influence dreams or narrate stories so vividly that they come to life," Enzo goes on. His features tighten as he adds, "There are also some very powerful and potentially very *dangerous* mental abilities, like being able to force people to do things against their will or suggest changes in thought patterns."

A shiver runs down my spine at the very idea of such abilities.

"Then there are mentals like Keeda here, whose words can have a hypnotic effect." Enzo turns to the paint-smeared girl, eyebrows raised. "Keed?"

Looking straight into my eyes, Keeda says, "You're so very tired."

A pulse of light shoots from her into me, and my sudden exhaustion is so crippling that I nearly collapse right onto the ground. A yawn overtakes me, then another, and my eyelids flutter shut before I hear a voice as if from far away saying, "Clear." I see a flash again, and the next moment I'm back to normal.

Keeda is still staring at me, and I hastily break eye contact, not wanting to see what other ways she might try to use her power on me. What if she can somehow force me to Speak without my consent?

I'm certain my face is an open book right now, my unease clear for all to see. Indeed, the blue-splattered girl shakes her head as if she can read my thoughts.

"Making Speakers say anything against their will, even just normal words, is one of our biggest limitations," Keeda tells me. "The kind of control it would require to break through another Speaker's natural defense mechanisms ..." She shakes her head again. "I don't know of anyone in either the Genesis or Exodus generations with that much control, that much power."

That, at least, brings me some relief.

"You still look worried," Keeda observes, and my eyes flick up to hers again. Big mistake. Because the moment they do, she cocks her head to the side and says, "Tell us your real name."

I see the flash and feel the hypnotic words wash over me, and just like the first time, they're captivating. I know I should respond, should open my mouth, but something is stopping me. Something inside me is saying I don't have to listen, that I can ignore, that it's my choice. I hold on to that something, I revel in the security it offers, and when the light that accompanies Keeda's quiet "Clear" comes, I blink quickly and look at her in amazement.

She sends me a half smile. "See what I mean? Natural defense mechanisms."

I return her smile tentatively, hoping she can tell I'm grateful she took the time to ease my concerns.

Enzo reclaims my attention by saying, "The last category is Speakers with emotional gifts. Some can manipulate the way others feel … make you happy, sad, angry, embarrassed or whatever. Some can give compliments and offer flattery so believable that you'll never doubt yourself again. Others can do the opposite."

I don't revel in the idea of someone influencing my emotions, but before I can linger too long on the negatives, Enzo continues.

"I'm in the emotional category, since I can use words to encourage others, to motivate and inspire people."

The teasing glint in his eyes makes my stomach plummet, and I brace for what he's about to say next.

"I don't think you need a demonstration, because I've been Speaking to you ever since we first met," Enzo admits, without the slightest hint of shame. "I may have … *encouraged* you to be more dedicated to your training than you would have normally been."

And there it is.

Here I thought I just enjoyed my personal training sessions because they gave me a modicum of control in my otherwise restricted life. But now I know that even those feelings were a lie. Or if not a lie, not entirely my own. I was *encouraged*.

Son of a —

"Hey, it worked," Enzo says, cutting into my thoughts after noting my stormy gaze. "You're fitter than Wonder Woman and pretty damn kick-ass these days. You can thank me later."

He's just taken away one of the only things that I considered mine. There will be no offerings of gratitude.

Ward makes a sound in the back of his throat, and Enzo seems to realize that he'd better hurry it along.

"Right," he says, pressing a hand to his still-bleeding arm. I feel myself soften toward him — but only slightly. "So, that's us. We're a talented bunch, sure, but there are other kinds of Speakers out there, too." He gestures toward the massive training room beyond these four walls. "There are some who can make you believe ridiculous lies, some who can command animals, some who can convince you that you played the leading role in a fictional story and heaps of others. Those are just a fraction of the Speaking abilities we've come across."

I can't even begin to process the scope of what he's saying. All these different abilities. I'm not — I'm starting to wonder if perhaps I'm not like them at all. Because … I don't fit under any of the categories Enzo has mentioned. Physical, emotional, mental … are they the only options?

"Every Speaker has strengths and weaknesses according to their type of ability, but all of us are limited to using words in one specific way," Enzo goes on. "There's only one kind of Speaker who has no limitations, and that's —"

"Creators," Ward cuts in, his eyes firmly fixed on me. "Creators have no limitations."

A chill slides down my spine.

"Creators have all the strengths, none of the weaknesses," Enzo states. "They don't fit in any of the three categories, since they can literally do *everything*. The only other kind of Speaker who has even close to that sort of power is a Destroyer, but there aren't any of those around anymore. And they still have nothing on Creators, who can do whatever they want with any words they want. They can create the unimaginable, unleash the impossible. They're the ultimate weapon."

The ultimate weapon. The ultimate monster. He couldn't be more correct.

"They're also power-obsessed psychos," Crew drawls.

Part of me marvels that this scary-looking, metallic-laden Slayer who can cause immeasurable pain with a single word has the audacity to call *anyone* a psycho.

"Maybe. Maybe not," Enzo says, plucking at his makeshift bandage. "There's only ever been one Creator on record, and since he died ten years ago, it hardly matters either way."

"After everything he did ..." Keeda actually shudders. "Ultimate weapon or not, that kind of power ..." She trails off again, lost to some dark memory. "We're better off without them."

I can still feel Ward's gaze on me, but I refuse to look at him. I'm waiting for him to speak up. To tell them what I am. For him to awaken in them the fear that lies just beneath the surface at the very idea of a Creator being in their midst. I want to know what happened to the last one ten years ago. I want to know what memory holds Keeda captive and what could cause Crew to label someone a "power-obsessed psycho."

I want to know so many things.

But mostly, I want to know why moments have passed and Ward remains silent. So I succumb to the temptation and look up at him. Immediately I become trapped in his bright-green stare, and everything around us fades away. He raises his eyebrows just slightly, enough for me to notice but not to draw attention from anyone else. Almost like he's challenging me to speak up for myself. To tell them my deepest, darkest secret. To share that I'm the monster they fear.

"So, that's the basic introduction," Enzo says, and I force my eyes back to him. "Lando, you need anything else from us? Or can we leave you both and go grab some grub?"

I try to pretend that my heart isn't thumping anxiously at the idea of everyone leaving me alone with Ward. It's a useless endeavor.

"You can go," Ward tells them, and my shoulders hunch in resignation. "Crew, you have tomorrow morning free, right? Swing by after breakfast and you can help out with a lesson on intention. Enzo, you up for being his punching bag?"

Enzo makes an unhappy sound. "As long as Cutter Freak over here —" he jerks his head at Crew "— controls his inner sadist, and someone makes sure Cami is nearby in case there are any 'accidents' —" he makes quotation marks with his fingers "— then sure, whatever."

At Ward's nod, the others turn to head toward the door. Keeda sends me a half smile and a wave goodbye, but Crew walks off without looking back.

Enzo seems torn about leaving us. Or that's what I guess, until he inexplicably says, "Sneak, buddy, you coming?"

I nearly jump out of my skin when a soft, disembodied voice responds, "Yeah, Enz. But I wanna meet her first."

Then I *do* jump in the air when a semitransparent boy materializes less than a foot away from me. I stumble backward, trip over my feet and start to fall, but Ward's hand snakes out to grab my elbow, and he hauls me back upright. I jerk my arm from his grip and sidestep away, not sure who I want to be farthest from — him, or the ghost boy.

"Hi," the boy says, with a timid wave.

He's still in that gawky-limbed growing stage, making me guess he's around fourteen or so. He has auburn hair layered like a bird's nest on top of his head. When I just stare at him, he glances bashfully at the ground, pushes wire-framed glasses up his nose and shuffles his feet uncomfortably.

"I didn't mean to scare you," he mumbles, looking like he wants to disappear again.

"This is Sneak," Enzo says, clapping a hand on the shoulder of the partially see-through boy. "His physical ability makes him like a human chameleon, since he can use words to blend into his surroundings or even disappear entirely."

"I'm still learning control," Sneak tells me, pink spreading across his cheeks. "Ever since I first Spoke, I haven't been able to turn back to fully solid." He flutters his hands downward to indicate his body. "This is the best I can manage for now."

"Don't worry, bud, you'll get there," Enzo encourages. "We all have to start somewhere."

Sneak nods his agreement and sends Enzo a small smile, pushing his glasses up again. "Do you think they're serving chocolate pudding in the mess hall tonight?"

Mess hall? Do the others not live in personal quarters like Ward and Cami? There is still so much to learn about Lengard.

Enzo laughs and slings his noninjured arm around the younger boy's neck. "Why don't we go and find out? Catch you later, Lando. And I'll see you in the morning, JD."

Whether he forgot Ward's order about my name or he just chose to ignore it since most of the others have already left, I'm not sure. I send him a tight smile, which he returns with a full grin, then he leads the ghost boy out the door.

The moment it seals behind them, I feel an acute sense of discomfort.

When the silence stretches on and finally becomes too much, I fortify myself and glance up, to find Ward watching me. I keep my expression open, hoping he can read the confusion, the frustration, the *wonder* I'm feeling bubbling up inside me. How can any of this be possible? And what, exactly, do they expect from me? To be trained as … one of their warriors? A limitless Creator — no wonder they kept me around for so long, waiting in hope that I might eventually prove my worth. The joke is on them, though, since I can't give them what they want. Limitless, I might be, but I won't risk the damage I could cause. The damage I *will* cause.

… The damage I *have* caused.

"There are two rules I expect you to follow," Ward tells me without any lead-up. "The first is that you'll tell no one that you're a Creator. You saw how they reacted just at the memory of one who has been gone for a decade. Your situation is complicated enough without others knowing the truth. Agreed?"

I grit my teeth but nod. I may be a monster, but that doesn't mean I *want* people to be afraid of me.

"The second is that you will commit yourself to the Exodus Project.

That means training, which in turn means *participation.* You'll be required to Speak. I can't teach you how to control your ability if you refuse to open your mouth."

I look at him sharply. Control? That's impossible. Monsters can't be controlled. They can only be caged.

Ward catches my look. "I'm not messing with you. You *can* learn how to control it. You just have to practice. If you submit to the training, you'll eventually be able to turn your power on and off just like the rest of us. You'll be able to have normal conversations, talk like a regular person. Isn't that what you want?"

Memories sail across my mind from a time long ago, a time of bubbly words and unending dialogue. When sentences fell freely from my lips only to be caught by the breeze, floating away into a harmless oblivion. Those memories are like dreams — impossible dreams of a long-distant past.

"I know you want that," he says, missing nothing. "I've seen you with Enzo and Cami. I've also seen you with Esther and the kids. You fight against forming attachments, but you still long for those relationships. It's natural, your desire for companionship. My uncle was right about that. And the more you've been letting them all in, letting *me* in, the more your walls have been breaking down."

I have to turn my head to keep him from seeing the pain flash across my face.

"I've seen you struggle not to talk," he goes on. "I've watched you open your mouth only to snap it shut again. Just imagine how liberating it will be when you can talk about anything you want, at any time, with no fear of consequences. You can't honestly tell me you don't want that."

I hate him.

I hate him, I hate him, I hate him.

Because he has me. And he knows it.

"One way or another you're going to be a part of the Exodus Project, because you know there's no real alternative. Falon won't allow it. *Lengard* won't allow it. The question is, are you going to cooperate? Will you dedicate yourself to the training and learn how to control your power?" He pauses for effect, then finishes, "Are you going to Speak?"

I know what he's after. I don't want to give it to him, but I need to know if what he's saying is possible. If it's true. Because I'd do anything to be a normal person again — even if that person is but a shadow of my old self. I've lost too much to ever be whole again.

Warrior, I am not. Nor will I ever be. But I would be a fool to ignore the offer before me. Not if there is the slightest chance that he is right. So I give him what he wants, hoping he was telling the truth earlier about the glossy black walls protecting the rest of the world from whatever I can conjure with my words down here.

"Yes, I'll cooperate."

My voice is brittle and weak from lack of use, but Ward's eyes flare with triumph, whether at my agreement or simply because I spoke out loud. He doesn't appear cocky, though, which surprises me. Instead, an echo of the warmth I'm used to lights up his features, almost as if he's pleased. Relieved, even.

I remind myself that it's only an act. I won't allow myself to forget that. Never again.

"Good," he says. "We'll start first thing tomorrow morning. What should we call you from now on?"

I lift my shoulders and drop them again. "Whatever you want."

Even just the few words I've said so far make my heart feel lighter. Down here, protected by the Karoel walls in this small, dark room, I feel freer than I have for a long time. Until —

"What I want is to call you by your real name."

Shaking my head, I quietly rasp out, "That's not going to happen."

Ward's voice is dangerously low. "Do I need to remind you that you just agreed to cooperate?"

My throat is already beginning to sting, but I manage to say, "And I will. I'll cooperate with whatever training you throw at me. But that's all you get, so you might as well stick with 'Jane Doe.'"

Before he can argue, I add, "Here's one last thing for you to think about, *Landon*." It's the first time I've spoken his name — the name he once told me to use, even if I've never considered him as anything other than "Ward." I find vindictive pleasure in seeing him flinch at my tone. "You once told me that's not who I am. That I'm not a Jane Doe. But like everything else you've said and done over the past month, I'm guessing that was a lie, too." He flinches again, his reaction telling enough to open a wound within me that will never heal. I swallow and finish, "You deserve a medal for your performance. I'd almost convinced myself that you actually cared."

I snap my mouth closed and ignore the raw, burning sensation from my screaming vocal cords. I won't let on that I'm in any kind of pain — physical or emotional. He doesn't get that from me, either.

I force myself to maintain eye contact. The emotions on his face appear for a fraction of a second, barely enough time to register and fleeting enough that I doubt what I see. I could swear I see remorse. But that's impossible, since he's been Falon's lapdog all along. *I'm* the fool here.

And what's worse is, from the very beginning, I knew better.

"You said we start training tomorrow," I say when it becomes clear that he's not going to respond. "Does that mean we're done for the night?"

His face is blank once more, but he nods curtly. "I'll take you back to your suite."

He turns, and I follow, releasing a silent breath of relief.

"Remember not to Speak once you leave this room," Ward says, stopping just before the door. "Until you learn how to control it, you still have to be careful."

As if I need the warning. Even if the impossible happens and I learn how to control myself, I'll still be careful. Words are too precious to throw around carelessly. I don't need to have a supernatural power over them to know that. I've *seen* it. Words demand respect. They are beautiful; they are terrible. They are a gift and a curse. I will never forget what they can do.

Because words have cost me everything.

CHAPTER FOURTEEN

"I'm sorry I left like I did."

Those are the words that greet me after Ward drops me at my suite and I step inside to find Cami curled up in a ball, nestled deep into the corner of the couch.

"I didn't — I couldn't —" She takes a deep breath and tries again. "I'm so sorry, Jane."

I cock my head to the side, wondering what, specifically, she's sorry about. There are so many possibilities.

"Someone should have told you. *I* should have told you."

At least if she's going to apologize for anything, she's jumping straight to the main event.

"Please, will you sit down and let me explain? I promise I'll tell you everything I know."

I'm standing just inside the doorway, tense as a brick wall. But at her begging tone, I make myself move forward. I feel a pang of distress when I'm close enough to see her puffy red eyes, and I have to resist the urge to reach out and comfort her. I still don't know if she was a part of Ward's act from the beginning. This could just be some kind of new performance.

"Do you remember that first day we met?" Cami asks, her voice quiet. "How we made pancakes and spent the day together? You were so guarded, Jane. So careful. You were damaged. You still are." She says the last as a whisper, her words hitching at the end. "It's this place. This stupid, awful place."

She scrubs a hand across her face, wiping away fresh tears. "Not the training rooms down below — they're actually okay, if you can believe it. It's everything up here that's like something out of a nightmare."

She inhales a wobbly breath and continues, "They call it an 'initiation,' but it's more like hazing. It's where they bring potential Speakers when they first arrive at Lengard, so they can force them into a stressful environment to see how well they adapt. The potentials are tested, mentally and physically, until they break. Usually it only takes a few days. On the rare occasion, a couple of weeks. The longest anyone has ever lasted was four months. Until you. You're … you're special."

Special. That's one word for it.

"I heard whispers about you, you know, before we ever met," Cami says. "All of us Exodus recruits knew about you — the silent girl who wouldn't Speak. You stayed quiet for so long that we all doubted you could even talk at all. When I learned that Landon was working with you, I knew I had to meet you. I wanted to know how anyone could survive in this place, survive *Vanik,* for as long as you did — and that was before I discovered you were working with him directly."

The way she spits out Vanik's name reminds me again that she has some kind of dark history with him. I want to find out what happened, but from my own experiences, I can already imagine what he might have done. I wonder how long Cami lasted before she "broke."

"You weren't what I expected at all," Cami goes on, still lost in her memories. "I thought you'd either be terrified of me or full of anger.

You should have been dangerous. Violent, even. But you were none of those things. Instead, you were amazed by chocolate chips. You helped stir pancake batter. You sat at a table and let me force-feed you enough food for an army. Then you let me comfort you after you ran to the bathroom. And we spent the rest of the day together — as *friends*."

Cami reaches across and takes my hands in hers. I don't return her grip, but I also don't pull away.

"That was real, Jane. All that was real. No matter what else you think, please, please believe me."

I don't say anything — but then again, I can't. Not without some kind of protection for my words. I'm not sure what I'd say anyway. I want to believe her. I really do.

"I went to see Uncle Rick after I left you downstairs tonight," Cami admits, her voice barely above a whisper. "He told me everything about what he asked Landon to do. I swear I didn't know. I mean, I knew my brother was spending time with you, and I knew it was because Uncle Rick asked him to, but I didn't know that it was all —"

She breaks off and bites her lip, but she doesn't need to finish the sentence, since I know exactly what she was going to say.

Fake. It was all fake.

"I know you probably think I was a part of it, too," she says, instead. "But I promise, I wasn't. I just wanted to be your friend. And I still do. If you'll let me."

I can't talk, but now more than ever I want to communicate with her. So I do something I haven't done in all my time at Lengard, something I've refused to do for fear that not only my spoken words have power. I pull my hands from hers and reach for the notepad and pen on the coffee table. I scrawl out a sentence for the first time in years, pleased when my muscle memory kicks in enough to make the words legible, and thankful that I now know nothing bad can happen unless I Speak the question:

Why didn't you tell me?

I watch her eyes travel over the ink once, then a second time. When she looks up at me, there is a slight wrinkle between her eyebrows.

"Why didn't I tell you?" she asks. "Do you mean about you possibly being a Speaker?"

I nod firmly, and she runs a hand through her hair.

"I know it sounds like a cop-out, but I wasn't allowed," she answers. "It's against the rules. Normally, those of us in the Exodus Project aren't supposed to have contact with potentials until they commit to the program — until they prove they can Speak. Enzo is the exception, since he can encourage newcomers to feel safe enough to reveal their powers. But your … *circumstances* … changed after Landon started working with you. If Vanik hadn't nearly caused you brain damage that day, you and I never would have met the next morning. And the only reason you were allowed to move in with me was because I swore I wouldn't say anything."

I make a face, unhappy with her answer.

"Please believe me, Jane. I had to follow protocol. But I want you to know, I argued with Uncle Rick. I didn't agree — I thought you deserved to be told the truth."

She shakes her head and finishes, "It's too late now, anyway. I can't take back the past, Jane. But I'm hoping you'll let me make up for it in the future."

As much as I'm afraid to believe her, I still do. She has no reason to lie to me, not anymore. I've already agreed to cooperate. That gives me the confidence I need to reach out and take her hand again. The moment I do, tears well in her eyes and she gives me a tremulous smile.

"I promise I won't keep anything from you again," she swears. "I love my uncle and I love my brother, but I don't agree with how they treated you. No one deserves that."

True. But I know that to make it through the next however long amount of training with Ward, I have to move past my hurt. If he can shut me out as quickly as he did, then I can do the same to him — or, at least, act as if I can. From now on, he means nothing to me. He's a means to an end — an end where I will hopefully learn to control the monstrous power in me so that no one ever gets hurt again.

Me included.

*

Cami and I stay up late, huddled on the couch, eating copious amounts of comfort food and watching chick flicks until we both fall asleep.

It's only when a pounding on the door reaches my ears the next morning that I wake up with a start, the shock causing me to tumble off the edge of the couch. My sudden movement has a domino effect on Cami, who fell asleep on the other end, and she topples, as well. Somehow we end up tangled in a pile of cushions and pillows, and the more we try to move, the more we become wedged between the couch and the coffee table.

I'm not sure if it's Cami or me who starts it, but one of us lets out a snort of laughter, and then we're both lost to the hilarity of the moment. I can't remember the last time I laughed so freely and completely. I'd forgotten how good it feels.

Cami and I are still on the ground, cheeks aching and tears streaming down our faces, when Enzo finds us, having let himself into the suite since neither of us were quick to open the door.

"Do I want to know what's going on here?" he asks, one eyebrow raised. "Or should I let my imagination run wild?"

"Neither," Cami gasps. "What're you doing here, Enz?"

"Just dropped by to make sure you got JD down to training on time. Lando's on a warpath, and he'll rip into all of us if she's late."

"What's his problem?" Cami grumbles, her humor dissolving. "He's acting like a —"

"Are you sure you want to finish that sentence?"

I bolt into an upright position at the newest voice and end up whacking my knee painfully on the coffee table. I wince and rub the bruised flesh, but my attention is focused on Ward's commanding presence as he strides into the room. Even Enzo appears startled to see him, but his expression swiftly turns into something that looks like a cross between apprehension and anticipation.

"I thought we were meeting you downstairs," Cami says to her brother, all traces of laughter gone.

"Change of plans," Ward replies simply. "Crew has something on after breakfast, so if we want to use him for our first lesson, it has to be now."

I look down at my pajama-clad body and wonder exactly what Ward means by "now."

"Time's wasting, Jane. Let's move."

A traitorous part of me is relieved that he called me "Jane" rather than "Six-Eight-Four," even if it still feels like a slap in the face coming from him. I cover my reaction by sending him an incredulous look, but he doesn't catch it since he's already turning and stalking toward the door. I swing my eyes to Enzo, and they narrow into a glower at the amusement I see him trying to rein in.

"You heard the man, JD," Enzo says, giving me a wolfish grin. "Chop, chop."

I stand to my feet but otherwise don't move. Cami rises beside me and mimics my body language.

"You, too, Cam," Enzo adds. "I'll need you to patch me up when Crew's through with me."

"We're not going anywhere, not until we've had a chance to put some proper clothes on," Cami says. "There's no way I'm walking the halls like this."

Ward prowls back into the room with a scowl on his face, having realized no one was following him. "What part of 'Let's move' did you not understand?"

"They're having a diva moment," Enzo drawls. "Looks like they want a few minutes to don their gowns and powder their noses."

Had I been closer to him, I would gladly have slammed my heel down on his instep.

Ward lets out a sound of irritation. "We don't have time for this."

In four quick strides, he's at my side with his fingers wrapped firmly around my wrist, dragging me forward. I let out a squeak of distress, but I won't risk vocalizing more than that. Instead, I pull against him, tugging back with all my might, but it's no use against the physical power he commands.

"Cam, you have ten minutes until I expect to see you downstairs," Ward calls over his shoulder.

"Wait! Landon, stop!" Cami cries out. "At least give her a jacket!"

Ward's steps falter, and he glances back at his sister with a confused frown. Then he turns his eyes on me and looks me over, finally noticing that I'm still wearing my sleeping attire — a pair of pajama shorts and a thin camisole. Despite being sure that his scrutiny can only be clinical, with the lack of genuine *anything* he feels toward me, I can still sense pinpricks of heat firing into every nerve ending his eyes touch.

I fight the urge to cover my body, no matter how uncomfortable I am from his perusal.

As if my touch suddenly scalds him, he releases my wrist and steps away. "Two minutes, Jane," he offers, looking past my head rather than at me directly. "Get dressed, and Enzo will take you downstairs."

With that, he whips around and disappears out the door again.

After quickly changing into jeans, a sweater and Esther's boots, I follow Enzo to the elevator Ward used to return me to my room last night — different to Falon's private one — and the nerves hit me like a freight train. If what Ward told me yesterday is true, there is a very real possibility that he'll be able to teach me how to control the monster in me. I haven't allowed myself even an inkling of hope for over two and a half years — it seemed futile, given my circumstances. But now …

Now anything could be possible.

"Penny for your thoughts?" Enzo asks.

I shake my head, knowing there's no way for me to communicate what I'm thinking.

Enzo forges on regardless. "Try not to worry about Landon. He's all bark, no bite. At least when it comes to you."

What is *that* supposed to mean?

"You definitely have him all tied up in knots, JD," Enzo continues, oblivious to my inner confusion. "He never stood a chance. Now he's just gotta figure that out for himself."

I blink, but the elevator door slides open before I can attempt to shape my expression into something depicting any of the three thousand, seven hundred and fourteen questions I want to ask.

"Enough of the deep stuff," Enzo says, stepping out into the corridor. "It's time to see what you're really made of."

He leads me down the dark hallway until we reach the entrance to the massive training room I saw yesterday. It's eerie to see it so still and silent this morning, with the other recruits either sleeping or in the process of getting ready for the day.

In between our movie watching last night, Cami shared that there are fewer than thirty older-generation Genesis Speakers who populate the facility, along with around fifty younger-generation Exodus Speakers — with that number growing as new teenagers are discovered. The Exodus recruits who have passed through initiation — the ones who survived Vanik's tests and Manning's psych evaluations before proving their suitability to join the Speaking program — are assigned to bunk-like dormitories, while the Genesis Speakers and their families live in private quarters. Like Cami and me. And Ward. And Falon's family.

Falon, Cami also shared, is not only the director of Lengard but also a Speaker in his own right. Esther, too, was one of the Genesis generation and has her own ability.

The surprises kept coming when Cami went on and I discovered that Falon didn't tell me the whole truth yesterday — that it's not *just* the Xanaphan drug that produces Speakers. They can also result when two Speakers reproduce. As such, Falon and Esther's children will one day have abilities of their own.

All this Cami told me freely, along with sharing that she and Ward aren't related to the Falons by blood but that the director and Esther took them in when their parents — their *Speaker* parents — died in a Lengard lab accident ten years ago.

Cami brushed over that part of her commentary, and I couldn't blame her for the lack of details she offered. She would have been only eight at the time — much too young for such a loss.

Unable — or unwilling — to linger on her memories, Cami had gone on to share that she and Ward aren't the only Exodus recruits born to Speakers — Keeda and Sneak were Xanaphan-free babies, as well, with their parents also tragically killed in the same lab accident. In the aftermath, Cami, Ward, Keeda and Sneak, along with a handful of others I haven't yet met, all grew up together down here, knowing long before puberty arrived exactly who they were and what they could do. It was hard to push aside my jealousy when I heard that.

Even now, looking around at the vast underground room Enzo and I are walking through, I know I have to put the past behind me in order to focus fully on what is ahead.

It's almost a relief to step into the smaller, Karoel-lined room, since it gives me a reprieve from the questions in my mind. But it also means I have to face Ward again and see the stone-cold look on his face as he stands there with the sadistic, metal-pierced Crew at his side.

"Cami?" Ward asks Enzo when the door closes behind us.

"You gave her ten minutes. She'll be here soon."

Ward nods and turns to me. "I've already told you this, but it bears repeating: Speaking isn't so much about the words we use as it is about the intent behind them."

I stand up straighter, realizing that he's jumping straight into lecture mode and I had better pay attention. I wish I'd had a chance to eat some breakfast or something first; even one of my old nutri-shakes would have helped me concentrate more on his words and less on my growling stomach.

"I've asked Crew to help with this lesson since his abilities will help you understand exactly what I mean — and hopefully they'll motivate you to learn quickly, especially if you don't want to see Enzo in too much pain."

"Don't worry 'bout me, JD," Enzo says. "I can handle a scratch or two."

Crew smirks. "Is that so?"

Ward holds up a hand before Enzo can reply, causing me to think their banter must be a common occurrence. "Unless you two can contribute something educational to the lesson, do me a favor and keep your mouths shut."

Enzo sends him a mocking salute. "Sir, yessir."

Ward's lips press into a thin line. "I figure we can start without Cami and she'll patch you up when she arrives. You good with that?"

Enzo answers with a nod.

"Good." Ward turns back to me. "You've already seen what Crew can do — that he can inflict physical injuries on people. Yesterday he used the word 'slash' to demonstrate. Today I want him to show you something different. Crew?"

At Ward's go-ahead gesture, Crew cocks his chin to the side and focuses on Enzo. "Avalanche," he says, and light streaks from him and slams into Enzo's cheek. Almost immediately the flesh swells to twice its normal size and a shallow graze opens, trickling blood down his face until it drips off his chin and onto the floor.

"Come on, man, not the face!" Enzo wails, slapping a hand to his bleeding cheek.

Crew just grins in response. "No one gave me any limits. If anything, I've made improvements."

The two of them descend into a verbal battle, but I turn my attention back to Ward, letting them argue it out in the background.

"As you heard," Ward says, "Crew didn't need to use a specific word to make his Speaking power work. 'Avalanche' has nothing do with 'face punch' or whatever he did to Enzo. So it wasn't the word itself that caused the damage — it was Crew's *intention*. What he imagined, happened. And he brought that imagination to life by focusing his mind and Speaking his intent into being, all in a tightly controlled manner."

I tilt my head to show I understand, at least in theory. The practical application of control still eludes me.

Ward notes my silent response and reminds me, "Don't forget, you can talk in here."

Strangely enough, I *had* forgotten that. The idea still makes me anxious, if I'm being honest. But that's also because with his words, I've just realized that the black Karoel might protect the outside world from whatever I can conjure down here, but what about Ward? What about Crew and Enzo? They're in the room with me, not outside its protective walls.

Without thinking, I move forward until there's no space between us. His body tenses at my proximity, but I'm too lost in my worries to care about just how close we are. Instead, I rise on my tiptoes to whisper in his ear, as if hoping my words will be less powerful since they're nearly silent.

"What about you guys?" I lean in even closer, my voice barely audible. "You're in here, not out there. What if I Speak something that can't be undone?" I hesitate and confess, "It's — it's happened before."

His hands move to my waist, and he pushes me back down so he can see my face again.

"That's what I'm here for," he tells me quietly but firmly. "Nothing will happen unless I allow it to."

He must read my skeptical look, because his hands on my waist — and I'm certain he doesn't realize they're still there, even if I'm all too aware of them — give a comforting squeeze.

"Think of me like a filter," he says. "You can't see it, but I'm using my ability to monitor the power behind every syllable that comes out of your mouth. And I'll continue to do so until you've learned enough control that I'm confident you're not infusing your words with unconscious intent. I wouldn't ask you to Speak if I thought you would do any permanent damage. You need to believe that."

I hold his eyes for a long moment, until I finally nod my acceptance and breathe out a single word: "Okay."

It'll be his fault if my training goes to hell — and takes innocent victims along for the ride.

"Okay," he repeats, and only then does he release me, take another step backward and return to his lesson on intention. "As I was saying, the words we use don't directly affect anything, but for Speakers like you who are in the early stages of learning control, they help provide a focus of sorts. For example, if *you* had used the word 'avalanche,' given the scope of your ability, I'd be willing to bet that the results would've been a lot different to what happened with Crew."

I look at him with alarm, afraid of what he's just so casually revealed, but he tilts his head toward where Enzo and Crew are still throwing insults at each other, oblivious to our conversation.

"When we say things, the language centers in our brain call forth visual imagery," Ward explains. "I say 'elephant,' and you automatically see an elephant. You don't see a spaceship or a tablecloth — you see a hulking gray beast with a long trunk and big flappy ears. That's just how our minds are programmed — to recognize and match what we say to things we imagine. And that's why, even though it's the intent that matters, often our words come automatically with their own pre-attached power. Are you with me so far?"

Am I with him? I'm practically hanging on his every word. Despite that, I play off my desperation with a flippant, "Say 'elephant' — see elephant. Got it." Before he can call me on my attitude, I add, "It's not rocket science, Ward, and I'm not an idiot. You're good to move on."

His face darkens, and he opens his mouth to respond, but before he can, Cami prances into the room.

"Looks like I arrived right on time," she says, moving directly over to Enzo.

She places her hand against his cheek and whispers something too low for me to hear. A soft light glows around her fingers, and when she pulls her arm back, Enzo's face is completely healed.

I'm staring at them in shock, more answers suddenly sliding into place. More questions, too.

Cami notices my wonder first and takes pity on me. "I can use words to heal physical injuries — some mental ones, as well."

A memory flitters across my mind from the morning I first met her. After I broke down and ran to the bathroom, she embraced me and told me everything would be okay. I remember that despite thinking she was wrong, her soft words still calmed me, offering an almost unnatural sense of peace.

"You've used your ability on me before," I guess.

Cami grins widely. "It's nice to finally hear your voice."

I send her a half smile in return but say, "No more messing with my head without permission."

She moves closer and pulls me in for a spontaneous hug. "No promises."

"As touching as this is, can we continue our lesson?" Ward interrupts.

"Spoilsport," Cami grumbles under her breath as she pulls away from me.

"What else do you need from me?" Crew asks Ward.

Ward considers for a moment before saying, "You're done. Jane says she's not an idiot, so I'm giving her the benefit of the doubt that she'll be a quick study."

I purse my lips, and Crew looks darkly entertained. "Sure, whatever. You know where to find me if you need me again." And with that, he saunters out of the room.

Enzo appears puzzled. "That was easy. I thought you were going to have him shred me just to make your point."

A shrug is Ward's response, along with the suggestive words, "Waste not …"

If Enzo catches the implication, he doesn't bite. Instead, he asks, "Does that mean it's breakfast time for us?"

"For you two," Ward says, indicating Enzo and Cami. "Jane has to earn her keep first."

Cami sends me a sympathetic look and promises to save me something for later.

I try to smile in thanks, but my stomach is in knots over Ward's statement. Just what does he have planned for me?

"Catch you later, JD," Enzo says, ruffling my hair as he walks past and pulling Cami out of the room with him.

I turn to Ward. "What now?"

He eyes me shrewdly. "You've heard the saying 'Practice makes perfect'?" At my nod, he tells me, "Consider that your new personal mantra."

I don't try to hide my apprehension. "I'm not sure I understand."

He smiles, his perfect teeth glinting in an almost predatory manner. "You will."

CHAPTER FIFTEEN

"We already know you're powerful," Ward states, striding into the center of the room and motioning for me to follow, "so this isn't the place to test the limits of your ability. Plus, you need to learn control before we even think of doing anything like that."

If what I've already learned about Creators is true, then there *are* no limits. I shiver just thinking about it.

"So that's what we're going to work on today," Ward continues. "Control."

"And how do we do that?"

"We're going to start by strengthening your mind." He taps a finger against his forehead. "You need to learn how to discipline your thoughts so that when you talk, you can *choose* whether you infuse your words with power or let them just be normal speech."

I nod vigorously, since that's exactly what I want to be able to do. "Again, how?"

"You're a unique case," he says, "so it's going to be a matter of trial and error until we figure out what works best. Then repetition is key until controlled Speaking comes as naturally to you as breathing."

I frown at him, unhappy with his lack of certainty. "I thought you knew what you were doing."

He raises one eyebrow cockily. "I do. It's you who's the wild card. All this depends on how willing you are to submit to instruction."

I resist the urge to pull a face at him and, instead, grind out, "Let's just do this."

He moves slightly, balancing his weight as if to be more comfortable on his feet. From that alone I get the feeling we're going to be at this for a while. "We'll start by putting into practice what you've just learned about intent. Think about a cat."

I'm caught off guard. "Sorry?"

"A cat," he repeats. "Close your eyes and imagine a cat."

I just look at him. "As in, meow?"

His return look is scathing. "What other kinds of cats are there?"

I clench my jaw, close my eyes and do as directed.

"Imagine a gray-and-white-striped tabby. Four legs, fluffy tail, soft coat. Can you see it?"

"Mmm-hmm," I murmur, seeing it as he described.

"Good. Now I want you to Speak it into being. You already know how. Just keep the picture in your mind and call it forth. It will be harder with the Karoel dampening your ability; you'll feel like you're trying to talk around a mouthful of honey. But you just have to push through the pressure and concentrate hard on what you want."

He makes it sound so simple, just like when we were up on Market Street. And really, it *is* unbelievably simple. Enough that I don't try to think about the impossibilities behind my ability, and instead, I just say the word, "Cat."

I understand straight away what Ward meant about the pressure in my mouth; it's an almost sticky, crowded feeling, like my gums are stuffed with cotton wool. It's as if something pushes back against the word itself, stopping it from forming.

And indeed, nothing happens.

As I gaze around in confusion, Ward says, "You have to force the word past the effects of the Karoel. Think of it like obedience training — you have to take command of the words you want to Speak, making them surrender to your will."

"I haven't had to do that before," I tell him, warily eyeing the glossy black walls. "Normally, I just open my mouth and whatever comes out is already powerful." Too powerful.

"And that's why we're in here," he replies, waving at the Karoel. "The mineral is a training tool that will help you learn how to actively control your words — as opposed to letting them control you."

Mentally comparing the task to adding weights to an already arduous workout, I nod.

Closing my eyes again, I think of everything Ward has told me. I focus on the cat he described until it is pictured perfectly in my mind, and when I'm convinced I'm ready, I purposefully push power into my word as I Speak, "Cat."

My eyes open just in time to watch the light fly out of me and a furry creature materialize on the floor in front of where I stand. I look down at the tabby and he looks up at me, each of us as shocked as the other, neither of us knowing what to do now. I jump a little when he opens his mouth and a soft, questioning *meow* comes out.

"Good," Ward says.

I jump again, turning back to him with what must be wide, incredulous eyes. Despite knowing what I can do, this is ... this is ... something else. Something beyond reason.

"Now, do it again. A long-haired white one this time."

I push past my shock and do as he says, forcing the word through the restrictions of the Karoel, and a Persian-like, squashed-nose cat joins the tabby.

At Ward's directive I create three more cats, until there are five pairs of feline eyes blinking in curiosity and confusion.

"Is there a point to this?" I ask, the words coming easily since I'm not attempting to power them. Impatience has begun to replace my shock, and I'm ready to move on from this strange cat-creating exercise. Or at least find out why Ward has me doing it to begin with.

My attention is pulled downward when an adorable black-and-white kitten rubs against my leg, a creature I took a few liberties with, making him younger than the rest just to test myself. It was a mistake, though, since I think I'm already half in love with the little guy. I draw him up into my arms, and he begins to purr contentedly, batting his paw at my hand for attention.

"Oh, you *are* cute, aren't you?" I coo at him, forgetting, somehow, that I've just asked Ward a question. When I look up at him, there's an unexpectedly soft expression on his face, but he masks it immediately when he catches me watching him.

"Of course there's a point," he states, annoyed. "Do it again."

Biting my lip to keep from snapping back at him, I keep the purring kitten in my arms and Speak another cat into the room. Then another. And another.

"At this rate I'm going to become known as the crazy cat lady," I mumble, absentmindedly stroking the kitten. I'm just about to create the ninth cat, when Ward stops me.

"Enough cats. Try a dog this time."

"Any preferences?" I drawl. This is getting ridiculous.

"German shepherd."

I picture the majestic dog in my mind, not even having to close my eyes anymore, and Speak it into being. "Dog."

"Good. Now a golden retriever."

I do as he says, and then when he asks for a border collie, I call one of those forth, as well. I'm beginning to get a little nervous about the dogs and cats in the same room, but so far they all seem too busy checking out their new environment to think about attacking one another.

"Now try a pony, one of those miniature ones so it doesn't take up too much space in here."

I regard him with wide eyes. "You want me to create a horse?"

"A pony," he corrects. Seeing my expression, he adds, "It's your imagination, remember? You can make it as big or as small as you want."

I bite my lip and concentrate on the image in my mind, thinking of a Shetland pony just a little larger than the German shepherd. When I say, "Pony," it appears, just like all the other animals.

After that, Ward has me create three baby goats, half a dozen chickens and a llama.

"It's like a petting zoo in here," I say over all the animal sounds. "I hope you're the one on clean-up duty."

His mouth curls upward ever so slightly. "Clean-up duty?"

I gesture around the room. "It's bound to happen sooner or later."

Before he can respond, the door opens, and Enzo and Cami walk into the room. They both stop dead and look around with astonishment.

"Please tell me you're seeing what I'm seeing," Cami says to Enzo, rubbing her eyes as if that will change the sight in front of her.

In her defense, in the hour she's been gone the room *has* filled up with farm animals. There's no way she could have anticipated that.

"I wish I wasn't, but I am," Enzo replies, warily eyeing the llama ambling over to them.

The fluffy white creature stops right in front of Enzo and nips at the brown paper bag he holds in his hands.

"Get this — this *thing* away from me," he says, using his free hand to push the llama's head away. But the animal is intent on its goal, still trying to nip at the bag.

Cami lets out a peal of giggles, and I feel like joining her, especially seeing the look on Enzo's face as he tries to shoo the llama away. But one glance at Ward's crossed arms and cold expression stifles my bubbling humor.

"Here, JD, take it," Enzo cries almost desperately, tossing the bag to me.

I catch it one-handed, careful not to drop the kitten now snoozing in the crook of my other arm. If Enzo's goal was to redirect the llama's attention to me, he failed, since the creature appears enamored with him, butting at his chest and rubbing its head along his arm.

When Enzo's attempts to shove the beast away only cause it to dig in its hooves and press closer to him, I'm unable to suppress my laughter any longer. Cami is now doubled over, with tears streaming down her face.

Enzo lets out a string of profanities. "Would someone —" he grunts "— get this —" he staggers back a step "— beast —" he pushes against it, but it doesn't move an inch "— off me!"

Now I'm the one with tears rolling down my cheeks.

"Jane."

Ward's sharp voice has the same effect as pouring water on a fire, and my laughter breaks off abruptly as I turn to him.

He gestures to the llama and says, "Do something about that."

It's my turn to raise an eyebrow at him. "Like what?"

"Get rid of it." He waves a hand around the room. "Get rid of them all."

Easy enough for him to say. I'm a Creator — not a Vanisher. I don't even know if there is such a thing. But then I remember that "Creator" doesn't just mean someone who creates something; it means someone who can use their imagination to make *anything* happen. What did Enzo say just yesterday? *They can do whatever they want with any words they want.*

Time to put that to the test. But ... there is just one problem.

"How do I get rid of the animals without getting rid of ... everything else in here?" I ask Ward, hoping he understands what I'm not saying. When he just looks at me blankly, I move closer and explain, "You, Enzo, Cami. How do I keep you from vanishing with the rest?"

Understanding lights his eyes. "Just don't let your mind go there."

I make a derisive sound, but I regret it when it stings my raw vocal cords. "I'm new to this, Ward. I've been at it for an hour, and all I've done is call some of Farmer Joe's friends into existence. Getting rid of them all at once *without* sending anyone else along for the ride —"

Ward cuts me off. "You can do this," he says. "And even if you can't, I won't let anything bad happen."

Right. He can protect my words. But I'm still not sure how he does that, exactly.

"Close your eyes, Jane."

I send him one last wary glance but do as he says.

"Imagine the animals disappearing one after another, vanishing like smoke. The chickens, the pony, the goats, the dogs, the cats, the llama."

"Sure, leave the llama till last!" Enzo cries out, but Ward shushes him into silence.

"Can you see that? All of them gone from the room?"

I can, but I'm also struggling to hold on to the image.

"Once you have it, Speak it out."

I take a deep breath and cross my fingers, hoping Ward knows what he's doing. "Go away."

Before I even open my eyes, I know it worked, because the shuffling animal noises have stopped. There are no more meows, woofs, chirps or bleats. No restless hooves or clawed feet scratching along the floor. The room is silent. Filled with trepidation, I open one eye and then the other, and finally release the breath I'd been holding. Ward, Cami and Enzo are all right where I left them.

"Did I do that or did you?" I ask Ward, wondering if he had to use his protective ability.

"Other than you trying to send me, specifically, away with the animals, that was all you," he answers with a hint of pride, not at all annoyed that I *may* have included him in my vanishing imagination. "But it looks like you missed one."

I cuddle the still-snoozing kitten closer to my chest and feign contrition. "Oops?"

Ward shakes his head, but somehow I get the feeling he's amused. As much as he will allow himself to be.

"If I told you to make him disappear," he says, "you'd just Speak him back later, wouldn't you?"

"I think I'll call him Schrödinger," I tell him by way of an answer. "'Dinger,' for short."

For the first time since he turned into cold Ward, his dimple comes out, and he releases a burst of laughter. "Schrödinger? How fitting."

Given the kitten's questionable state of existence, I couldn't agree more.

The humor still lights Ward's features as he turns to Cami and Enzo, but his smile quickly disappears, and he bites out a quiet curse.

I'm not sure what the problem is, until I notice the way they're staring at me.

I open my mouth to ask what's wrong, but then it hits me and I realize *I'm* what's wrong. They weren't supposed to learn what I can do, about the power I wield. They weren't supposed to know that I'm a Creator. Not yet, at least. But maybe — maybe we can still salvage this. Maybe there's some other kind of Speaker who can call animals forth and make them disappear again.

I look hopefully at Ward, expecting him to have some kind of cover ready. But all he does is open his mouth and say, "Best not to tell the others about this. Not until she has enough control to not freak them out too much. Agreed?"

Enzo just continues to look at me, his face a mask of disbelief. "She's a Creator?"

"She is," Ward confirms. He doesn't seem worried about Cami and Enzo knowing the truth, so I can only assume his earlier rules were never meant to apply to them.

"All this time?" Enzo asks.

"All this time."

Enzo shakes his head. "That's not possible. We would have known."

"How would we have known?" Cami cuts in. She doesn't seem as incredulous as Enzo. Compared to the reactions from the others last night, now that she's shaken off her shock, she appears not to be concerned at all. "She didn't say a word to anyone for over two and a half years. She gave no indication of any kind of Speaking ability, let alone the rarest one."

"This is crazy," Enzo states. "I don't believe it."

I feel a sting of hurt, like his adamant words are some kind of personal rejection. Despite him keeping his distance as my evaluator, I still grew to care about him enough to consider him a friend.

"I'm sorry," I whisper, unable to meet his eyes. "I can't help what I am. But I'll do whatever it takes to learn how to control it. I promise I won't become someone you have a reason to be afraid of."

"Jane, you don't have to —"

"You're seriously a Creator?" Enzo interrupts Cami.

Something in his tone causes me to glance back up at him. He baffles me completely when a wide grin stretches across his face.

"This is *wicked*!" he exclaims. "Seriously — I don't believe it."

He said that before, but I now realize his reaction isn't negative.

"This is the best news *ever*," he declares. "It's too good to be true." He shakes his head again, laughing to himself. "Little JD — a Creator! I never would've picked that!"

He takes five quick strides across the room and gathers my startled self into his arms, lifting me clean off the ground as he draws me up in a massive bear hug. My eyes nearly pop out of my head with surprise, and I let out a gasp of pain when tiny kitten claws dig into my arm, telling me Schrödinger isn't a fan of being squished.

When Enzo releases me to the ground, still beaming, I grin back. Deciding to give an impromptu demonstration — and trusting that after my morning of practice I can pull it off — I look down at the kitten again. I make sure to imagine the picture of what I want clearly in my mind, then I send a quick warning glance to Ward — just in case he needs to step in — and I say, "Schrödinger, to my bed."

Immediately the kitten disappears from my arms, hopefully to rematerialize in my room as I imagined. I'll find out later if it worked, but at least for now, I no longer have him scratching my flesh off.

Seeing the damage, Cami dances over and places her hand on my forearm. With a quietly Spoken word — "Heal" — and a touch of light, my skin mends in an instant.

"Thanks, Cam," I say gratefully. I'm amazed to discover that my throat doesn't feel as strained now, either.

"That's one of the funny things about Creators," she says, smiling softly at me. "You can do pretty much anything, except heal yourself. No one knows why that's the case. It's the same for me, though — I can heal anyone except me."

"Too much power," I suggest. "If we could heal ourselves, then we could live forever."

She nods seriously. "Yes, I think you're right."

"Was there a reason you two came by?" Ward interrupts.

"We brought some cookies for JD," Enzo says, pointing to the brown bag. "She didn't get breakfast, and while they're not exactly nutritional, she still needs to eat."

Mmm. Cookies. My stomach grumbles with anticipation, so I open the bag. Inside I find a pile of gooey chocolate chip cookies.

"Fresh out of the oven, direct from Aunt Esther and straight to you," Cami says. She snakes her hand into the bag and pulls a cookie out for herself, then takes a bite. "And lucky for me, you're good at sharing."

I roll my eyes at her but pass the bag around to Enzo and, reluctantly, Ward. After they each take one, there are still plenty left.

"Better get your strength up, Chip, since we still have a lot to do today."

I freeze in the act of raising the cookie to my mouth, but Ward doesn't seem to notice — nor does he seem to realize that he just slipped up and called me "Chip."

Taking a deep breath, I nibble on my cookie, deciding it's best to act as if the verbal slip never happened.

CHAPTER SIXTEEN

It's been two days since I discovered what I am and began working with Ward to control my Speaking ability, but it's as if he's communicating in a foreign language.

I can comprehend what he's *trying* to have me do. Everything he's said about intent makes sense — it's more the practical side of things where I ... lose my way.

After the success with the farmyard animals, my hopes had risen, and I'd wondered if perhaps it wouldn't be so hard to learn control. As if sensing my growing confidence, Ward has since found a way to smash me back down to reality, and today he is particularly brutal.

"You need to do better than this, Jane," he growls when I ask for a break.

Leaning over with my hands braced on my knees, I look up at him through my hair, trying to catch my breath.

"I'm *trying*," I say. I have no idea why the effort of just forming words is so hard on my body. Part of it is from pushing through the added pressure of the Karoel, but still. All I'm doing is *talking*.

"Not hard enough," he replies.

I manage to raise myself into a standing position and glare at him. "It would help if you offered more instruction than 'Just do it, Jane.'"

He returns my glare and snaps, *"Just do it, Jane."*

I look around the room for evidence of my multiple failed attempts. The problem is, I have summoned nothing yet. Other than Ward and me, there's nothing else in the black-walled room. And that's because Ward has tasked me with summoning objects from my past. Items of significance, items of nostalgia.

"How hard is it for you to create your favorite childhood book?" he asks. "Your favorite pair of shoes, stuffed bear or piece of jewelry? These should all be vivid in your mind — this should be *easy*, Jane."

He's right. And he's wrong. They *are* vivid in my mind. But what he's asking is not at all easy.

I can clearly see my ragged old copy of Lewis Carroll's *Alice's Adventures in Wonderland*, the cover worn by time, the pages nearly torn from the spine that is strained from countless readings with my father.

I can clearly see my ballet slippers, the pink satin in perfect condition because it only took one lesson for me to realize I preferred watching the dancers with my mother than being one of them.

I can clearly see Pink Bear, the stuffed teddy I was given by my father during a hospital stay after a swarm of bluebottles became tangled in my hair while I was swimming at the beach.

I can clearly see the diamond ring my mother always wore, the ring that was still on her finger when —

I suck in a heaving gasp, close my eyes tight and draw air carefully through my lungs.

Ward is right. It's easy for me to visualize all the things he's asking me to create. But seeing them in my mind and bringing them to life are two different things. I can barely handle the images — I know the physical evidence of them would be more than I can take, and the last thing I need is to break down in his presence again.

The Ward who held me in the bathroom is a long-distant memory. This Ward in front of me is more likely to snap at me than to hug me. So I refuse to give him the opportunity.

"Maybe I don't remember," I say. "I've been locked down here for so long — maybe I've just forgotten. Give me another task."

"That would defeat the point of this exercise," Ward says, unyielding. "To create an object with personal meaning from memory alone."

I raise an eyebrow as I consider his words. "Why didn't you say that was all you wanted?"

Immediately I create three things one after the other: The book Ward threw at me to read the first day I met him. The woolen socks I found on my feet after spending the night in his bed. And the ice cream he bought me during our trip topside.

The book and socks I hand over without looking at him. The ice cream I keep for myself, not letting on how amazed I am that it's edible. I swipe my tongue over the chocolate scoop, the coolness bringing relief to my throat.

Ward regards the book and the socks with an unreadable expression, but there's something working in his eyes — an emotion I can't interpret — before his face blanks again.

He holds up the objects in his hands. "This isn't what I asked you to do."

"I created three objects from memory alone," I say, "just like you wanted."

"They needed to have personal meaning."

I almost laugh, because he knows damn well that they do.

Reading my expression, he practically barks, "Personal meaning to you, Jane. Not to me."

I reel backward, unable to control the reflex action. But before I can pull apart his words or their meaning, the door to the room opens and Dr. Manning strides in.

I haven't seen him for three days, not since Falon ended my morning therapy sessions — sessions that were a ruse all along.

"I hear congratulations are in order, Jane," Manning says as he approaches, his partially balding head gleaming under the halogen lights.

"Congratulations, commiserations, take your pick," I reply, not caring that the first words I've ever uttered to him are brimming with attitude. He's yet another person who should have told me the truth — *years ago.*

"We're in the middle of something," Ward tells Manning.

"The director sent me," Manning says. "Jane no longer needs to see me regularly, but Falon wants me to have a follow-up session with her now that she's ... openly communicating."

I suppress a snort. Is that what they're calling it now?

"Are you even a real therapist?" I ask. "Or were you just another Genesis Speaker tasked with trying to get me to reveal my ability?"

"Both," he says without guile.

I have to admit, I'm surprised by his admission. Maybe not *everything* down here is a lie.

To Ward, Manning says, "Falon wants to see you while I speak with Jane. I'll escort her back to her quarters when we're done."

Ward shakes his head. "She's not ready to talk without me covering her words."

I've only been training for two days, so he's right. The idea of him leaving fills me with anxiety.

Straightening his white lab coat, Manning says, "I can hardly expect her to feel safe enough to share if you're in the room."

"And you won't be safe at all if I'm not," Ward shoots back.

I flinch, knowing he speaks true.

"What about the Karoel?" I say as a compromise — and a reminder. To myself as well as them. "As long as we stay in here, it'll keep me aware enough not to consciously push power into my words."

Manning's eyebrows lift, and I'd say he was agreeing with me if he didn't look so puzzled. But it's Ward I'm focused on, waiting to see what he says.

He cocks his head to the side and asks, "You're confident the Karoel will be enough to stop you?"

"Considering it's a pain in the backside to Speak around, yeah," I answer truthfully. "It's much easier to talk normally in here than it is to use my ability."

With his hands tightening around the book and socks, Ward gives a brusque nod. "Dr. Manning is experienced enough to take care of himself if you do slip up, since despite what you say —" he raises the objects in his hands "— you can work around the restrictions of the Karoel easily enough. So be very careful not to power your words with intent."

Manning still appears bewildered, but then his face pales as he peers at the walls and understanding hits him — a delayed recognition of my Creator ability and exactly how dangerous I am without the power-dampening black mineral surrounding us.

"Just to clarify," I say, "I'm *not* allowed to accidentally turn my therapist into an otter?"

Ward doesn't respond, not verbally, though that strange light does enter his eyes again. It's there for only a fraction of a second before his lips tighten and a muscle ticks in his jaw. He leaves the room without another word.

"So, Jane, how are you feeling?" Manning asks me, drawing my attention to him.

How are you feeling? Four words that he used to ask me every morning, four words that I never answered. Now, in the safety of the

Karoel room, I can actually reply. Not that I know how to respond. *How am I feeling?* The truth is impossible to articulate.

"Fine, thank you," I say, as if I'm speaking politely to a stranger — which I guess I am. "And you?"

His beady black eyes narrow slightly. "Perhaps we should sit."

After standing for hours with Ward, I'm happy for the reprieve as I fold my legs under me and sit cross-legged on the ground.

Manning looks down at me, one dark eyebrow raised. "I thought perhaps you might like to produce chairs."

My first reaction is to feel embarrassed for missing his implication, but I rally and say, "You heard Ward. I have to be careful with my intent. Unless you want to risk *becoming* the chair, I suggest you make do with what we have."

I don't know why I'm so flippant with him. Perhaps it's because I spent years in his presence and he never once shared that there were other people like me — and that he was one of them. Protocol or not, as my *therapist,* he should have realized how much I needed to know.

Lowering himself to the floor, Manning says, "You seem agitated."

"You don't say."

"Would you like to talk about it?"

A therapist's perfect opening line: *Would you like to talk about it? No, Dr. Manning. I would not.*

"You know what I'd like to talk about?" I say, instead, but I don't wait for him to ask. "I'd like to talk about Lengard."

His expression sincere, Manning invites, "What would you like to know, Jane?"

And just like that, the floodgates open. Questions I haven't been game to ask Ward, questions I haven't had the opportunity to ask anyone else. But with Manning in front of me, one of the original Genesis-generation Speakers, I take full advantage of everything he's willing to share. And that turns out to be a surprising amount.

I learn that to survive down in this underground bunker, everything needed comes from Speakers with mental abilities similar to telekinesis — like my Creator ability but with much stricter limitations. They are able to summon food, clothes, money, *whatever,* from a storage bunker located topside and deliver it to Lengard as required.

I learn that when new potential Speakers are discovered, a team is sent out to bring them here so they can learn how to control their power. They each spend time in a cell as a "test subject," just as I did, but the initiation process — which Cami already described for me — only lasts a short time, unlike in my case. As soon as they reveal their Speaking ability, they are moved into the dorms so they can commit themselves to the program.

I learn that their training is mostly covered by the Genesis Speakers, the ones who aren't out scouting for new teenagers. Those older-generation Speakers — many of whom comprised my bevy of floating evaluators before Ward came along — are tasked with teaching the Exodus recruits control, just like Ward is attempting to teach me.

I learn that they're training — *we're* training — so that when the time comes for the government to announce our existence to the world, the military can call on us to use our abilities for everything from international political negotiations, to conflict resolution, to encouraging peace during times of war.

Everything Manning tells me lines up with what Falon said about us being the perfect weapons. No need for ammo, just a pointed syllable or two from a Speaker with the desired ability and the world could be brought to its knees.

Manning's willingness to share all this blows my mind. But he saves the best until last. Because after nearly an hour of unending conversation, I learn that there are other Speakers out there; an offshoot group who once lived at Lengard but now ... don't.

"They call themselves the 'Remnants,'" Manning says, giving a distasteful sniff. "They're made up mostly of Genesis Speakers and their children who, after learning how to control their abilities, chose not to remain in Lengard any longer."

There's something about the way Manning's eyes avoid mine that prompts me to look at him more carefully.

"They were ... allowed to leave?" I ask. "Just like that?"

"The Remnants are rebels," he states, straight up. "They are a terrorist group who disagree with the values and ideologies that Lengard adheres to."

By this, I assume he means they didn't want to take part in the government's "super soldier" program.

"A few of the early dissenters managed to escape a decade ago, taking their families with them. Their numbers remain small, but they are growing, since they, too, are actively searching for new breakout teenagers, convincing those they find before us that Lengard is the enemy to be feared."

Manning gives a sad shake of his head. "One in four new Speakers ends up being located by the Remnants before we can get to them. They're then deceived into believing they are a part of something special, when really they're training to become the very terrorists they've been brainwashed into fearing."

There is so much in this information that I don't know where to start. I focus on what I believe is the most important thing: his repeated use of the word "terrorist."

"These Speakers — these Remnants — are they dangerous?"

Manning's eyes don't leave mine as he says, "More dangerous than you can possibly imagine."

A shiver runs down my spine.

"The director told you about the military's early experiments on Genesis Speakers — what my generation went through in those initial testing days," he goes on, without any hint of the trauma he must have experienced.

"Falon said the tests were unpleasant," I say carefully. "That not everyone … made it."

"They *were* unpleasant," Manning agrees, again without any sign of distress — or resentment. "But they were also effective, and most of us came to see that — at least, after a time. Regardless of the methods, we learned how to control our abilities, and that was more important than anything else. However —" he shuffles into a more comfortable position on the hard ground "— even after the testing changed to actively *help* us utilize and strengthen our powers, some of those in my generation weren't able to appreciate the lengths the military went to in order to reach their goals."

"And a rebel group banded together," I guess.

Manning's face is grave. "They waited many years, carefully stirring up discord and whispering about the need for vengeance, before they made their escape."

Holding my gaze, he goes on, "The Remnants threaten everything we are trying to achieve here. Once their numbers are strong enough, I fear it will only be so long before they reveal themselves to the world — in a way that no one will ever forget." He pauses. "And in a way that no one will ever recover from."

*

Late that night I lie awake in bed, staring at the dark ceiling, trying to comprehend everything I learned today.

Manning didn't attempt to play the therapist card after sharing his bombshell. He seemed content that I'd been "openly communicating" with him for the duration of our conversation. Or perhaps he'd merely noticed my ashen features after hearing about the rogue group of

Speakers with nefarious intentions. I, more than anyone, know exactly how dangerous our powers have the potential to be. So the idea that there is a rebel group out there — a *terrorist* group — knots my stomach and makes me break out in a nervous sweat.

Needless to say, I didn't have much of an appetite for dinner, and after watching a movie with Cami but not actually *seeing* any of it, I silently excused myself and headed to bed.

It's now hours later, and I'm still tossing and turning — something that is not ideal, since I know Ward will be relentless in my training tomorrow, and I need a good night's sleep before I have to face him again.

With a frustrated sigh, I push my covers aside and stand to my feet. A glass of warm milk used to settle me before bed when I was younger. Perhaps the nostalgia will be enough to do the same tonight.

But when I reach the kitchen and turn on the light, I jump backward in fright at seeing the figure on the couch in the adjacent sitting room. My hand goes straight to my chest, and I release a terrified squeak before I press my lips together to keep anything more disastrous from leaving my mouth.

"It's just me," Ward says.

As if there's anything "just" about him at all.

"Sorry if I scared you."

The defiant part of me wants to tell him he didn't, but even if I were willing to risk saying so, we'd both know it was a blatant lie. My heart is *still* pounding from the shock of seeing him in the shadows, and I'm sure that's clear from the rest of my body language.

Remaining seated, Ward tells me, "I just got back."

I presume he means from his meeting with the director, though I'm surprised, since he left me alone with Manning hours ago. But then I take a step closer and see that his hair is windswept and there's a flush to his features as if he's been outside. Perhaps Falon had him out searching for a new breakout teenager.

Ward scrubs a hand over his face in agitation. His body is tense, his eyes downcast, as if he's trying to keep me from reading his expression.

"I thought I'd check on Cami before heading to bed," he explains when the silence drags on between us. "I didn't realize how late it was."

All I can do is look at him with raised eyebrows, wondering why he's telling me this. And why, upon realizing the lateness of the hour, he decided to camp on our couch in the dark rather than return to his own suite.

Rising to his feet abruptly as if hearing my unspoken questions and wondering the same, Ward gives me a stiff nod and strides quickly to the door.

Given how odd he's acting, I half expect him to walk straight through without so much as a "Goodnight," but he doesn't. Just before he disappears, he turns back to me, his face not blank in the way I've come to despise over the past few days. Instead, he looks … he looks … There are no words to accurately describe his features. If I had to go with anything, I would say he seems agonized and uncertain … but also *determined*.

"Everything will work out," he whispers. His voice is so quiet that I have to strain to hear him. "Just know that."

And then he's gone.

My eyes wide, all I can do is stare at the now-empty doorway and wonder what *the hell* that was all about.

CHAPTER SEVENTEEN

Three weeks later I collapse to my knees, unable to support my weight any longer. There are tears brimming in my eyes from the sandpaper feeling that comes when I try to swallow, but I push them back, not allowing Ward to see that I'm in any kind of pain — physical or mental. It's not usually this bad; I've been using my voice for the past twenty-four days, enough that it's become normal again, but today's Speaking tasks have been more arduous than usual. Ward's demands haven't eased up for hours.

"Back on your feet, Jane," he barks at me. "And do it again."

I stagger up into a standing position, breathing hard from the effort it takes to concentrate while fighting against the limitations of the Karoel.

"I need to rest," I rasp out. "Something to eat, some water. Just a moment to recover."

"Three more and then we'll stop for the night."

I shake my head, wanting to argue with him but unwilling to waste the words.

"I need a break," I semi-repeat, and embarrassingly, my request comes out sounding like a hoarse whine.

"Three more," is his unwavering response. "Cat!"

After so many days of this, I act on autopilot and open my mouth, ready to repeat the word. But as Ward has slowly disciplined me into doing over the past few weeks, instead of conjuring a feline, my true task is to create something different. In this case, in the microsecond before I Speak, I let my weary imagination run wild as I picture a king-sized bed, complete with feather-down quilt and fluffy pillows. And when I finally rasp out, "Cat," it's not a four-legged creature that appears but, rather, the most comfortable-looking bed I've ever seen.

Ward sends me a dry look. "I know you're tired, Jane, but really?"

I just shrug, too exhausted to respond.

After my failure when Ward wanted me to create nostalgic items, we went back to animals, but with him teaching me to separate my words from my thoughts. It was only when he decided I wasn't learning fast enough that he chose a new way of motivating me — and that was by calling out the names of deadly creatures. After a close encounter with a saltwater crocodile, a polar bear and a rabid wolf, I finally managed to Speak the word "lion" while imagining something harmless — a fluffy white bunny. A hint of approval had lit Ward's eyes, there and gone in an instant.

We've now moved on from animals, but that's because last week Ward barked out "honeycomb" and I accidentally summoned a swarm of bees. The two of us were stung multiple times, and when I pointed out that Ward was partially to blame for not protecting my words, his response was so biting that I almost called the bees back into the room.

Fortunately, Cami stopped by around mid-afternoon that day to check on our progress, and after stifling her laughter at the sight of our swollen, stung selves, she quickly used her gift to heal us.

Since then, I've been very careful to create only inanimate objects.

And while I'm making progress with my training, I'm still a danger to myself and others — something that became clear when Ward decided to test my boundaries.

At least he'd had the insight to experiment while all the other Speakers were off at lunch, so the huge, non-Karoel-lined training cavern had been empty. But catastrophe had struck when my innocent statement, "It's as hot as hell down here, don't you think?" ended up sparking a raging inferno that roared to life. My higher functions had dissolved at the sight of the flames, so the best I had managed was to scream, "Water!" which brought a torrent the size of a small ocean rushing into the underground cavern.

While no longer at risk of burning to death, Ward and I had struggled against drowning from the tsunami that enveloped us. It was only when my head was above water long enough to splutter out a nonsensical, "Freeze!" that our situation improved — *slightly*. The new problem was, while the water had indeed stopped pummeling us from all sides, that was only because we were encased in ice.

Had we not been frozen solid, the look on Ward's face would have been enough to start a fire again.

"I panicked, okay?" I said by way of apology.

Fortunately, those three words had been tightly under my control, so they had prompted nothing more than a clenched jaw and glower of frustration from Ward, along with some terse instructions from him for getting us out of our predicament. I then had to erase all evidence of the natural disasters so that when the other recruits returned to the training room, they had no idea what had happened.

In my defense, I *had* warned Ward that I wasn't ready to be tested. It wasn't my fault he'd chosen not to listen, just as it wasn't my fault he'd chosen not to use his protective power on my words.

Natural disasters aside, the last three weeks have been a mind-numbing repetition of Ward drilling control, control, control into my head during every waking moment. And the results *are* there — as witnessed by the king-sized bed in front of me — but my consistency is unreliable. Sometimes I can keep hold of my mental images and my intent, but other times I become distracted and am incapable of controlling my thoughts. Because of that, I'm still not safe to speak freely like a normal person — or even just like the other recruits, all of whom are able to carry on casual conversations. They have the opposite problem in that they struggle to infuse power into their words, so they have to actively practice to make their Spoken words work.

This little room is still the only place I can talk without consequences — unless Ward is with me. But he avoids me when we're not working — *especially* since that night I found him sitting in the darkness of my suite — so I still spend plenty of time in silence, longing for the day when I won't have to fear opening my mouth.

"Twice more, Jane," he says, pulling me back to the present. "Then we're done. Pillow."

I sigh loudly and force myself to move beyond my exhaustion. Obediently I rasp out, "Pillow."

A boulder the size of a basketball appears, *thunking* onto the floor in front of me.

"Good," Ward says. "Last one. Chocolate."

That was cruel of him, because now all I want is chocolate. And that makes it harder for me to picture anything else. But I know if I don't get this right, he'll make me do it again. So I take a breath, scrunch my forehead in concentration, imagine a piano — because, hey, why not? — and call it forth by saying, "Chocolate." All that is done in a matter of microseconds, barely enough time for Ward to scold me for taking too long, which he has done a number of times in our sessions.

"A baby grand?" Ward looks equal parts amused and dubious. "High aspirations, Jane. You play?"

I shake my head, not wanting to aggravate my throat further by answering verbally.

"Interesting," Ward says. "Well, you never know. Perhaps one day."

Something I've noticed about Ward is that right at the end of our sessions together, after the training is complete for the day, a hint of his old self shines through. He's a little more pleasant, a little more talkative. A little friendlier. I don't understand why. But on days like today, I don't have the patience for his mood swings, not when all I want is to get back to my suite, take a hot shower and have Cami heal away my aches and pains.

Already eager to leave, I release a groan when the door opens and Crew walks in, followed closely by Keeda, Enzo and Cami. I also see a slight distortion of a blurred body, telling me that Sneak has joined us, as well.

In the last three weeks, Crew, Keeda and Sneak have dropped in to see me almost as often as Enzo and Cami, the three of them unendingly curious about what Ward and I do in here each day. They don't know I'm a Creator — we've managed to keep that secret from everyone but Enzo and Cami — but they don't seem to mind the mystery. I'd even go as far as to consider them friends now: Crew and his abrasive personality, Keeda and her snarky attitude, and Sneak and his shy vulnerability.

"What's up, JD?" Enzo asks, walking straight over to me.

I send him a quick smile, again trying to save my throat. But all it takes is one pleading glance for Cami to dance over to my side, curl her cool fingers around my neck and whisper a quick, "Relieve," before I'm as good as new.

"Sorry I didn't come earlier." Her tone is apologetic. "They had a mock Genesis-versus-Exodus battle and some of the Speakers —" she shoots Crew an irritated glance "— were a little overenthusiastic with their intentions."

"Those Genesis Speakers bleed a lot," Enzo says, flexing his arm muscles. "It's unnatural."

"Or maybe Crew just hacked into them more than was necessary," Keeda counters around a mouthful of chewing gum. "He practically aimed straight for their arteries."

"No pain, no gain," Crew says. "We were told to win at all costs. I was just following orders." He lowers his voice to a mutter. "Like the good little puppet I am."

My interest is snared by his bitter-sounding words, but before I can ponder his attitude further, Cami intercedes.

"Maybe so, but I was the one who had to clean up the mess you made." She shudders dramatically. "I can't count on both hands how many injuries I healed today, mostly thanks to you. It was icky. People are gross."

Good thing Cami doesn't have her heart set on becoming a doctor. Her bedside manner leaves much to be desired.

"I take it you've finished for the day?" Ward says to them, moving to stand beside me.

"All done," Enzo confirms. "We wanted to check in and make sure JD was still alive. I've gotta ask, though, do you two need more time alone?"

I frown a little, not sure what he means. But when he sends a look over my shoulder, I follow his gaze and see the king-sized monstrosity of a bed that I called forth.

"I was just practicing." I frown even more at how that could be interpreted, so I quickly add, "Control. I was just practicing my control. My *Speaking* control. You know, like every other day." When not just Enzo but all of them look at me with amusement, I blurt out, "It's a cat."

Cami gasps. "You turned Schrödinger into a bed?"

Understandably, my roommate has come to love my adorable

kitten, so I can appreciate her horror at the idea of my having turned him into an inanimate object.

"No!" I promise. "I mean, it's meant to be a cat. But it's not — it's a bed. Which is good, since it wasn't supposed to be a cat at all, really."

There's silence for a moment, until Keeda says, "Did you mess with her brain when you healed her, Cam? 'Cause something's not right in there."

Considering the nonsensical babble that just came out of my mouth, I can't blame her for wondering. "Never mind," I mumble. "It doesn't even matter."

"Whatevs," Keeda says, blowing her gum into a bubble large enough for it to burst with a *pop*. "None of us have any idea what you do down here all day, and I for one am good to keep it that way." She eyes the bed as she says this, then turns her gaze to Ward, before settling it back on me with a sly wink.

"This sure is one comfy bed," comes Sneak's timid voice.

I hear a rustle of material and watch as the feather doona indents with the weight of what I'm guessing is his body.

"Hey, Ward, can I sleep in here tonight?" he asks. "This is way better than having to listen to Crew's snoring."

The glare Crew shoots toward the indented quilt is powerful enough to make me want to back up a step. At the same time, I feel the inexplicable urge to jump in and take the Slayer's attention from the innocent younger boy, so I blurt out, "I had a sinus problem as a kid, and my dad used to joke that I snored like a congested walrus."

The moment the words are out of my mouth, I want to snatch them back. But for all that I can do with my Creator ability, for all the lack of limits I supposedly have, there are still things I can't do. Anything that goes against the natural order of the world is impossible for me — things such as bringing people back from the dead or creating something that doesn't belong, like a dragon. I'm also incapable of reversing time, which is unfortunate, since I would *very much* like to go back a few minutes and seal my lips. But no Speaking ability, Creator or otherwise, will allow me to do so.

I don't meet anyone's eyes, and I pray they will let my comment slide. I haven't spent enough time with Crew, Keeda and Sneak yet for them to realize the importance of what I just gave away, but Ward, Cami and Enzo all know by now that there are certain things I don't mention. Things like my past. Things like my parents.

A loaded silence falls upon us, until Sneak — God bless him — says, "That's really gross, Jane."

A breath of laughter leaves me, and suddenly everything is all right again. Ward is watching me, but Cami and Enzo are giving me space. I love them both a little more for that. They must know there is a reason I refuse to talk about anything before Lengard, yet they have never once pressed me. Not even Ward has tried to make me talk about the past, for which I am grateful.

"Does one of you want to share the reason for your visit?" Ward asks, bringing the conversation back to where it started. If I didn't resent him so much for all he has put me through, I would be grateful for that, as well.

"Aunt Esther dropped by earlier," Cami says. "She's booked the kids in for a special night-safari event at the zoo but forgot that she and Uncle Rick have dinner plans, so she asked if we can take them. These guys —" she indicates Enzo, Crew, Keeda and the invisible Sneak "— invited themselves along, so I figured it might be fun if we all go. Jane's training is going so well — she deserves to be rewarded with a night out."

Topside again. I experience a flare of envy at the freedom these other Speakers enjoy, yet I also revel in the idea of leaving Lengard once more.

Until Ward says, "Out of the question."

Cami's brow furrows. "Why?"

"Because I already have plans. A group of Genesis Speakers are briefing me on their recently failed mission to collect a new Exodus recruit."

"What does that have to do with Jane?"

Ward leans forward slightly. "If I don't go, she doesn't go."

His declaration doesn't surprise me, but it still leaves me feeling hollow.

"That's stupid," Cami argues. "Why do you have to be there for her to come?"

"You know why." His glance at the others reminds Cami not to mention — but also not to forget — my Creator ability. Yet again I am reminded that, friendship or no, they would consider me a monster if they knew the truth.

Cami doesn't back down. "You told me yourself, she's developing control way faster than you anticipated —"

This is news to me.

"— but even if she wasn't, she doesn't even talk unless she's down here. She knows it's not worth the risk. Right, Jane? If we take you out with the kids, you'll be a walking mute?"

I nod quickly, even if I'm not thrilled about the way she describes me.

"We're all gonna be there, Lando," Enzo says.

His tone is encouraging, enough for me to wonder if he's infusing a slight amount of Speaking power into his words.

"Nothing will happen that we can't handle," Enzo adds. "She'll be safe with us."

"It's not her I'm worried about," Ward mutters, too low for anyone but me to hear.

"Cuff me if you want," I tell him, even though I hate the idea of being bound after not having seen the metallic restraints since I was officially accepted into the Exodus Project. "Gag me, too, if it'll make you feel better. And if I so much as sneeze wrongly, have Crew on standby to take me down."

Ward looks so repulsed that something inside me loosens.

"Seriously, Lando," Enzo says. "She'll be fine with us."

Soft waves of light tell me he's *definitely* using his Speaking ability now.

Ward sighs and rubs his temples, fending off Enzo's words. "Give us a minute," he says, and leads me to the other side of the room. When we're far enough away to not be overheard, he quietly asks, "How confident are you that if something like Market Street happens again, you'll be able to handle the clean-up without me?"

I'm shocked that he's asking me, shocked that he's willing to consider my opinion, shocked that he might trust me. I know I have to give him the whole truth.

"I'm not sure. I want to say I'll be fine, but honestly, I don't know."

He looks into my eyes for a long moment and then nods. "That's good enough for me. You can go, but *please* try to keep your mouth shut unless it's absolutely necessary. You're still new to this, remember."

"Wait — I can go?" When he nods again, I have to ask, "Why?"

"Because you're not confident," he says. "That means you'll be extra careful. If you were overconfident of your control, you'd be more likely to test it out. And I don't want you testing it anywhere if I'm not around. Let's not forget the fire-water-ice disaster, yeah?"

I look forward to the day we can move past using that as a reminder.

When we walk back and share the news with the others, they respond with an embarrassing amount of enthusiasm. I feel like a kid being allowed out for a sleepover for the first time.

"Don't worry, Ward. We'll look after her," Sneak promises quietly, slightly more visible now.

Ward looks at the younger boy and his expression softens. "Sorry, buddy, but you can't go with them. You know that."

Sneak's face falls.

"What's the harm in the kid coming?" Crew asks, smoothing his red Mohawk. "It's not like anyone will see him, especially if he turns his ghost-o-meter up to full."

"Even invisible, he could still bump someone in the crowd," Ward points out. "And with Abby, Ethan and Isaac there, he wouldn't be able to communicate with any of you. Can you imagine the kind of chaos that could come from someone hearing a disembodied voice?"

I recently learned that while Falon's kids will one day embrace their own Speaking abilities, they're not yet old enough to fully understand what happens at Lengard. Other than the actual initiated recruits, no one aside from the military higher-ups and the gray-uniformed, non-Speaker guards who once manhandled me through the corridors knows the truth about us and our under-*under*ground training area. That's why Esther is a medic on-site, even though Cami can heal people with just a word. Visiting militia and other nonessential personnel have to be treated without the slightest hint of the supernatural.

"But, Ward —"

"I'm sorry, Sneak," Ward interrupts, his tone unwavering. "But there's something I need you to do for me while they're gone. It's really important, and you'd be doing me a huge favor."

Downcast, Sneak shuffles his feet and fails to make eye contact, but he still answers, "Sure."

"Good man." Ward claps him on his semivisible shoulder. "We'll talk while the others get ready to leave."

"You have to let us into the topside elevator, Lando," Enzo says. "Neither Cam's clearance nor mine will allow us out this late."

I glance at them both, then at the others, my eyes questioning.

"We're the untrustworthy nobodies," Keeda informs me, blowing another gum bubble. "Cam and Enz can leave during the day, but the rest of us aren't allowed to go anywhere without a Genesis babysitter."

Crew's face is dark. "And they wonder why we love it here so much."

There's that bitterness again, and again I'm intrigued to know why it's there. I thought the Exodus recruits were content to spend their days learning how to control their abilities so that they can go on and use them for the greater good. The idea of being a warrior for the government still doesn't appeal to me, but I can't deny that the concept has merit. Crew's attitude, however … I don't understand what I'm missing.

"Easy, mate," Enzo says. "It's not like it's hard to get authorization to leave. When have you ever been denied a pass?"

"That's not the point," Crew replies, and he leaves it at that.

He's right. But in defense of everything Lengard makes claim to, allowing any kind of Speaker out into the world without some contingencies in place would be risky at best, catastrophic at worst. While I can certainly relate to Crew's dislike of being locked up, I can't say I blame the security measures the facility has in place. I do, however, have one question:

"Will I have to be blindfolded this time?"

Keeda raises her eyebrows at Ward and then me. When she quietly mutters, "Kinky," I shoot her a glare.

"I think we're past that," Ward answers me. "You now know what Lengard really is and your place in it. We've gone beyond keeping you here against your own volition."

They have? Since when? I want to ask if they would let me leave should I choose to go, but I'm also aware that I have nowhere else *to* go. So I keep my mouth shut, practicing the silence that I'm determined to keep for the rest of the night.

CHAPTER EIGHTEEN

There are only two ways to reach Taronga Zoo from the city: by road or by water. Since the ferries at Circular Quay are within walking distance from Lengard's exit at Centrepoint Tower, it's from there that we jump on a boat and catch a ride straight across the harbor. It's twilight when the vessel delivers us to the tail end of the zoo, and we head straight to the Sky Safari, a cable car that offers a bird's-eye view over the whole park as it carries us directly to the entrance.

Bundled up against the brisk weather, I rub my hands together as the others decide where we'll start. Winter begins officially in less than a week, but as I stand waiting to hear their decision, it feels as if it's already arrived. The children, however, look as if they were born for this moment, and they're ready to embrace every second of our evening expedition, bitter wind or not.

When a direction is finally agreed upon, Cami turns to the kids and asks, "Are we ready?" At their vigorous nods, she says, "Then let's go have some fun!"

As we walk along a path, following instructions from the map-wielding Keeda, I'm caught up in all the sensations I'm experiencing. I hear birds jabbering to one another as they settle down in their nests for the evening, the distant sound of screeching monkeys, then a strange, deep groan from far away that raises the hairs on the back of my neck.

"Did you hear that?" Abby asks, her voice filled with wonder.

Enzo scoops her up until she's piggybacking across his broad shoulders. "Sure did, baby girl. Sounds like the lions are hungry."

I'm just as much in awe as she is. Years and years ago, when I was about Abby's age, my parents brought me here to this zoo. That was back when we lived in Sydney, before they packed us up and we moved to the other side of the country. I remember being amazed by the animals and throwing the biggest tantrum when we had to leave. The only way my parents could get me to go was by promising that we'd return someday.

That never happened.

But here I am, fulfilling that promise on my own. And the place is just as wonderful as I remember, if not more so in the fading light. I refuse to let my mind wander down a path best not traveled *ever,* let alone right now. All that matters is that I'm here. Even if my parents can't be.

Guided by Keeda, our group heads to the reptile enclosure first, and the kids are delighted when a keeper allows them to stroke the scales on a large diamond python. Once we're outside again, Abby runs ahead with the two boys, zipping forward and back and calling out, "Hurry up, or we'll miss all the good aminals!"

I have to hide a snicker of amusement when I hear Ethan's long-suffering sigh.

"Animals, Abby, not aminals. *An*imals."

Abby stomps her foot. "That's what I *said,* Ethan! Aminals!"

I actually need to walk a short distance away to keep from laughing.

And I'm not the only one, since even Crew sidles along beside me, his normally fierce eyes crinkling with humor.

Over the next two hours we watch elephants spraying water through their trunks, we mimic meerkats posing on their back legs, we're entertained by playful spider monkeys, we feed giraffes and we cuddle koalas.

The animals come alive as the darkness descends, and they go about their lives as if they're not held captive behind glass windows and retaining walls.

They're utterly magnificent.

It's while we're watching the chimpanzees bed down for the night that something strange happens. With everyone's attention on the mischievous creatures, I seem to be the only one who hears the whispered murmur and sees the soft flash. The next moment, something slams into me from the side. I stumble a few steps before I regain my balance, but when I do, I don't understand what I'm seeing.

Because I'm looking at me.

An exact copy of myself stands right where I was before I stumbled.

Alarmed, I raise my hand to gain the attention of the others and point out the *Twilight Zone* scene in front of me, but I gasp in horror when I can't see my own arm. A glance down is all I need to discover that from head to toe, I'm entirely invisible.

Panicking now, I open my mouth, certain Ward would call this "absolutely necessary." But before I can utter a single word, an invisible hand clamps over my lips, muffling any cry, while a strong arm wraps around my midsection from behind. Shocked, it takes me a moment to get my wits about me enough to struggle, but all the self-defense moves I've learned from Enzo fly from my mind as I'm dragged backward by my captor's unyielding grip.

We scuffle invisibly past the giraffe exhibit, and we're nearly down past the empty cafeteria, when I find the first opening to thrust my heel down on my assailant's foot. At the same time, I sink my teeth into the fleshy palm covering my mouth. I hear a satisfying grunt of pain, but then the arm around my waist tightens enough to force the breath out of me.

"Stop fighting me," a male voice demands. "I just want to talk."

His words offer me little comfort. But I also know that despite my many hours of sparring practice, I can't fight him, not with the hold he has on me. So I force myself to relax; my feet cease kicking, and my arms stop trying to gain an advantage over him.

My sudden passivity allows him to wrestle me onward again. I know better than to continue resisting, since I need to save my strength for the right moment. But when I see that he's dragging me past the sun bears and toward the tiger exhibit, I begin struggling anew, until I'm pulled off the main path and brought to a halt beside the rock wall enclosing the big cats. The arm around my waist disappears for a second, and I try to twist away, but I'm not fast enough before he latches on to me again, squeezing the breath out of me.

"Don't even think about it, princess," he hisses into my ear. Then, louder, "Jet, can you —"

"I've got it," replies a second voice, belonging to a young girl.

My body stills, and I wonder just how many other people are invisible to my eyes. But then my attention is snared when part of the rock wall slides open, revealing a secret doorway. It leads into an old elevator, the kind found in decrepit mine shafts. The kind that calls to mind images of trapped miners and deaths from asphyxiation.

I make a fearful noise in the back of my throat, but there is no savior nearby to hear my muted cry, nor anyone to stop me from being shoved forward and into the elevator.

I am alone with my kidnappers … and completely at their mercy.

CHAPTER NINETEEN

The elevator lowers us down, down, down, creaking and groaning the whole way, shaking almost as much I am. It comes to a jarring halt at the bottom, the clunking boom echoing in my ears. The rusty grate is lifted to reveal that we are in some kind of long, flame-lit tunnel.

Panic awakens every cell in my body, and I start thrashing again. I claw at my captor's arms, I push against his grip, I struggle with all my might to get away.

"Stop it," he hisses at me, giving a firm shake. "Just stop."

I don't stop. I fight even harder, desperate not to find out where this tunnel leads. But his grip on me tightens, squeezing the air from my lungs. I have to stop, if only to breathe.

"If you're going to fight me every step until we reach the catacombs, I'll knock you out and haul you over my shoulder," he threatens. "It's your call."

Catacombs? Beneath the zoo? Despite my overwhelming fear, some small part of me is intrigued. Another part is curious why he didn't just knock me out to begin with. There's a strange tone in his voice, almost like he doesn't *want* to hurt me. He's giving me the choice.

All I know is, if I'm unconscious, I won't be able to escape. So I do the only thing I can: I stop resisting and force my body to be still.

"Good decision."

I grit my teeth but remain compliant in his arms.

"Jet, you can stop hiding us now."

Two things happen at once.

First, I become visible again, as does the hand covering my mouth.

Second, a girl appears in front of me. She's young, maybe thirteen, with owlish eyes and freckles covering almost every inch of her skin. She looks at me with undisguised curiosity.

"She sure doesn't seem to want to be here," the girl — Jet — says.

Everything about her is innocent. I can't fathom what she is doing in the company of my captor.

"She'll be fine once she understands," he replies shortly.

What could they possibly want me to understand? And why did they go to such extreme measures to get my attention?

The hand over my mouth disappears — not because it's invisible again but because it releases me. The one at my waist remains in place, but I can now open my mouth. Not waiting another second, I do exactly that, infusing my words with as much power as I can, heedless of control.

"Let me go!" I demand.

Nothing — absolutely nothing — happens.

"Sorry, princess, not until I'm certain you won't do anything stupid."

I tug against his grip, pull in a deep breath and assert very clearly, "*Release me.*"

Even though I can *feel* the power of the words as they leave me — as well as the perfectly controlled intent behind them — my captor's arm remains in place.

"I actually feel sorry for her," Jet says, but there's a wide, mischievous grin spreading across her face. "I'm confused just thinking about how confused she must be."

I barely hear her over my turbulent thoughts. Why can't I Speak? I'm a Creator — my words have the potential to make or break the *world*. Surely I should be able to loosen a single unwanted arm from my midsection. But it's like there's something … *blocking* me.

"I'll let you go if you promise not to run," my captor tells me, baffling me further. "But you have to give me your word. You of all people know that words hold power. We Speakers have to be careful with the promises we give."

We Speakers.

I now know exactly who I'm dealing with. Manning's fractured voice floats across my mind: *They call themselves the "Remnants" … a terrorist group … more dangerous than you can possibly imagine.*

I am in worse trouble than I thought. And yet, survival instincts tell me to cooperate as much as I can and wait for an opportunity to escape. To do that, I need to be able to move freely. I make the obvious choice.

"I promise not to run away," I tell him, while mentally adding *yet*.

He holds me close for a long moment, but then his arm slowly untangles from around me.

I immediately take a large step away and spin around until I'm facing him. When I do, I can't keep my eyes from widening slightly before I lock down my expression.

As much as I wish it weren't true, my captor is, well, *captivating*.

He is, undeniably, dangerous. But with hair just two shades lighter than pitch-black and eyes so dark that it's like staring into an unending midnight, he is also, undeniably, gorgeous.

"Who are you?" I croak out, watching the light from the flames flicker over his skin. "And where are you taking me?"

"Why don't we get there and you can see for yourself."

He strides forward, brushing straight past me with the young girl at his heels, and I realize I'm expected to follow without question.

I look back toward the elevator, wondering what my chances are of making it rise again on my own, but it's so ancient that I wouldn't know where to begin. I doubt I'd even have the grate back down before my captor followed through on his promise to throw me over his shoulder.

I trudge after him, saying, "At least tell me your name."

His steps don't so much as pause, but to my surprise, he does answer.

"Kael. My name is Kael."

I wait, hoping he'll say more, but he remains silent. My fear is dissolving, with frustration taking its place.

"How about telling me why I'm here?" Still no response. "Come on. Give me something. *Anything.*"

I'd particularly like to know why my words aren't having any effect. I can talk normally down here, just like when I'm in the Karoel-lined training room. But I see no hints of the glossy black mineral coating the underground corridor. There has to be something else disabling my ability.

"Jet, why don't you run ahead and make sure the others are ready for us," Kael suggests.

She smiles at me over her shoulder and says, "See you soon!" before sprinting off down the dark tunnel. As she passes Kael, he reaches out and musses her hair, which earns him a playful scowl in return.

The affection in his action gives me pause, since their warm interplay doesn't scream "terrorist" to me. But perhaps that's what they want me to think. They obviously know something about me and staged my abduction for a reason. If they really *are* terrorists, then having access to my Creator ability could be what they've been wanting all along.

On that worrying thought, Kael and I continue forward in silence, with me having realized he's not going to answer anything until he's ready. I scout the path, searching for an exit, but the stone walls offer nothing until we reach a fork in the road. Three paths lie before us, with Kael leading us to the left. I'm curious about the other two — especially the middle path, which, unlike the others, is consumed by darkness. When I ask where they go, I again receive no answers.

We continue onward for a few more minutes before our path opens into an empty but vast underground chamber similar to Lengard's main training room but also … *not*. I can understand Kael's earlier use of the word "catacombs" now, since it's the perfect description for what I'm seeing. Lit by yet more flaming torches, the huge open space calls to mind images of ancient civilizations buried deep beneath the earth. It's like I've entered another world, another time, another life.

Even knowing my questions have gone unanswered, I still can't resist asking, "Where *are* we?"

"Don't tell me Kael forgot his manners again."

At the sound of the smooth new voice, I turn to see that we've been joined by a dark-skinned guy with short dreadlocks. He appears to be around the same age as Kael — perhaps a year or so older than me.

"There's nothing wrong with my manners," Kael says. He faces the newcomer and asks, "Where are the others, Dante? I thought we were meeting here."

Dante shrugs. "Liana saw something. We need to swing by her room first to remedy a … complication. The others are waiting for us in the control room."

Kael looks like he wants to ask more questions, but even I notice the brisk head shake Dante sends him, and I wonder what that's all about. I don't have time to dwell, however, since they turn and stalk back along the tunnel we just came from.

"We're on the clock," Kael says to Dante. "We have less than an hour before we need to get her back topside and swap her out with Shae, or they'll take the wrong girl back to Lengard."

Relief floods me at the realization that this abduction is only tempo-
rary. Confidence, too. Enough that I'm about to try another round of
questions, when we arrive back at the fork. This time Kael leads the
way down the right path.

Unlike the first tunnel we traveled along, this one has multiple
offshoots, like one huge underground maze. With each new turn, my
hope of escape dwindles. But Kael's mention of returning me topside
helps keep me calm, even if I'm yet to discover why I've been taken
captive in the first place.

The two boys stop in front of a closed door embedded in the rock
wall, and Kael rattles off a knocking sequence before latching on to my
arm and tugging me through.

It's dark inside the room, and it takes a moment for my eyes to
adjust, especially when Dante enters and seals the door behind us.
Only a solitary candle lights the space, held by a wisp of a middle-aged
woman with luminescent white hair so long that it trails down past her
hips. I stifle a gasp when she moves the candle high enough for it to
reveal her face. Her eyes are almost as colorless as her hair, with large
black pupils keeping her from looking like she's possessed.

"I am Liana," she tells me in a voice that is somehow both deep and
high-pitched at once. "Your future is cast in shadow and song, your
destiny filled with echoes."

A shiver trails down my spine. I have no idea what her words mean,
but I'm unnerved by the soft light I saw flare when she uttered them.
I glance around at the others and note that while Dante seems unper-
turbed, Kael appears more alert than ever.

"Do you feel it now?" Dante strangely asks.

Kael gives a slight nod, his eyes roaming the darkened room. I don't
know how he can see anything, because I sure can't. The candlelight
picks up a vague shape of a bed and an outline of some other large
piece of furniture, but everything else is hidden from sight.

Dante moves to lean against the door. It's a casual movement, but I sense there is purpose in the action.

"He was keeping his distance before," he says, "but there's not enough space to hide in here. Plus, I'm guessing his energy is crashing from having to maintain it at full for so long."

Unable to curb my irritation, I demand, "What's going on?"

Kael's eyes narrow in on the space directly to my left as he says, "We're not alone in here."

And with his declaration, Liana blows out the candle, and the room goes dark.

CHAPTER TWENTY

I'm pushed into the wall, and I hear a scuffle in the pitch-black room that barely lasts seconds before another flame is lit. What it illuminates causes my eyes to widen and my heart to drop.

"*Sneak?*"

The young boy is trapped in Dante's arms, and he looks terrified. I feel for him, I really do, but I'm also struggling to understand what I'm seeing — because he's not transparent at all. He's not even semi-transparent. He's completely solid, something I know he's not capable of controlling on his own yet. Like my Speaking ability, something is blocking him. Or perhaps, some*one*.

I turn to Kael and demand, "Are you doing this?"

He doesn't take his eyes off the white-faced Sneak. "I'm afraid you'll have to be more specific, princess."

I frown. "Stop calling me that. And answer my question."

"The time for your questions is later." Kael takes a menacing step closer to Sneak. "What are you doing here, boy?"

I move forward, ready to jump in if needed. "His name is 'Sneak,' not 'boy.'"

It hits me suddenly how ridiculous I sound, since I doubt his real name is "Sneak."

"I don't care what his name is — just that he knows mine," Kael says. "And you do, don't you, *boy*?"

I clench my jaw but keep silent this time.

"You're Kael Roscave," Sneak says, his fearful voice barely above a whisper. "Everyone knows who you are."

Everyone?

"I am," Kael confirms. "And I want to know why you're here."

I can see Sneak trembling from where I'm standing, and my protective instincts want me to close the distance between us and demand his release. But I have no power here — that much is clear.

"I'm not — I won't —" Sneak takes a fortifying breath and stands up a little straighter. "I don't have to tell you anything."

Kael cocks his head to the side. "You're right. You don't." To Dante, he asks, "You getting anything?"

It's only then that I realize Dante's lips have been moving the whole time in a silent litany and a soft glow is emanating from around him. His gaze is unfocused, but when Kael addresses him, he seems to snap out of his thoughts.

"Ward sent him to keep an eye on her," Dante says, gesturing to me. "He made it look like the kid had to stay behind, but he's been tailing her ever since they left Lengard."

I suck in a sharp breath, the only outward sign of how much this news rattles me. Sneak has been *following* me? *Spying* on me? But … that doesn't make sense. Ward was the one who told Sneak he couldn't come with us. He's the one who —

There's something I need you to do for me … It's really important, and you'd be doing me a huge favor.

I shut my eyes tight against the memory of what Ward said to the younger boy. He never intended to keep Sneak from the outing

— he just didn't want any of us to know we were being followed.

He didn't want *me* to know.

That stings more than I would like. More than it *should*.

Craning his neck to get a better look at his captor, the young boy breathes, "You're Dante Oberon."

"Smart kid," Dante says. I can't tell if he's being sarcastic or not.

"Wait a second." I hold up my hands. "How do you know he's been following me?"

Dante's shoulders lift and fall. "My Speaking ability — I can read people."

"As in … their *thoughts*?" At his second shrug, I close my eyes again, wondering if this day could get any worse. A real mind reader? I wouldn't believe it if I hadn't just seen him use his ability for myself.

A soft touch on my hand makes me jump. Liana is directly beside me, her gaze unwavering in its intensity.

"Your future is cast in shadow and song, your destiny filled with echoes," she repeats in the same eerie voice as earlier, but no light flares this time. "No one knows what lies ahead. But more than any path I've ever seen, yours is hidden most of all."

Like the first time, the power in her words makes me shiver. "What —"

"Liana has a rare ability," Dante interjects. "She can Speak news of the future into the present, warning us of what may be coming."

I swing back around to gape at Liana. First mind readers, now people who can see the future. What's next?

"She's the reason we knew to expect your bodyguard here," Dante continues. "Not to mention," he adds, "she saved the kid's life, since she saw that he was gonna run off in a panic and get lost down here. He wouldn't be the first person to never make it out again."

Sneak swallows. "You mean …"

Dante sends a wolfish smile down at him. "Better stick with us, kid. You'll never find a way out on your own."

Sneak's pupils are huge, his fear tangible. Despite him being sent here to spy on me, I still feel protective of him.

"What are you going to do with him?" I ask the room. "With me?"

"We don't have time to do anything but bring him along," Kael says. "We'll figure out the rest as we go."

He moves toward me, and I automatically back away, but he reaches out and wraps his hand around my wrist.

"We've wasted too much time," he says, dragging me toward the door and out into the tunnel. "We brought you here for a reason. Now you need to learn what it is."

Well, *finally*. But as relieved as I am, I'm also apprehensive. Because if my captors are as dangerous as Manning claimed …

"You didn't answer me before, so I'm just going to ask straight out," I say as Kael drags me along. "You're the Remnants, aren't you?" I look over my shoulder, to see Liana following with Dante and Sneak. "The rebel group of Speakers who broke away from Lengard. The terrorists."

"We are many things, known by many names," Liana answers.

"Renegades, fugitives, deserters," Dante offers. "Insurgents, revolutionaries, anarchists."

Kael's grip tightens, and I hear him add, "Survivors."

"If there's one thing we *aren't*, it's terrorists," Dante says as we step out of the tunnel onto a ledge that overlooks another immense catacomb chamber, this one even larger than the first.

My feet stop without my permission as I take in the sight. I feel as if I've stumbled upon another ancient archaeological wonder. But it's not just the expanse of the cave, with its flame-lit torches lighting up stone walls, archway exits and labyrinthine pathways. No — it's the *people*. They're everywhere. Walking, talking … some of them sitting, eating, reading, laughing.

… *Living*.

Are they *living* down here?

Is this place their *home*?

"Survivors are what we have to be."

Kael's voice comes to me as if from far away while I stare at all the people spread out beneath us.

"Because it's those at Lengard who are the real terrorists. And soon enough, Alyssa Scott, you'll understand why."

Two words.

That's all it takes for my heart to stop and the walls to close in around me.

CHAPTER
TWENTY-ONE

"How do you know that name?" I whisper, my voice barely a breath of sound.

"All in good time, princess," Kael says.

How — *how* — can he possibly know that name?

I'm too afraid of what his answer might be, so I don't ask again. I keep my lips sealed and try to steady my raging thoughts, bracing myself for whatever might come next.

We traverse a spiral path downward until we're walking through the center of the cavern. Some of the inhabitants glance at us as we pass. They are all different ages and genders and cultural backgrounds — as diverse as the people of Sydney itself.

"This way," Kael says, yanking me through an archway and down another tunnel. At the end is a single door that he opens with his free hand and pushes inward with a booted foot.

"It's about time you guys got here!" Jet cries upon our entry. "We've been waiting for*ever*."

I glance around the room and take in the large, semicircular desk facing what appears to be live newsfeeds broadcasting across numerous screens mounted to the stone walls. Other screens show real-time surveillance of the zoo, and I immediately hone in on the footage of Abby sitting in my replica's lap and watching the after-dark seal show. I want to shout at the imposter to take her hands off the child, but I know there's no point. Even if I could Speak, she still wouldn't hear me from here.

"Jet's right," says a new female voice. "I was beginning to doubt you'd made the swap, despite what she claimed."

The owner of the voice is someone I haven't yet met. The girl is a few years older than me, but she barely reaches five feet. Purple hair parts in the middle to form pigtails on either side of her asymmetrical face, with a nose too small and eyes too large, adding to her childlike appearance.

"What's up, Creator girl?" she says with a wonky grin. "I'm Pandora. It's about time you stopped by for a visit."

Fear creeps along my spine at the casual way she mentioned my Speaking ability, proof that they all know what I can do. None of them seem afraid of me, but Sneak … he lets out a strangled-sounding gasp at the revelation.

"You make it seem like I had a choice in coming," I say to Pandora, ignoring Sneak's reaction. If Ward didn't want anyone else at Lengard to know about me, then he shouldn't have sent along a spy.

I nod to the screens and ask, "If you can run electricity down here, then what's with all the fire?"

"We don't exactly want to broadcast our position to Lengard," Pandora answers, as if the answer should be obvious. "This room is tapped into the zoo's electricity feed, and its output is low enough to travel under the radar. But to light up the entire catacombs? For sure someone would be sent down to investigate."

That makes sense. It's also unfortunate, since I wouldn't mind

Lengard knowing about this place and swooping in to retrieve Sneak and me right about now. Despite what Dante and Kael both said about *not* being terrorists, I know better than to trust them. Manning even told me that's what the rebels say to the new breakout Speakers they find first — that Lengard is evil and the Remnants are good.

"Take a seat, princess," Kael orders, and if that's not enough, he shoves me into a chair. "Judging by the look on your face, it's time to correct your education."

Liana, Jet and Pandora fan out around the room, taking up positions around us, while Dante continues to keep a grip on Sneak.

"I'm going to jump straight in here," Kael says, straddling a chair backward and resting his arms across the top. "Lengard has lied to you."

I raise my eyebrows and barely hold back a snort. "It's a secret government organization. Emphasis on the *secret*. And on the *government*. Of course they've lied to me, even if I don't know the specifics."

He shakes his head. "Lengard's not a branch of the government — secret or otherwise."

I just look at him, not comprehending. "Of course it is."

"I'm guessing Falon told you that once the first round of Xanaphan teenagers began exhibiting supernatural powers, the government rounded them up and locked them away to carry out tests on them." I nod, and he admits, "That part is true."

"Then why —"

"It's everything else he told you that's a lie."

I'm willing to hear him out, if only so I know exactly what kind of brainwashing threat I'm dealing with here. "Go on, then. Set the record straight."

He doesn't react to my tone, just continues his story. "The testing the military carried out on the first-generation Speakers was highly trial and error, since supernatural abilities were — and still are —

beyond the scope of human understanding. The experiments were painful, violating, and more than once resulted in death."

"I know all this," I say. "Falon told me. Manning, too."

Kael continues, "When they'd had enough of the routine electro-shock sessions and waterboarding —" I wince at this, since I've experienced both at the hands of Vanik during my time at Lengard "— and when they were sick of mourning their friends and wondering if they would die next, the Speakers rallied together under the leadership of a man named Jeremiah and planned a coup. Together they managed to overthrow their guards and take control of the facility."

"Jeremiah," Sneak whispers, and I turn to find his face ashen. With wide, terrified eyes he repeats, "Jeremiah! He's —"

Dante's arm moves in a flash until his meaty hand covers Sneak's mouth. "It's rude to interrupt, kid."

Kael's voice pulls my attention back to him.

"Jeremiah was charismatic. He had influence, but more than that, he had power — the kind of power most Speakers can never dream of commanding. Whatever his mind could conceive, he could achieve. He was the ultimate weapon."

Remembered words invade my thoughts: *They can create the unimaginable, unleash the impossible. They're the ultimate weapon.*

I gasp with realization. "Jeremiah was a Creator? As in, *the* Creator — the power-obsessed psycho everyone fears?"

Kael's expression seems to close off. "I see you've heard of him."

"Of him, yes, but not about him," I answer, my mind spinning. "All I know is that it's because of whatever he did that people will panic if they discover I'm a Creator, too." I glance at the others in the room and amend, "Well, the people at Lengard. You all seem to be the exception."

"Or perhaps we're the norm, and your pals at Lengard are the exception," Pandora offers, finger-combing her purple pigtails. "Just a thought."

"The coup may have freed the Speakers from their immediate prison," Kael goes on, "but they were still just a lost group of teenagers at the time, and they had the full force of the Australian military beating down on the door to the facility. They were trapped, and they knew it. And that forced them to carry out some desperate measures.

"Among the Genesis Speakers, there were two others Jeremiah was close with — Maverick Falon and Kendall Vanik."

I give a small jolt at the familiar names, my attention now piqued.

"Falon's Spoken words were supernaturally wise, so he assisted with insight, logic and strategy when it came to complex reasoning and decision making. As for Vanik, he was able to read minds like Dante can, but his ability was phenomenally powerful. He was also considered a genius, and he managed to convince Jeremiah to act out against the military, to cut them off from ever being able to regain control of Lengard or the Speakers inhabiting it."

I'm fascinated by his version of Lengard's history, and I find my categorization of good versus evil beginning to blur.

"Vanik told Jeremiah that the only way they would all be safe was if they were forgotten. That anyone who had ever heard so much as a whisper about the existence of Speakers needed to have his or her memory erased."

Ward's voice sweeps through my consciousness: *Just center your thoughts on Abby, and imagine the people who watched that happen forgetting what they saw. Then Speak.*

I know the kind of power Kael is talking about. I've experienced it myself.

"Jeremiah followed through with Vanik's advice," Kael says. "In a matter of seconds, any knowledge of Lengard disappeared from the minds of anyone without a Speaking ability. Jeremiah and the others were free."

I lean back in my seat, having moved to the edge of my chair at some stage during the story. "I'm sensing a 'but' here."

Kael nods once. "The 'but' is that the military's initial testing on Vanik made him crazy. As in, clinically insane."

This description is not news to me.

"His condition deteriorated as the years passed, and Falon and Jeremiah's concern grew, until everything came to a head about a decade ago," Kael says, his eyes unfocused, as if looking into the past himself. "That was when the second round of Xanaphan children began entering puberty and awakening their Speaking abilities, meaning it wouldn't be long before the government swooped in to repeat their actions with a new generation of Speakers. Jeremiah and Falon — even Vanik, in his sane moments — wouldn't allow that to happen.

"So, while Jeremiah and Falon concocted a strategy to reach the newly Speaking teenagers and get them safely to Lengard before the military stepped in, Vanik went about his own, separate mission. He figured that if *everyone* had the capacity to Speak, then the military wouldn't care about a rogue group of supernaturals living underneath the city. They'd be considered the same as everyone else. So he decided to make it so everyone, *anyone,* would be able to Speak."

Kael says nothing more, and I cross my legs, uncross them. Cross them again. The whole time, he watches me silently.

When I can't handle waiting further, I say, "How did he plan on doing that? Didn't they get rid of all the Xanaphan research? And didn't Jeremiah wipe the memories of anyone who knew anything about it?"

"Yes, to both," Kael confirms. "But Vanik didn't intend to recreate Xanaphan and replicate it for mass development."

"Then what —"

"Insane or not, he was still a genius," Kael interrupts. "He'd had years to read the minds of everyone he had contact with, acquiring more information than you could possibly imagine. Information like complicated, experimental medical practices and dangerous, risky procedures."

Still unsure what he's getting at, I just look at him and wait for him to explain.

"When two weeks went by without anyone seeing Vanik, Falon and Jeremiah went to visit him in his lab," Kael says. "What they saw …" He shakes his head and tries again. "On one side of the lab were Speakers lying on examination tables, and on the other side were some of the non-Speaking military guards who had been captured in the coup but were offered positions in security after their memories had been wiped. Each of the bodies Vanik had in his lab were in various stages of … testing."

I narrow my eyes. "Testing?"

Kael's expression is hard, like he's repulsed, horrified and enraged all at once. "They were his lab rats. Whatever you can imagine he might have done to them, it was worse. Dead or alive, the tests were —"

He doesn't finish. It's almost like he *can't* finish.

He swallows and simply says, "Only a few remained alive, but by that stage, they would have been wishing for death."

My overactive imagination fills in the gaps of everything Kael refuses to share, as I vividly picture the horrors that occurred within Vanik's laboratory.

"Jeremiah and Falon were horrified when Vanik tried to explain himself and his desire to share the 'gift' of Speaking with the world. Stem cell cloning, he said. That was how he was going to make it happen. But he didn't know enough about where the genetic anomaly was rooted in the DNA of Speakers, so he had to experiment with different … tissue samples … until he figured it out. It was all in the name of the greater good, he claimed. In his delusional mind, he considered himself a hero of the people. The Speakers' savior. He was going to bring them freedom."

I'm shaking my head, appalled, yet morbidly engrossed in the tale. "What did Jeremiah do?"

"He did the only thing he could," Kael answers, his tone almost regretful.

My eyes widen. "He tried to kill him?"

Kael jerks back in shock. "Of course not."

"It would have been better if he had!" Sneak cries, managing to get the words out around Dante's hand, which is still clamped over his mouth. "And then he should have done us all a favor and killed himself, too!"

I don't understand Sneak's vehemence against Jeremiah, when clearly Vanik is the villain of the story.

"Shut it, kid," Dante says, giving Sneak a warning shake. "You have no idea what you're talking about."

The look on Kael's face arrests me, since it's like he's been physically struck. But he rallies and continues with his story.

"Caught up in the trauma of what he was seeing, Jeremiah tried to Speak too many things at once, and he lost control," Kael says.

I dig into my palms to stave off my own similar memories.

"He tried to save them all — Speakers and guards alike. But instead of healing them, somehow he managed to heal *Vanik,* curing him of his insanity. However, in doing so, Jeremiah also took away Vanik's Speaking ability."

I gasp, not realizing such a thing was possible.

"It's true," Kael says. "Vanik hasn't been able to read anyone for ten years."

I can't believe it. I've never once considered that I might be able to get rid of my Speaking ability. I wonder —

"I can imagine what you're thinking, princess, but don't bother. Speakers can't use their power on themselves. At least, not in that way."

Cami already told me that. But, oh, how I wish it weren't true.

Because other than saving Abby that one time, nothing else about my ability seems worth it.

"What happened next?" I ask, glossing over Kael correctly guessing my thoughts.

"Knowing something had gone wrong with his intent, Jeremiah — with Falon — tried everything possible to save the victims," Kael says. "But Lengard's only Speaker with healing abilities was lying unconscious on one of the lab benches, and Jeremiah refused to use his Creator ability again in case he caused more damage. Vanik, back in his right mind, was calling out instructions but also saying it was better to put them out of their misery, and Jeremiah believed him. Before he was willing to admit defeat, however, he tried for one last-ditch miracle, asking for assistance from the healer's young daughter."

My entire body stills at the mention of a child. And then the air rushes out of me with Kael's next words.

"A girl you know as Camelot Ward."

CHAPTER
TWENTY-TWO

"Sometimes Speaker-born children manifest the same ability as one of their parents," Kael tells me while I struggle to regulate my breathing, "so Jeremiah hoped Cami had inherited her mother's healing affinity. But at only eight years of age, Cami hadn't yet awakened her Speaking gift, and all she could do was watch from Falon's arms as the life drained out of her parents. All the while, Vanik stood over their bodies, remorseless, cold and analytical until the end as he helped expedite their deaths. To that little girl, he was the stuff of nightmares, and in one swift moment, he effectively ruined her life."

I now understand my friend's hatred toward Vanik, and my heart breaks for what she went through.

"Jeremiah begged for her silence, but Cami ran from the laboratory, screaming at the top of her lungs. The news spread throughout Lengard, but it also became twisted, until everyone believed that *Jeremiah*, their benevolent leader, had sanctioned the experiments and allowed a well-known madman to carry them out. Not only that, Jeremiah hadn't used his all-powerful Creator ability to save the victims. Instead, he helped kill them."

I'm seeing now how Keeda, Crew and Sneak might consider Jeremiah a power-obsessed psychopath. Their reactions to the mere memory of a Creator are beginning to make sense.

"Jeremiah didn't defend against the accusations thrown at him. In his mind, he *was* guilty. As leader of the Speakers, he was responsible for Vanik. That meant Vanik's actions and the resulting deaths were Jeremiah's burden to bear. He also failed to regain control of his Creator ability, which meant he couldn't protect his people anymore."

That's a lot of guilt for one man to hold, especially when, from my perspective, it wasn't as if Jeremiah had experimented on the victims to the point of torture and death — that was all Vanik.

Kael slides his chair back and leaps to his feet, startling me. He begins pacing like an agitated panther.

"With half the Genesis Speakers afraid of him and the other half unsure what to believe, Jeremiah knew Lengard needed a smooth change of leadership and that the best thing for everyone was for him to leave and let Falon take over. So he readied his family, and with Falon's help, they disappeared."

Clenching his hands as he continues to pace, Kael says, "The idea of a sadistic Creator being loose in the world brought alarm to the Speakers, so Falon enlisted a trusted Speaker with manipulative abilities to convince everyone that Jeremiah had somehow absorbed Vanik's insanity and he'd accidentally Spoken words that ended his own life, as well as the lives of his wife and only child." Kael's voice turns bitter. "They all believed the lie. What's more, they celebrated. Lengard was safe again, with a new leader, and they were content to stay cocooned in their underground utopia."

"I'm sensing another 'but' here," I say quietly, feeling uneasy. "Can you sit down again? You're stressing me out with all the pacing."

Kael halts mid-step and seems surprised for some reason. Then the impossible happens, and I swear his eyes lighten just a shade and the corner of his lip twitches.

"As you wish, princess," he mocks.

I blow out a huff of annoyance.

"You're right about the 'but' — and it's Vanik again."

Of course it is.

"In the aftermath of the lab incident, the Speakers ended up pardoning Vanik, since their fear and ire were mistakenly directed toward Jeremiah. Amid all that, it took a while for Vanik to realize his Speaking ability was gone for good and not just a temporary lack of control. More than ever he was determined to identify the genetic Speaker anomaly — this time so he could replicate it for himself. His experiments started all over again, with him spending every spare moment in his lab."

My body shudders as I think over all the experiments Vanik has carried out on me. But none of them were as invasive as what Kael implied. As far as I know, he hasn't taken any … tissue samples.

As if reading my thoughts, Kael says, "He had to be careful to not let anyone know what he was doing, so there was nothing outwardly intrusive, nothing resulting in more fatalities. But over the next few years, he had Speaker friends summon specific and complex medical equipment for him, as well as anything he needed to carry out more tests. On the surface, the tests seemed reasonable enough that they became standard protocol for any new Speakers who arrived at the facility, considered as part of their initiation." He pauses, then clarifies, "The noninvasive tests, at least."

They call it an "initiation." Cami's voice travels across my mind. *The potentials are tested, mentally and physically, until they break.*

I swallow, thinking of my years spent in initiation, but before I can muster my next question, my attention is caught by Sneak and his haunted words.

"I was four years old."

The young boy's voice trembles as tears pool in his eyes. Dante moves to cover his mouth again, but Kael shakes his head, allowing Sneak to continue.

"Four," he repeats, a whispered breath of sound. "But I remember all of it. I remember Cami running through the halls, screaming for help, more scared than anyone I'd ever seen. I didn't know you could be that afraid."

Sneak's voice is barely audible when he repeats, "I was four years old." Then he says, "Cami was eight. Landon nine. And Keeda seven."

The look on his face hurts my heart.

"We lost our parents that day. The four of us, instant orphans."

Understanding hits me — the tragic lab accident ten years ago that killed all their parents in one fell swoop. Now I know it was all because of Vanik — that those people were all killed *by* him. And it was no accident.

"We lost our parents," Sneak says again. Then his voice hardens and his teary eyes narrow into slits aimed at Kael. "And it's all his dad's fault."

I feel as if I've missed a step, but no one else in the room seems surprised by Sneak's accusation.

"I thought I recognized you, kid," Kael says to him. "You were really young back then. Sylvia and Pierre's son, right?" At Sneak's tight nod, Kael softly says, "I liked them. I'm sorry."

"D-Don't you dare!" Sneak cries.

His teary-eyed fury startles me. I can see he's barely holding on to his emotions, so I whisper, "Sneak," but I have no idea what else to say.

He moves his fiery gaze from Kael to me. "I was trying to tell you earlier, Jane," Sneak says, desperate to get his words out before he's silenced again.

But Dante makes no move to stop him this time.

"Jeremiah — as in Jeremiah *Roscave* — is Kael's *dad*."

I sense that this is supposed to affect me more than it does, but the reveal about Kael's heritage isn't all that shocking compared with everything else I've learned today. Next they'll be telling me that since Jeremiah had a Creator ability, which had the potential to be passed on genetically, I'm actually his illegitimate child, and Kael is my brother. On that thought, I can't help peering at him curiously, but I already know there is little resemblance between us. And besides, my family …

Stop.

I can't go there. Instead, I focus on Sneak and try to understand his biting accusation.

"I don't get it," I say. "Why do you blame Jeremiah if you know it was Vanik all along?"

"Because Vanik was crazy back then, but Jeremiah wasn't," Sneak spits out. "Jeremiah should have paid more attention to him. He should have known. He should have *stopped* him. And when he couldn't, he should have — he should have been able to heal them. He had the power. Why didn't he use it? He could have saved them!"

Ah. There it is. A four-year-old's perspective is hard to argue against. But I more than anyone know that having an ability and controlling it are two entirely different matters. I could no more justifiably blame Jeremiah for what happened — or didn't happen — in that lab than I could blame myself for —

NO!

STOP!

I'm breathing heavily from my turmoil, choosing to ignore the wary glances being passed around the room as the others take in my wavering composure. I briefly wonder how Dante's reading ability works and if he has to be touching me to hear my turbulent thoughts. Then I wonder if Liana has seen what future lies in store for the next few minutes, and whether I'll survive it.

"Give us a moment, guys," Kael says. Other than Sneak, who struggles against Dante's hold on him, they leave the room without objection.

"You okay?" Kael asks me once they're all gone.

Not in a sharing mood, least of all with him, I say, "I'm fine," and I jump to my feet. I'm now the one pacing, needing to release some restless energy.

"Good," he says, though it's clear he doesn't believe me. "Because there are a few more things you need to hear before we're done here."

My temples pound, and I let out a quiet groan, not sure how much more info dump I can take right now. But still I say, "Go ahead."

"You might want to sit back down for this," Kael suggests. I ignore him, and he adds, "Don't say I didn't warn you."

I let out a deep sigh and take my seat again.

"I'm hedging a guess you know from personal experience that Vanik is pushing the boundaries with his experiments, right?"

I can only nod at his understatement.

"Well, what you don't know — what we think even Falon doesn't realize — is that Vanik *hasn't* stopped his invasive practices. He's just hidden them."

CHAPTER
TWENTY-THREE

Not understanding Kael's declaration, I ask, "What do you mean?"

"Vanik is still experimenting on Speakers today, just like he did ten years ago," he answers. "Only, now he's more careful about how he does it. He makes sure to cover his tracks so that no one knows."

My eyes narrow in question. "If that's the case, how do *you* know?"

Kael chooses his next words carefully. "I'll admit, most of it is guesswork. We have a few people on the inside, but even they can't get close enough to confirm anything."

"Then how —"

"Because I've seen the failed attempts," Kael interrupts. "I've seen the non-Speakers he's practiced on and what's become of them. I've seen the results of him needing ever more Speaker test subjects to experiment with. And I've seen what happens when he's close, but not close enough."

"What —"

"Ebola, 2014," Kael interrupts again. "Did you hear about the outbreak that happened back then?" He swivels his chair around and clicks away at a keyboard until the screens fill with news footage of the hazmat-suited medics and the rising numbers of dead. "That wasn't an organically occurring event. For decades, Ebola was contained within small pockets of Central Africa, but suddenly it was crossing state lines and international borders. Hardly anyone knows this, but it was all because of a non-Speaker guard named Quentin who Vanik was *convinced* he'd transferred a healing-ability gene to. He thought being in a remote village with the worst kind of infectious disease imaginable was an ideal testing ground for Quentin to prove himself, but he was wrong. Quentin's DNA *had* taken on some small part of the Speaking anomaly, but it wasn't that of someone who could heal. Instead, it was a mutated gene that degenerated exponentially. Within days of his arrival at the isolated little village where, at that stage, the virus was contained, he managed to Speak the wrong word at the wrong time with the wrong intent, sparking the pandemic that sent the world into a panic. He himself caught the disease and died a horrible death before Vanik could even try to extradite him to the safety of Lengard's walls."

I know my face must be showing my dismay, but I can't help it. What he's saying …

"That's just one case of Vanik's failed attempts at cloning Speakers, but it's nothing compared with the times when he more or less succeeded," Kael says. At my perplexed look, he explains, "Vanik *did* correctly isolate and replicate the Speaking gene, eventually. But while he could make normal people gifted for short amounts of time, it always wore off. Even so, he still utilized their abilities while they had them, with terrible consequences."

A few more swipes of his keyboard and the screens change to show more news coverage, this time of planes vanishing off the face of the earth, missing without so much as a hint to their whereabouts. Earthquake victims never found among the rubble. Trains derailing.

Nuclear reactors failing. Tsunamis, volcanoes, super-cell storms — all headlines from the past few years that I missed while being locked away from the world. Everywhere, people missing, missing, missing.

"There are only so many brainwashed, non-Speaker guards at Lengard," Kael says quietly, likely noting my horrified expression. "Vanik needs a constant supply of … fresh subjects … and he also needs opportunities to test his genetically modified Speakers. To him, it makes sense to kill two birds with one stone, so to speak. His tempo-rary Speakers cause the catastrophes — accidental or not — and any live casualties are collected by Vanik to … recycle."

I didn't think it was possible to be more repulsed by his actions, but I am. "That's — that's — I don't know what to say."

"It is what it is," Kael says, his voice low. "But it's not all bad news. We've managed to build something good here, where we try to hunt down the new-generation Speakers before Vanik can get his hands on them, and we free others from his clutches. The catacombs are our haven, a place for us to come and go as we please. It's our sanctuary. And more, it's our base of operations for anyone wanting to be part of the defense *against* Lengard."

There's a lot to address in what he's just said, but there's one thing I have to know: "Is Jeremiah — is your dad — is he here?" I was told he died ten years ago, but I'm not sure what to believe anymore.

Kael gives a swift shake of his head, telling me all I need to know. "He's — he's no longer with us."

"I'm sorry," I offer quietly, and I am. I know what it's like to lose a father. I wouldn't wish that on anyone. But I'm also sorry because a small part of me feels connected to Jeremiah on a level I haven't been able to establish with any of the other Speakers. As a Creator, he of all people would understand my inner battle. My constant struggle for control. The reason I can't talk freely, unlike —

"Wait a second." I glance around the room, again noting the

distinct lack of Karoel. "I know that there are more important issues, but I need to ask — why can't I Speak down here? How am I talking like a normal person?"

"Ah," Kael says, leaning back in his seat. "That would be because of me."

I raise my eyebrows in question.

He offers me a strangely smug look. "You might be a Creator, princess, but me? I'm a Destroyer."

It's Enzo's voice that comes as a memory this time: *Creators have all the strengths, none of the weakness ... The only other kind of Speaker who has even close to that sort of power is a Destroyer, but there aren't any of those around anymore.*

Clearly, he was mistaken.

"And that means?" I ask.

Kael watches me for a long moment. "I'm only going to answer because I realize that after hauling you down here as I did, you might appreciate a show of faith."

I withhold my "You think?" glare and wait for him to share.

"I can destroy words," Kael says. "I can effectively nullify the words uttered by a Speaker, stopping them from having any effect — which is what I've been doing with you."

I marvel at this new information. While I, as a Creator, can do almost anything, and Ward, as a Protector, can control the intent of words that are Spoken, it would seem as if Kael's Destroyer ability means that he can effectively ... *dissolve* words, stripping them of their power entirely.

"But here's a bonus most people don't know," he adds. "More than just destroying the power of words, I can also change the intent behind them."

I struggle to understand what he's saying, still trying to wrap my head around the differences between Speakers.

"Your Slayer friend, Crew, right?" Kael asks, reading my confusion. "He might Speak to open a gash on someone's knee, but I can redirect the intent behind his words, breaking the person's arm, instead. My only limit is that I have to stay within the boundaries of a Speaker's own Speaking ability. I can't change Crew's intent to heal, for example, any more than I could use Cami's words to injure someone."

"That's insane," I whisper, overwhelmed by the possibilities. And then my breath hitches, and I jump out of my seat again, backing away from him when I realize what that could mean for me.

He watches me with a furrowed brow. "What's going through your head right now?"

"I'm a Creator. I have no boundaries," I say, telling him something he already knows. "You could do anything you want with me — with my words."

He stands and moves one step, two steps, three steps closer, until I'm pressed up against the wall and he's right in my space.

"I could," he admits, his voice quiet. "Or I could choose to gain your trust by *not* doing exactly that." He leans in even closer, if that's at all possible, and his breath flutters across my skin when he says, "Remember who my dad is, princess. I witnessed his struggle, watched him fight for control every day. He wouldn't let anyone help him, but I'm hoping you'll be different. I want you to discover the full scope of what you can do with your ability. In return for my guidance, I want you to help me stop Vanik from hurting anyone else."

Silence gathers around us while I rally my thoughts enough to frame a response. But I can't. I don't know where to begin. As much as I wish it weren't true, I'm tempted by Kael's olive branch. Ward drew me in under false pretenses, stealing my trust and throwing it back in my face. Kael, however, literally kidnapped me and gave me every reason to *dis*trust him — but as far as I can tell, he hasn't once lied to me. And because of that, it's almost as if, with something as important as this, I *can* trust him.

Before I can get my head around that enough to reply, Kael jumps in again.

"You've been given a lot to think about, and I'm guessing you're near the limit of what you can take right now," he says. "I'm also aware that when you leave here, you're going to see the happy, smiling faces of your Lengard buddies, and you'll start doubting everything I've said. So instead of me telling you anything more, you've reached the part where you need to see proof for yourself."

He leans into me anew, close — way too close — and my lungs constrict when I fail to offer them more oxygen. But all he does is knock twice on the door beside my head. He pulls me toward him when it opens outward — saving me from landing on my backside — and the others stream back into the room.

"Dora, you're up," Kael says to Pandora, as if she's supposed to know exactly what he's talking about.

"Hmm," she says, walking over to the center of the room. "Let me see what I can find in my little box of goodies."

Dante groans. "Seriously, how many times do we have to hear the 'Pandora's box' gimmicks before you realize they're not the least bit funny?"

"We have new ears," Pandora says, motioning to Sneak and me. "Let me have my moment."

"Dora, we're tight for time here," Kael says, reminding me that soon we will be returned to the surface.

"All right, all right," she snipes, reaching for a box hidden beneath the semicircled bench. She rifles through it and pulls something out, then passes it to me.

I turn it over in my hands and say, "It's a glove."

"Ten points, genius," she responds with a snicker. "We'll work on identifying socks next."

"What I meant is," I say through gritted teeth, "*why* are you giving me a glove? And just one?"

Pandora flicks her purple pigtails over her shoulders and eyes Kael furtively. "Didn't you tell her anything?"

"I told her enough," he says.

"Clearly," Dante mutters, amused.

"Here's the dealio, Lyss," Pandora says.

I jerk violently at the nickname.

"I have a Speaking ability that allows me to infuse — or transfer — matter into other objects, such as replicating a certain director's DNA and handprint particulars into a glove just like the one you're holding."

My eyes light with understanding when I realize she's just given me an all-access pass to Lengard. All except for —

"And here, you'll need these, too," Pandora adds, handing me a pair of gaudy, purple-and-pink-framed glasses. "Put them on and they'll help you cheat the retinal scanner. The infusions will only last three days, but you'll be able to go wherever you want in that time so long as you don't get caught."

"But where —"

"Falon has a hidden doorway in his office," Kael says. "Did you know that?"

I nod, fiddling with the objects in my hands. "When he first took me down to the real training rooms and told me all about Speakers, we went through that door and along a hallway until we reached a secret elevator."

"That's where you need to go," he says. "Slip through his office and get to that elevator, but instead of going down, go up. It'll take you directly to Vanik's hidden lab. It's there you'll find evidence that we're not the terrorists in this equation, and you'll see you can trust us with whatever comes next."

"I thought you said Falon doesn't know what Vanik's doing," I say, ignoring his comment about trust. Evidence or not, that will still need to be earned. "How can that be true if all he has to do is take the elevator to the lab and see for himself?"

Kael shakes his head. "I didn't say Falon doesn't know — I said he doesn't *realize*."

"We think Vanik has someone who can modify memories," Pandora explains, noting my confusion. "Someone he keeps handy for any ... unexpected visitors."

Dante jumps in. "That's how we think he's kept Falon in the dark for all these years. Because while the director certainly has his faults, he'd never allow Vanik to carry on his experiments if he knew how far he was really going with them still."

I wait for someone to tell me more, but no one offers anything else, so I say, "I'm sorry, but if Vanik has access to a Speaker with that kind of ability, what's to stop him or her from modifying *my* memory?"

Pandora snorts. "You're a Creator. Be creative."

Looking around at the faces all watching me — and with expectation — I realize they have a lot more faith in my ability than they should.

"I may be a Creator," I say slowly, "but my control is scattered at best. I'm certainly not competent enough to go up against another Speaker and *be creative* enough for us to both come out in one piece."

With a laugh, Pandora says, "Don't be ridiculous. Kael, tell her."

I turn to Kael, fully expecting him to back me up, since he's had to destroy the power of my words the whole time I've been down here.

"Dora's right — you'll be fine," he says.

My mouth drops at his quick, unconcerned agreement.

"No, seriously," he says. "I'm hardly destroying any of your words now — you're doing most of it yourself. As long as you're careful with your intent, you shouldn't have any problems with your control."

My hands tighten around the glove and glasses. "But what if I come face-to-face with this memory Speaker?"

Pandora grins and says, "I suggest you turn whoever it is into a frog. That'll teach 'em."

She's not taking this seriously. None of them are. But none of them know exactly what I'm capable of. If they did, they wouldn't be so relaxed around me. Not even with Kael here to keep me in check.

"Aw, come on," Pandora says, laughing again. "Lighten up, Lyss."

I'm so anxious about it all — the expectations, the misguided faith, the joking frog suggestion that would be all too easy for me to carry out — that I can't keep from snapping at her. "Stop calling me that. 'Lyss' — 'princess' — I don't know why you're calling me that."

Pandora looks taken aback. Hurt, even. "Um. Maybe because that's your name? Well, not the princess part — that's all Kael, and I'll admit, that's weird. But the Lyss part …"

I shuffle my feet, shift my eyes and wonder how I might escape the room and everything I've learned in the past hour. And yet, I still hear myself summon the courage to ask, "How can you possibly know that?"

It's not Pandora who answers, but Kael. His voice is strong and steady. Calm, even. Perhaps too calm.

"We've been watching you for years, Alyssa Scott."

My breath freezes in my lungs at the name I've heard only twice in over two and a half years, both times from his mouth. But he's not finished, and I know this because the words he utters next shatter me from the inside out.

"We've been watching you since long before you killed your parents."

CHAPTER
TWENTY-FOUR

I need air.

I need air, and I need it *right now.*

Heedless of what I'm doing or where I'm going, I tear out of the room before anyone can catch me. I hear cries of alarm from behind me, but I can't stop — I won't stop — *I can't stop — I won't stop —*

I run and I run and I run, following the flame-lit corridors of the underground labyrinth, not caring how lost I become or if anyone will ever find me. I just need to get away.

"Alyssa, stop!"

I can't stop.

I won't stop.

I can't stop.

I won't stop.

"Lyss! Would you just wait a second!"

My lungs are burning. I have a cramp forming in my calf and a stitch in my side that feels like I've been stabbed. But it's nothing compared to the pain I'm really feeling. The pain that I know no amount of stretching or breathing will make go away. So I keep running, blurring my way through the unending tunnels and deep into the depths of the underground maze.

"*Alyssa*! Enough!"

Arms like steel bands wrap around me from behind, yanking me back in a violent halt. The abrupt stop pushes the little remaining air from my lungs, making me realize just how hard I've been breathing, with unnaturally short, sharp breaths. My pulse is skyrocketing, too.

I have no control over my reaction. All I know is that something is keeping me from running. And I *need* to be running. So I spin around and lash out like a cornered animal, punching, kicking, clawing my way to freedom. The arms only tighten, pulling me so close that I'm trapped against a hard, warm chest, barely able to wiggle, let alone maneuver myself free. Even so, I don't give up. I fight. *I fight.*

It's only when I begin to lag with exhaustion that I hear a deep, soothing voice as if from far away, and I realize the owner has been talking for a while, telling me some kind of story.

"… and then when I was fourteen, I rode my bike into a parked car — don't ask how — and I fractured it *again*. I felt so stupid that I didn't tell anyone for days. I waited so long that they had to stick a metal plate along the bone to get it to set right. Remind me to show you the scar next time you're not trying to scratch my face off."

The fight leaves me and I slump against Kael as the haze of terror clears from my mind.

"I-I-I'm s-s-s-sorry," I stutter through chattering teeth. I don't know if I'm cold or if it's just my body's way of dealing with what happened. "I d-didn't mean t-to —"

"Don't worry 'bout it, princess." Kael's arms are still supporting me. "Do you want to hear about the next one?"

"The ne-next one?"

"My next trip to the emergency room."

That's what he's been sharing with me?

"Why're you telling me about your hos-hospital visits?" I'm pleased that I almost manage to get the whole sentence out without chattering. My heart rate is calming now, too, and my breathing is almost back to normal.

I feel Kael's shoulders move in a shrug. "You were panicking. It used to happen to my dad. The only thing that helped was if I gave him something else to focus on. So I would tell him stories — real ones, made-up ones, it didn't matter. Just something for him to listen to. It helped draw him back, pull him out of his fear."

My body tenses again, but Kael tightens his hold on me and says, "It's nothing to be ashamed about. It happens to the best of us."

I finally push away from him. My legs wobble, but I'm able to hold myself up without his help. "I bet it's never happened to you," I say, unable to meet his eyes.

"Doesn't mean it won't one day," he replies. His voice holds no judgment, no pity. "Now, are we going to talk about why it happened?"

"No," I say quickly. Too quickly.

"I'll rephrase," he says firmly. "We're *going* to talk about what just happened. I've seen anxiety attacks before, but that was extreme. And as much as I don't want to worry you, you should also know you were screaming 'I can't stop — I won't stop' over and over, with powerful intent behind your words. If I hadn't been chasing after you and nullifying your ability, you would have literally run yourself to death."

I flinch, knowing he's right. And more than that, I could have screamed anything in my panicked state. If he hadn't followed me and destroyed the power of my words … I don't want to imagine what I might have said. What I might have *done*.

"I'm sorry," I say quietly. "I don't know what happened."

"Sure you do," he replies. "You lost it because I mentioned your parents."

I flinch again, this time much more violently.

"It was years ago, but you still haven't dealt with it," he continues, not noticing — or not caring — that every word he says is like a knife slicing into my flesh. "You're still holding on to that guilt. You have to let it go before it destroys you."

"I can't do that," I force out. "I don't know *how* to do that."

"You're going to have to figure it out," Kael tells me. "Because next time something like this happens, it might not end so well for you — or for the rest of the world."

He's right — again. I have to get control of my thoughts. Maybe then I'll find it easier to get control of my Speaking ability. Perhaps the two are connected somehow. But I'll be damned if I run that theory past Ward in our training sessions. No way will I tell him about my past, about what happened, about what I did. I still refuse to give him my name, let alone anything else.

"How do you know?" I ask Kael. "How do you know about me, my parents, *any* of it?" I step forward, closing the space between us again. "You said you were watching me since before — since before it happened. But how? And why?"

Before Kael can answer, his phone makes an obnoxious alarm sound, and he pulls it from his pocket, cursing when the display lights up.

"Time's up, princess," he says, turning the screen around to show me the clock.

I hadn't realized it was so late; the zoo's after-hours event will be finishing up in a few minutes, and any remaining visitors will be kicked out of the park.

Kael gently grabs my upper arm and starts retracing our steps along the tunnel. "We've got to get you topside before your Lengard crew takes off," he says, each of his steps requiring two of mine, "and since we're halfway to hell down here, we're going to have to hurry to get you back."

"You haven't answered my questions," I say, skip-jogging beside him. "How do you know about me?"

When he doesn't say anything, I dig in my feet, halting us both. "Kael. Tell me."

Every muscle in his body is locked tight. "We don't have —"

"We don't have time, I know, I know," I interrupt. "But you need to *make* time. I need you to explain how you know who I am and what I've done, when no one else in the world knows."

He lets out a surprised laugh. "You're kidding, right?"

I'm not kidding, but I *am* confused. And Kael must see that, because the smile drops off his face, replaced by an incredulous expression.

"You really have no idea, do you?" He shakes his head. "I hate to be the one to tell you this, but almost everyone at Lengard knows who you are, Lyss. At least in the Genesis generation. They've known all along."

I suddenly find it hard to breathe again and wheeze out, "What?"

"In the history of Lengard, very few Genesis Speakers have left the facility permanently, and only two families managed it on their own without needing to be smuggled out. The Roscaves ... and the Scotts."

He pauses to let that sink in, but all I hear is a ringing in my ears until he continues, "You were just a baby when your parents packed you up and took off, but my dad — and later Falon and Vanik — kept an eye on you all. Your whole life, they've been watching you. Even longer than we have. How else do you think they found you in some backwater psych ward?"

Feeling slightly ill, I say, "Falon said that their scouts found my brain scans or something in the system after I checked myself in, and that the readings matched what they were after so they picked me up."

"You seriously believed that?"

It does sound far-fetched. "But if my parents were at Lengard, then that means —"

"They were Speakers, too? Yep. You're Xanaphan-free, princess."

Overwhelmed and frustrated by everything he *hasn't* explained, I demand, "Why do you keep calling me that?"

He rubs the back of his neck and releases a sigh filled with impatience. "Look, there's lots I haven't yet told you, including how Liana has kept an eye on you over the years. But I'm not kidding, Lyss — if we stand around and chat just to appeal to your curiosity, then you're going to miss the ferry." ·

I open my mouth to argue, but he places a finger over my lips, keeping me silent.

"I promise you'll hear from me again soon. And I'll explain everything then. You have my word."

For some inexplicable reason, I believe him. That, and I don't want to get stuck down here and allow copycat me to go back to Lengard to carry on with the ruse. So I nod and follow after he drops his hand from my mouth, flashes me a small but dazzling grin and leads the way back up the tunnel again at a pace so fast I'm nearly sprinting to keep up.

CHAPTER
TWENTY-FIVE

It's surprisingly easy to get back aboveground.

After retrieving the glove and glasses I'd dropped and hiding them in my coat, and after saying goodbye to Pandora and Liana, who are both staying behind, I hurry with Kael, Jet, Dante and the still-restrained Sneak back to the ancient elevator.

Jet keeps the five of us cloaked once we're out of the catacombs and walking along the zoo's paths again, but it's not as much of a fright this time, since I now understand why I'm transparent. Strange, yes. Terrifying, no.

Invisible, we hurry toward the ferry terminal, having received an update from Pandora that my Lengard friends are getting ready to board the boat back to Circular Quay.

We're almost to the dock, when Kael pulls us all off the path and into a grove of trees swallowed by darkness. Only the faintest trace of moonlight filters through.

"Jet," Kael says.

Whether he destroys her cloaking or she cancels it herself, either way, the five of us become visible again. Due to the limited light, I can make out little more than the shadowed outline of their bodies.

"I don't need a reminder," I say, assuming that's why we've paused here. "I know I only have three days to use the glove and glasses to see if you're right about Vanik's secret lab. I won't forget."

"That's not why we've stopped," Dante says, pushing Sneak in front of him and closer to me.

There's meaning in the move, but I'm not sure *what* meaning.

Not until Kael explains, "You have to wipe his memories, Lyss. He can't go back to Lengard knowing everything he heard and saw tonight."

I'm taken aback by his words, even if on some rational level I know he's right. But I can't get a single word out — whether to agree or disagree — before Sneak starts to struggle.

"No!" he cries out. "Don't listen to them, Jane! I don't — You can't — Please, don't —"

"Easy, kid," Dante cuts him off, holding him tighter. "She's not going to hurt you. You won't even know anything has changed."

Sneak's face looks positively ghostly in the moonlight. "She doesn't have any control! She could do anything to me!"

He's correct, but that doesn't stop me from recoiling at his words.

Kael doesn't miss my reaction, and his face hardens. Even in the low light I see him narrow angry eyes at Sneak.

I reach out to touch Kael's arm. "No, he's right," I say. "I've only wiped memories once before, and that time I had Ward keeping me in check."

"And this time you have me," Kael points out. "Not that you need my help."

"You have too much confidence in me," I murmur.

"No, I just have more confidence in you than *you* do," he replies. "Now, hurry up or you'll both be camping here for the night."

Still unsure, I tentatively ask, "How much do I try to modify?"

"Take him back to the chimpanzees and wipe everything from then on," Dante says. He has a hand on Sneak's temple again, and a soft light glows around them both. "He was hungry and considering leaving you quickly to go grab some food, so make him think that happened and that he wandered on his own for a while before meeting up with the group for the seal show. Make sure he has no suspicions. Everything was normal, and you were with the others the whole time."

"No! No, Jane, don't do this!" Sneak cries.

He is terrified — of me.

I look to Kael, and he gives me a single nod.

"Careful now," he warns. "Watch your words. Watch your intent. But also trust yourself — you can do this."

"And if I can't?"

"Then like I said, I've got your back, princess. The kid'll be fine either way," he answers. "Now, do it. Quick. The moment you're done, I'll stop blocking him so he'll be back to his invisible self, and Jet'll cloak us again to keep him from seeing us. You'll have a few seconds where he'll be disoriented, and that's when you need to get out of here, but don't worry, we'll push him in the right direction for him to stumble out and meet you on the boat."

His confidence starts to rub off on me, the plan clear in my mind.

"Shae — your doppelgänger — will be waiting in the bathroom on the ferry to swap places with you," Kael finishes. "Now, hurry — because by the sounds of it, they're getting ready to cast off."

Feeling the stress of the moment but also knowing how important it is to concentrate, I take a deep breath, ignore Sneak's pleas, trust Kael's promise and focus my thoughts on a single-minded intention. "Forget," I whisper, seeing everything in my mind exactly as Dante suggested.

I don't need to watch the soft light flow from me or hear Kael's quiet, "Nice work, princess," to know I managed to do it all on my own. And I feel a little bit of pride at that, even as we all disappear again and I hurry out of the trees, down to the dock and over the gangplank onto the ferry.

Jet must know exactly when I enter the bathroom, because the moment I do, I become visible again.

"Thank *God*! I thought you'd never get here!"

I stop short at the sight of — *me*.

Stunned, I can only watch as my copycat, Shae, says a few quiet words and, with a flash of light, transforms into a young man wearing a smart business suit.

Only then does she — now *he* — catch my gaping self and push me toward the door. "What are you waiting for? Seriously, Lyss — go!"

It's only when I'm seated at the back of the ferry with Abby asleep on my lap and my Lengard friends arguing about whether the penguins or the crocodiles were more interesting that I try to gather my thoughts. But everything Kael told me is too fresh. I need time to get my head around it all, time to see for myself if he was telling the truth. Time to decide what to do.

For the rest of tonight, at least, I won't think about Vanik's lab or Lengard knowing who I really am. I won't think about my parents being Speakers, why they left Lengard and why they never told me about their ability — or thought to warn me about mine.

Instead, I close my eyes, lean my head back and focus on clearing my mind.

Everything can wait until tomorrow, I tell myself. I'll deal with it all then.

CHAPTER
TWENTY-SIX

In my defense, my intentions were good. I *planned* to follow up on what I learned yesterday first thing this morning. But before I could do so, I was called to an unexpected — and early — training session with Ward. Hours later, I'm blurry eyed and have a stress headache verging on migraine status, with it taking everything I have to concentrate on his lesson.

It doesn't help that Ward is edgier than normal today. Last night he stopped by our quarters after we returned from the zoo, and I struggled being in the same room as him, wondering if he knew the truth about Vanik. If he knew the truth about *me*.

… And fearing his level of involvement with what might truly be happening here at Lengard.

This morning's session has given me no further insight into what he might know. The only way I'm able to remotely focus on the tasks he's setting is by suppressing everything Kael said yesterday. It's the only way I can listen to Ward, look at Ward, be anywhere *near* Ward.

"Where's your head at today, Jane?" Ward barks.

I drag my eyes to him.

Standing in the center of the Karoel-lined training room with his jeans and white T-shirt in stark contrast to the black rock, he glares at me.

It seems like forever ago that I last saw his dimpled smile.

The moment that thought crosses my mind, I shove it away.

I don't want to see Ward smile.

I *don't*.

Not at me. Not at anything.

He manipulated me. He *betrayed* me. And, quite possibly, those are the least of his offenses, if even a fraction of what Kael claims about Vanik is true — and especially if Ward, the director-in-training, has been in on it all along.

"I didn't sleep well," I mumble out my excuse, forcing myself to ignore the way his features soften at my admission. "And I have a headache."

He walks toward me, his steps deliberate. "Something on your mind?"

I nearly laugh at the loaded question. But perhaps … "Can I ask you something?"

I see it happen immediately. His face shuts down, his body tightens. His reaction makes me want to throw something at him.

To my surprise, however, he says, "Of course."

I remind myself that he didn't promise honesty. He has no qualms about lying to me. But this is an opportunity I'm not willing to waste.

"Why two and a half years?"

"What?"

I know I have to tread carefully. "Cami and Manning both told me that when new Speakers arrive at Lengard, they go through an initiation period, but it doesn't last long before they're moved down here to begin proper training."

Ward nods, his eyes wary but not as shuttered as they were before.

"Why did Falon wait over two and a half years with me?" I ask. "Why wait so long and then suddenly threaten to kill me if I remained uncooperative?"

Ward straightens. "Falon never threatened your life."

I cross my arms. "The implication was there. Come on, Ward. What do you think he was going to do once my month was up? Let me go on my merry way?"

"He wasn't going to *kill* you," Ward says firmly. "My uncle is many things, but he's not a murderer. That's not what happens here."

I wonder how he can say that to me with a straight face after what happened to his parents. Sneak confirmed it, so I know at least that part of Kael's story must be true.

"Then explain it to me," I challenge. I was never brave enough to ask before, but now I have to know. "Justify how I was locked up, imprisoned in an unending routine, until you came along and I was given a month to live."

A muscle in his jaw twitches. "I'm telling you, Jane. That part you misunderstood."

"Did I misunderstand the rest?" I ask, eyebrows raised. "Did I imagine the years of electroshock and everything else? Is torture considered a normal hazing practice for Lengard's new Speakers?"

I know I've scored a point when Ward is unable to hold my gaze.

"Vanik took liberties with you beyond what was acceptable," he admits. "He's been reprimanded for his actions."

My reply is caustic. "I'm sure that will stop him from hurting anyone else."

"He's the reason Enzo was working with you."

My forehead crinkles. "Come again?"

"Exodus recruits aren't supposed to have contact with those in initiation," Ward reminds me, "but Enzo was with you from the very beginning to monitor your well-being, making sure you were staying physically healthy — and mentally healthy."

An image of my hot-pink gloves comes to mind, the only splash of color in my otherwise whitewashed existence, and Enzo's words from that night whisper across my memory: *You can survive this ... Just don't give up.*

Was he playing me all along, too? Just like Ward?

I hear Enzo's voice again, remember more of his words: *It's about time you joined the fold. I thought you were never gonna Speak.*

I close my eyes and turn away from Ward, certain he'll be able to read the question on my face if I don't. The question of whether they all know who I really am. Whether they all know the real reason I didn't Speak for so long. Whether they know my name ... Whether they know I killed my parents.

At least I'm certain Cami doesn't know. She would have told me. I'm sure of it.

Having confidence in my friend helps loosen the ugly feeling in my chest a little.

"It was my uncle who tasked Enzo with watching over you," Ward says, drawing my eyes back to him. "Enzo grew up as a military kid, his parents both highly decorated officers. In the years before he began Speaking and was brought here to Lengard, he was schooled in all kinds of physical training, which made him the perfect person to keep an eye on you."

I roll that over in my mind. "Why was Enzo in place to make sure I survived the initiation if Vanik wasn't supposed to take things so far?"

"Given your background, my uncle figured it was better to be safe than sorry."

My breath hitches, and I squeak out, "My background?"

I wonder if this is it. The moment that I'll discover just how deep his betrayal goes.

"You checked yourself into a psychiatric institution," Ward says.

I relax — slightly.

"No one had any idea how you would react to being here. And when you didn't Speak for so long ..."

He trails off with a shrug, so I finish for him. "When I didn't Speak, they decided to just keep waiting to see if I would."

"Yes," he confirms. "It was important that you revealed your ability of your own free will and didn't feel pressured into working with us."

At that, I can't hold back my incredulous laugh. "I guess two and a half years was enough for them to give up on that, huh?"

"No one forced you to Speak that first time, Jane," Ward says, his voice hard. "You did that on your own."

"If I hadn't, Abby would be six feet under right now."

He has the grace to flinch — violently.

Running a hand through his hair, he says, "Look, there's no point arguing about this."

"We're not arguing," I, well, argue. "We're discussing the justification for my imprisonment." Never mind that I *wanted* to be locked away from the world. That part doesn't need to factor into our narrative right now.

"I don't know what you want me to say, Jane," Ward declares, throwing his arms out in an uncharacteristic show of frustration. "Do you want me to admit that I don't know why they kept you in that prison cell for so long? Do you want me to tell you that I think what Vanik did to you was unforgivable? That he should be punished for his actions and made to endure the same horrific tests he carried out on you? Do you want me to say I wish my uncle had sent me to you sooner? Is that what you want from me?"

I'm trying to keep my expression blank, but it's taking everything in me to do so. I haven't seen him so emotional since before he turned into cold Ward. But there's nothing cold about him now. His eyes are burning, his hands are clenched and every line in his body is strained with tension.

It might make me a coward, or it might make me an angel, but either way, I don't think either of us can handle taking this conversation further. Not right now. My headache has only increased during our discussion, and my temples are throbbing so painfully that it's a miracle I can see straight.

At least, I convince myself that's the reason I feel tears coming. Not because he's just shown me a glimpse of the Ward I remember. The Ward I miss.

"Why don't we just —" My voice comes out hoarse, so I clear it and try again. "Let's just — let's just get back to training."

I watch as he visibly relaxes, a short nod of agreement all he offers me. The transformation of his features is instant, with all signs of emotion gone and his walls firmly in place once more. It makes me wonder if I imagined his outburst. If I read more into it than what it actually was. If it, like everything else with him seems to be, was an act.

With a sigh, I return my attention to the ground, and piece by piece I focus on building the haystack Ward directed me to create earlier. I put aside our discussion and lose myself in the task, moving the golden straw into position with my words and imagination. Only when I'm done do I turn to Ward again.

I'm not surprised when I can't read his face. I can't ever seem to read his face anymore.

When he continues to just look at me, I wave my hands, a gesture that appears to startle him, as if he hadn't realized he was staring at me.

"Good job," he says, taking in the haystack that I shaped roughly into the form of the Eiffel Tower. If you squint, tilt your head and turn all the lights off.

"One more activity, then we'll call it quits for the day."

My shoulders slump, but I show no other resistance — even as I ignore the pounding across my forehead that has yet to ease.

"You've been handling things well lately, so I thought we'd try something different this afternoon, out in the main room again," Ward says, moving toward me.

Without being told, I banish my sad attempt at recreating the iconic French landmark and turn my focus back to him, wary but also curious about what he might have in store for me next.

CHAPTER
TWENTY-SEVEN

Ward asks me to hold out my hand, so I tentatively do so, and he places something in my palm. It's not heavy, nor is it light. What it is, is invisible.

I ignore the tingles that wash over my skin as he uses his fingers to wrap mine around the object, then squeezes them until whatever I hold is secure in my hand.

"Um," I say as he puts three deliberate steps of distance between us, "do you want to maybe explain?" I wave the invisible object I can feel but not see.

"The first day you were brought down here, there was a paintball skirmish going on outside."

I remember that. The memory is vividly burned into my brain.

Reading my face, Ward continues, "You're currently holding an unloaded paintball gun."

"It's invisible."

Sadly, those are the exact words that come out of my mouth, which is why I find Ward's response to be generous.

"Very astute, Jane."

I can practically hear his unspoken "dumb-ass" tagged on the end.

"The weapon you're holding has been cloaked by a Speaker to make it invisible, but nothing more."

I automatically think of Jet and her ability, wondering who in Lengard has a similar power.

"The weapons your opponents will be using are also invisible, but they're infused to generate and release paintballs at the Spoken word 'bang.'"

His use of the word "infused" calls to mind Pandora's transferring ability and the objects I have hidden in my wardrobe. Three days. I still have time. "My opponents?"

"You can't play skirmish with only one person, Jane."

Ward's dry response irks me, but I'm guessing I'll find out for myself soon enough.

"If my gun isn't loaded like theirs, how am I supposed to shoot anyone?"

He peers at me for a long moment before inhaling and looking upward, staring at the ceiling as if seeking divine patience. "You're a Creator, Jane. *Use your imagination.*"

Oh. Right.

Ward shakes his head and reaches into his pocket. He pulls out a strip of blue material and throws it to me. I catch it with my free hand.

"Your task is simple," he says.

As he speaks, I wedge my invisible gun between my knees so I can tie the makeshift armband around my left biceps. When I'm unable to manage such a coordinated feat on my own, Ward sighs heavily and strides forward to secure it in place for me.

"I'm listening," I say as he retreats once more. I attempt to figure out if, after reclaiming my gun, I'm holding it the right way or at risk of shooting myself in the face.

"I don't care if you're on the winning team or the losing one, just as long as you maintain control of your ability," Ward tells me. "All you have to do is create paint, using the same 'bang' word as everyone else so no one realizes your gun isn't infused like the other guns. Think you can do that?"

"I'm assuming if I can't, you'll protect them from me?"

"That's not the point," he argues.

"But it's still *a* point," I say. When his eyes narrow, I roll mine in return and confirm, "Yes, Ward. I think I can keep enough control to create a little bit of paint. But just to be sure …"

I can't ignore the opportunity he's presented me, so I raise my hand, tug on what I think is the trigger — not that it matters, since the gun isn't really loaded — and say, "Bang!"

A flash of light appears with my Spoken word, and, at seeing the results of my command, I have to lift my free hand to cover my mouth, holding back laughter.

"You, uh, didn't think to protect yourself?" I ask Ward, my voice bubbling with humor as I take in his rainbow-splattered chest.

I'm half expecting him to yell at me, so it comes as a surprise when his eyes brighten and his lips twitch before he shuts down his expression.

"You didn't lose control, so there was no reason for me to inter-vene," he responds. "Plus, from this you can now tell if you need more or less creativity with your intent. I suggest you visualize a touch less paint next time." His mouth quirks as he adds, "And you could prob-ably leave out the glitter."

So I *may* have let my imagination go a little wild. But it was worth it just to witness his lighthearted reaction. It's been so long since —

I stop my train of thought before it gets away from me.

"And remember, you're on the blue team, which means —"

I raise my gun and shoot him again before he can finish, this time swapping out the rainbow with plain blue splatters. "Blue paint only. No glitter. Got it."

"For the record, it's not pleasant being shot at close range, imaginary paintballs or not," Ward says, rubbing a hand against his chest and smearing the paint there. "And while I know you kept your impact soft since my ribs aren't crushed right now, feel free not to do that again."

I'm not proud of my lack of sympathy, but … I *did* get to shoot Ward. *And* see him splattered with rainbow glitter. It was worth the minor bruises he can easily ask Cami to heal later.

Before I can muster a response — or attempt some kind of contrition — the door opens, and Enzo walks in.

"We're all ready out there," he says. "Just waiting on you two."

Ward turns to him. "Thanks, Enz. We're coming now."

Enzo's face breaks into a brilliant smile when he sees Ward's torso, and he looks at me. "Getting in a few practice shots?"

"Can you blame me?" I say, though with a whispered word, I vanish the paint from Ward's chest before anyone else can question the source of the rainbow glitter.

Enzo barks out a laugh. "Glad you're on my team, JD. We'll put you to good use."

Cami, Keeda and Crew are all waiting for us outside the Karoel room, and I can just make out the blurred image of Sneak, as well. With Ward and Enzo, that makes seven of us in total. Three of us wear blue armbands: Enzo, Crew and me; while Ward, Cami, Sneak and Keeda are all wearing green. I have to do a double take when the green team walk away and huddle to discuss strategy, knowing what I now do of the tragic event that made them all orphans.

"Yo, JD, you feel like adding anything here?"

Enzo's question makes me focus on my team again. Four against three doesn't seem like fair odds, but then I remember that I'm a

Creator, Enzo has military training and Crew is ... aggressive. It should even out the playing field, especially since I assume neither Cami nor Sneak will be particularly ruthless. Keeda, however, is no pushover, and I'm certain she and Ward will present the biggest threats.

Being careful with every word I say, I share my thoughts with Enzo and Crew — leaving out the part about me being a Creator — and when I'm done, Enzo nods with approval.

"Nice deductive reasoning," he praises.

Ever the pessimist, Crew tugs his eyebrow piercing and says, "Let's hope your aim is as good as your judgment."

"Want to try me?" I challenge, pushing the imaginary safety off my gun.

Crew's surly attitude dissolves into a grin, and I understand why when Enzo says, "There's, uh, no safety on paintball guns."

Heat touches my cheeks, but I'm saved from having to respond when the green team return.

"Are you done discussing how you'll lick your wounds after we beat you?" Keeda asks.

"We thought it was more important to be realistic," Crew shoots back.

"Shut it, Slayer boy," she says. "Your team is going down."

As if those words hold magical properties, I take my lead off the others, and we all scatter, running to find shelter behind the pillars of the room as the skirmish begins in earnest.

It takes the length of three heartbeats for me to realize that I'm going to pay immensely for shooting Ward earlier — twice. And I know this because in that short amount of time, he's already shot me — *twice.*

And it *hurts.* Enough that I want to exact retribution.

So with a war cry that mingles with those from my allies and enemies, I throw myself into the skirmish, shooting left, right and center.

And I miss, left, right and center.

Part of that is because the green team have clearly done this numerous times before, and they're frighteningly quick to duck and dodge my attacks. But most of that is because I'm so acutely wary of my intent. While outwardly I only have to say the word "bang," in the back of my mind I have to focus on at least four different things all at once: shooting a paint pellet from the nozzle of my invisible gun; making it burst with the same shade of blue produced by the rest of my team's weapons; being sure it doesn't have too much or too little pressure to differentiate it from the shots the rest of them are firing; and aiming the line of fire at a specific target.

Skirmish is challenging enough *without* having to concentrate on all those things at once, let alone while doing them *and* making sure I don't lose control of my intent. Without the dampening effects of the Karoel, there's nothing pushing against me to limit my power, so I have to keep a tight rein on my words — something that I struggle with at the best of times.

Five minutes in and I realize I need a new plan. I haven't managed to hit anyone yet, but I've taken a number of paintballs to my torso and limbs, smearing me in green. My teammates are starting to notice how little I'm helping, whereas Ward, Cami, Keeda and Sneak work together like a well-oiled machine. I wonder how many times they've played this game over the years, and I sullenly acknowledge that their close history gives their team another advantage that I hadn't considered earlier.

But ... observing the way they carry out their attacks gives me an idea.

I've been so focused on creating paintballs that shoot from my gun that I haven't stopped to consider that the normal rules don't apply to me. The others are all limited to using the physical ammo infused into their weapons. But I'm creating my own — and the paint doesn't need to come directly from my gun.

Gleeful at my out-of-the-box thinking, I wait until I have a clear line of sight at Keeda, who is engaged in a fight against Crew. Then I raise my weapon vaguely in her direction and say, "Bang!"

It doesn't matter if my gun's aim is true or not, because *my* aim is. I could have been facing my weapon to the ceiling and still splattered the paint across her thigh, just as long as my intent was on the result I was after and not the complex process of making it happen.

And suddenly, it's like something clicks in my brain.

For so much of my training with Ward I've been focusing on *how* to make my ability work, all the little things I've had to concentrate on with my intent. Really, it's much simpler than that. I don't need to focus on the *how;* I only need to focus on the *what.* On the actual *result.* Just like my first day with him when I said "cat," and a cat appeared. I don't know where Schrödinger came from — whether he was someone's pet or a stray, or whether he didn't exist at all until I created him. All I did was call him into being, and he came.

With a smile stretching across my face, I raise my eyes around the room as I realize I can do this. I can keep control because I only have to focus on one thing. Not my aim, not my ammo creation, not my pressure … just my targets. And with an elated feeling, I take off again, shooting left, right and center once more.

This time I hit Cami, Keeda and Sneak, one after the other. Blue paint bursts onto their clothes, and I run and duck and hide as they retaliate. I can't resist the temptation when I see Ward across the room in a skirmish with Enzo, and while I know he's too far for anyone else to target, I don't have the limitations of a normal gun. So I sneakily whisper, "Bang!" while he's hiding around a pillar with no weapons trained on him, not even mine. His body gives a jerk when my light hits him and blue smears him, and he looks around in puzzlement at his lack of enemies in range before he glances farther across the room in realization.

I give a cheery wave. He never said I couldn't cheat, just that he wanted me to keep control.

And right now, I feel more in control than I've ever been. It's exhilarating. Breathtaking. Empowering … *Intoxicating.*

Unfortunately, it doesn't last.

As the time flies by with me running and laughing and shooting — and, admittedly, being shot — I start to grow tired. Physically, yes, but also mentally. It becomes difficult to keep my concentration, my aim going wide more often than not, or just not resulting in paint at all. The light stops bursting from me consistently, and the effects of my ability become scattered, to the point that I'm once again a liability to my team rather than an asset.

I'm beginning to become legitimately concerned, when Ward calls a halt to the skirmish.

The match is declared a tie — despite objections from both teams — and everyone disperses to go clean up, leaving me alone with Ward again. I follow him back into the Karoel room and don't hesitate to ask what's wrong with me, explaining how I was doing so well and then … not.

His answer surprises me.

"You got tired, Jane. Plain and simple. It's harder to do anything when you're tired — Speaking included."

I almost want to laugh at how normal it makes me feel, to have a weakness that is so commonly shared by everyone in the world.

"It's not a good thing," Ward says, reading my expression.

I shrug, aware that he's probably right, but still pleased.

"You need to take this seriously," he says. "Fatigue makes you lose concentration — which means you, especially, become more dangerous than normal. Sometimes, like today, your ability will stop working consistently. Other times your intent could become muddled, producing unwanted and potentially disastrous results. You need to recall the signs and keep them in mind for the future." He looks intently into my eyes. "You know how they say not to drive a vehicle while tired? The same goes for you and Speaking. Be alert to your body and recognize when you need to avoid using your ability altogether."

I give him the nod he expects.

"Good," he says. "Then on that note, we're done for the day. You did well — even if you cheated."

I wish his praise didn't make me feel so warm, but it does.

"You say I cheated. I say I *used my imagination*."

CHAPTER
TWENTY-EIGHT

By the time Ward escorts me back up to my suite, my headache has returned with a vengeance. Even after Cami heals me, I'm so exhausted from the strain of the past few hours that I drop right off to sleep without eating dinner.

The next day passes in a similar manner, without the skirmish action but with the addition of a few nagging worries. I wonder when, how and even *if* I should try to verify Kael's story. It's not like I don't believe him. His story was so complex and full of detail that I'm sure some of it has to be right — or at least based on some form of the truth. But no, my hesitation is because I know that if I do find evidence to corroborate his tale, there will be no coming back from it. And what will I do then? Prison or haven, Lengard is my home. And if Kael is right — that will change everything.

To avoid planning my infiltration of Falon's office, after I finish training for the day I crash on the couch for a movie night with Cami. Keeda shows up carrying two bags stuffed to the brim with junk food, and we welcome her with open arms. We laugh and chat — or they chat, since I'm still not confident enough away from the Karoel or Ward to join in — and we have a perfectly relaxing night.

I need a night without responsibilities. And I take it.

But the next day is harder. Because today is the final day Pandora's gloves and glasses will work, so I actually have to make a choice.

It's quite simple, really.

Do something … or don't.

Investigate … or ignore.

Summon courage … or submit to fear.

While I try to create a miniature landscape in the training room, with a forest-bordered river and a snow-dusted mountain range half the height of my body, I'm distracted. Enough that I make fresh snow fall from invisible clouds above us, rather than have the snow already stuck to the peaks of the chair-sized Alps. Ward isn't impressed, so I quickly vanish the icy flakes now covering us both and construct a miniature ski village at the base of the mountains, chairlift included. All the while, my mind is repeating a litany: *Go, don't go. Do it, don't do it. Go, don't go. Do it, don't do it.*

When I'm back in my room later that evening, acutely aware that it's now or never, I still lack the motivation to make my move. Lying on my bed with Schrödinger curled up at my side, I am paralyzed. I know there's no choice, really. Not if I want to know the truth. But still …

I

    don't

        know

            what

                to

                    do.

Frustrated by my inability to gather the courage and just *go,* I'm interrupted by the most unexpected of voices.

"What the hell are you waiting for, princess?"

I bolt upright, only to see Kael standing in front of me — *in my bedroom.*

I half wonder if I'm hallucinating. But seeing his agitated expression, I know I couldn't have summoned a face so accurately — and *vividly* — demanding an explanation for my delay. Even so, I'm frozen in place, because I suddenly hear voices floating through my closed door from farther down the hallway, telling me that Cami has returned. By the sound of it, she has company.

When Kael draws in a breath to speak again, I do the only thing I can think of: I launch myself off the bed and straight at him, intending to slap my hand over his mouth to keep anyone from hearing.

I don't proceed with caution; I propel my entire weight at his body. But instead of slamming into his torso and silencing him, I keep going, straight *through* him, until I crash noisily into the wardrobe behind him.

Ow, ow, ow, ow, owwwww, I mentally complain, but then I hear hurried footsteps approaching my room, and I frantically try to untangle myself from the clothes at the base of my closet.

I come unstuck just as my door bursts open. Ward rushes into my room, followed quickly by Enzo and Cami. I know I have approximately one-point-five seconds to come up with a valid reason for Kael's appearance — not to mention, my current position — but when I notice that all three of the new arrivals are staring only at me, not him, I flick my eyes to where he was standing, only to find that he's no longer there.

"What happened?" Ward demands, following my gaze with clear suspicion.

Cami pushes past her brother to help me out of the closet and to my feet.

"Are you okay?" she asks, concerned.

"You can talk," Ward quickly adds. "I'm covering you."

Something about his assurance prickles me. It's frustrating that after all the training I've endured, including playing skirmish outside the safety of my Karoel room, he still doesn't trust me to talk without leaking power. What's the point of him teaching me control if he's always going to insist on protecting my words, regardless? It's no wonder I have trouble believing in myself, when it's clear he doesn't.

"I'm, uh, not sure what happened," I answer Cami, rubbing my throbbing shoulder. "I just … tripped."

Enzo laughs. "Clumsy much? This is what happens when you stop training with me and start training with this brute." He elbows Ward, whose only response is a slight narrowing of his eyes.

"Thanks for coming to check on me," I tell them all, feeling embarrassed — and acutely confused. Where *is* Kael?

"No problem, Jane. Glad you're okay," Cami says.

She reaches out to touch my shoulder, taking away the throbbing with a quiet Spoken word and a quick smile, before she ushers Ward and Enzo out of my room.

I follow them to the door and close it behind them, then bang my head softly on the wood. "I'm going mad," I whisper, making sure to keep a tight hold on my intent since they're the first words I've uttered outside of the Karoel room without proper supervision. But if ever there was a time to express myself freely, it's now.

"I sure hope not. The last thing we need is to have a mad Creator running around."

I spin, and there's Kael again, this time leaning over my bed and teasing my kitten. Schrödinger's black-and-white paws are batting at the hand Kael waves just above him, his little claws going straight through the noncorporeal flesh. He's purring up a storm, the traitor.

"Your kitty likes me, princess."

I don't know which to address first: the fact that Kael is somehow magically in my room and speaking to me and yet he's *not*; or the fact that he, in all his badassery, just used the word "kitty."

"Dinger's a bad judge of character," I say, carefully monitoring each word and keeping my tone low so as to not draw attention from the others again.

"Dinger?" Kael stops teasing my kitten and stands upright. "What kind of a name is that?"

"Short for Schrödinger," I explain, though I'm not sure why I bother. It's not like he'll —

"Schrödinger?"

Kael releases a quiet burst of laughter. I've never seen him laugh before. It transforms his whole face.

"Now, *that* is a great name for a cat. Especially one I'm guessing you created."

"Would you keep your voice down," I tell him, stepping toward him and glancing nervously at my door. "The others will come barging in again."

"Ah, yes." He nods at the wardrobe. "Not your most graceful moment."

I wonder if throwing something at him and having it go straight through his body would feel as cathartic as if it actually hit him.

"How are you *here*, Kael?" I bite out. "And ... not?"

"Put up a soundproof wall and I'll explain everything," he says. At my questioning look, he adds, "Are you a Creator or not? Just imagine a sound-blocking bubble or something around the room, keeping anyone out there —" he gestures to the door "— from hearing what we say in here."

"But ..." I chew my lip and fidget with a loose thread trailing from the hem of my shirt. "Despite you being here, I'm guessing you're not *actually* here, so you can't destroy my words. I'm being really careful not to throw power around right now, but if I deliberately try to Speak, what happens if I accidentally turn the whole world silent or something?"

Kael sends me a "Seriously?" look. "Have a little faith in yourself, Lyss. You'll be fine."

I'm surprised by his quick response, by how different he is compared with Ward. Surprised but flattered.

Taking a deep, fortifying breath, I decide to trust his confidence in me and whisper, "Block." Perhaps I concentrate a little *too* hard on my imagery, because when the flash of light bursts out of me, so, too, does an actual multicolored, bubble-like sphere. It circles the boundary of my room, with us in the middle.

Kael looks a touch too amused for my liking. "Let no one say you're unimaginative."

He uses a normal volume, and making sure not to power my words again, I say, "Keep it down — what if it didn't work?"

Sending me a pointed look, in a voice so loud that it could raise the dead, he bellows, "HELP! HELP ME! HELLLLLLPPPPP!"

I jump a foot in surprise and spin around, waiting for Ward, Enzo and Cami to come running. But they don't.

"Convinced?" Kael asks smugly. "Told you you'd pull it off."

I'm on edge despite his belief in my control. But so far nothing catastrophic has happened. I feel strong. I feel powerful. I also feel contained — like my ability is ... *waiting*. Like I could use it if I wanted, but it would only happen because I made the deliberate choice to do so, rather than it being an accidental slip with disastrous consequences. And because of that, I decide to trust — or at least *hope* — that I'm not making a mistake by engaging Kael in conversation; my first completely unprotected exchange since awakening my ability.

Taking a deep breath, I carefully ask him what he's doing in my room — and *how* he's actually here.

"One of the Remnants, a guy named Smith, he can project an image — or, say, a person and their consciousness — to another place," Kael answers. "I needed to talk to you, and this was the easiest way to make that happen."

"That's incredible," I murmur, forgetting that I should hold some kind of negative emotion toward him for showing up out of the blue and scaring the living daylights out of me.

"It is," Kael agrees. "What's *not* incredible is that you only have a couple of hours left until Pandora's infusions won't work anymore, and you still haven't gone to check out the lab."

There's a question in his tone, and my immediate response is to form some kind of defense, to claim that he arrived just as I was about to leave. But instead, I trudge over to my bed and collapse across it, not caring about my lack of grace as I admit the truth: "I don't want to go."

"Of course you don't," Kael replies instantly, to my surprise. "No one normal *wants* to see what you might find there. But the question is, can you live with yourself if you decide not to go? Regret's a fickle mistress, especially when it comes from fear. And don't forget, princess, 'the truth will out,' regardless of your involvement."

"Ugh. Shakespeare."

Kael laughs. "I take it you're not a fan."

"I can hardly judge someone so highly regarded."

"You're entitled to an opinion," he points out. "Everyone is."

"Okay then, my *opinion* is that I don't want to go to the lab." I force myself to slide back off the bed and to my feet again. "But I also know you're right. I won't be able to handle the regret of not going just because I'm dreading what I might find."

Kael's look is approving — almost proud. "I have it on good authority that Falon will be away from his office in ten minutes, so I suggest you go then."

"Good authority?" I repeat, skeptical.

"The kind of authority responsible for causing a diversion to call him away and distract him, just for you."

"Your people on the inside?" I guess.

Feigning innocence, he says, "I don't know what you're talking about."

My lips quirk into a smile without my permission, and something in Kael's eyes shifts as he looks at me.

"There she is."

I raise my eyebrows in question.

"You want to know why I call you 'princess'?" he asks.

"Uh — sure. I mean, I thought you were just trying to annoy me. But, yes, of course I want to know."

"One of my earliest memories of seeing the world outside Lengard was on my seventh birthday," he says.

I have no idea where he is going with this.

"My parents took me to the aquarium. I thought it was just to cele-brate, but it was also so they could meet up with some old friends. Some old Speaker friends."

I brace myself in preparation for what I think he's about to tell me.

"You wouldn't remember me," he says quietly. "You were with a group of people at a different party, so even though your parents were able to duck out for a few minutes to speak with my family, you never saw me. But I saw you."

My breath stutters in my chest because I *remember* the day he's talking about. I remember the aquarium party, since it was my friend's sixth birthday. She insisted on a fairy-tale theme, requiring that we all had to dress up.

"I was a princess," I whisper, vividly recalling the sparkly gown that my mum made for me and the diamanté tiara that I refused to take off even to sleep.

"I only saw you for a moment," Kael goes on, "but in that moment, you were twirling around with your hair flying out behind you, laughing like you didn't have a care in the world. To my seven-year-old mind, you looked like you were born to be a princess. And a moment ago, when you smiled, you looked just like that again."

I honestly don't know what to say. But Kael must read something on my face, because he laughs suddenly.

"Don't get too excited. I'm stating a fact, not hitting on you."

I smile again — fully this time. "I didn't think you were," I tell him truthfully. "But you did surprise me. I was just caught up in the memory."

"I saw you again a few other times over the years until your family moved away," he says. "Our mums were best friends, if you can believe it. But once my family left Lengard, it was always yours who came to visit mine, not the other way around."

I shake my head, marveling at this unknown fact, wondering yet again why my parents never told me about the Speaking world. Why, if Kael's parents were so close to mine, did I never meet them, never even know they existed? What were my parents keeping me from? Or perhaps … what were they keeping from *me*?

"You were always smiling, always happy," Kael goes on, drawing me back to him. "That said, I never saw you in that ridiculous dress again. I still don't know how you managed to walk in it."

I laugh at that, and his eyes light with triumph.

"My dad ended up carrying me home," I share, letting the memory wash over me. Rather than feeling the usual ache and the blinding panic that come with thinking about my parents, all I feel is a wistful melancholy. "It may have been pretty, but all those layers were heavy."

"I'll bet," Kael says, grinning. "I have one at home just like it myself."

"Sure you do," I say, laughing again. I wonder how I can be so relaxed around this guy, who only a few days ago kidnapped me and held me captive, who has shown up unannounced and left his body behind. But the truth is, I'm more content right now than I have been for *years*. And that's with us reminiscing about my parents, two people who I haven't been able to think about in all that time without spiraling into an anxiety attack. Somehow Kael has achieved the impossible with me. He's also given me the confidence to be an active part of our conversation. Nothing bad has happened. I'm speaking — but not *Speaking*. And it feels *wonderful*.

"Thank you," I blurt out.

Fortunately, I don't have to explain, since Kael seems to know exactly what I'm thanking him for.

"Anytime, princess," he says meaningfully. Then he glances at his watch. "Our ten minutes are almost up. Are you ready?"

"Nope," I answer, but I still move to my wardrobe and start digging through the mess that I made when I fell earlier, searching for where I hid the glove and glasses. "But I think we're beyond me being ready. Turn around, will you?"

When he doesn't move, I say, "It's either you turn around to let me change, or you un-project yourself out of here and back to your little cave. No peep show for you tonight."

"Just tonight?"

He puts his back to me, but not before I catch the smirk on his face.

"Careful, Lyss," he adds, "or I'll start to think you're hitting on *me*."

I ball up a pair of socks and throw them at his head. Even though they go sailing through him and hit the wall on the other side, I still feel better afterward.

Ignoring his chuckle, I make sure his back remains facing me while I quickly change into something more appropriate for the mission ahead. When I'm done, I say, "You can turn around now."

Kael cracks up upon seeing my new outfit. "What, no balaclava?"

I glance down at the jeans-and-black-jacket combo that covers me from head to toe, having finished the look off with Esther's boots that I've yet to return.

"I was going for clandestine," I respond, gesturing to my dark clothes. "I want to avoid being noticed."

Still laughing, Kael says, "You failed. Miserably."

I'm not sure how to take his comment, so I busy myself with tying my hair back.

"Best if you just aim to stay out of sight completely," he adds, saving me from having to form a response.

"That's the plan," I agree.

"Then go get 'em, tiger," Kael says, shooing me toward the door. "I'll have Smith project me back here in an hour to find out how it went."

Something about those words helps loosen the tension knotting my stomach. Knowing that Kael will check in with me later — it's comforting.

I'm still afraid of what I might discover tonight, but I meant what I said earlier — one way or another, I need to know the truth. I'm determined to see this through, to seek out the answers that have eluded me, to uncover Lengard's deepest secrets.

Or, preferably, *not*. Because part of me still hopes that Kael is wrong and that I will find nothing.

But I'll never know for sure unless I go and see for myself. So with a farewell wave to Kael, I step through the soundproof bubble and out of my room, ready to face the future and whatever it might reveal.

CHAPTER
TWENTY-NINE

The good thing I discover while leaving my suite is that Cami, Ward and Enzo aren't around anymore, so I don't have to think up some excuse for my late excursion — or my attempt at a stealthy outfit. In fact, when I pass Cami's room, the door is open, and I can see that it's empty. I spare a thought to question where she could be, before I realize that I don't have time to wonder about that right now. Instead, I head out into the hall, and blending in as well as a hippopotamus wearing a bikini, I make my way along the whitewashed walls until I reach Falon's office.

As Kael's "good authority" promised, there is no answer when I knock lightly on the door. So, after a less-than-subtle glance over my shoulder, I place my infused glove on the scanner until it opens with a *click*. With my heart pounding in my ears, I push my way into the room and close the door quickly again behind me, then move straight to the inner touch screen panel.

I pull the gaudy glasses from my jacket and use them along with the infused glove again; it only takes a second before the secret wall exit hisses open and I slide through it.

Feeling distinctly edgy now, and very much just wanting to get back to the safety of my room, I half jog down the declining path, noting again that the walls steadily darken to charcoal by the time I reach the elevator. Now, at least, my outfit blends in better.

Once I'm in the metal box and the doors close behind me, I just stand there for a moment, bracing myself. This is as far as I've ever come. From here on out, not only am I on my own but I also have no idea where I'm going or what I may find. What if I *do* come face-to-face with a Speaker who can modify memories? What if I have to follow Pandora's advice and "be creative" to stop them from stealing *my* thoughts?

My fears spiral until I'm verging on panicking and I decide that enough is enough. I've chosen my path, and I will see it through, come what may.

Determined, I lean forward until the infused glasses are scanned, and I quickly follow with my glove against the panel. Once the access light shows Falon's ID is accepted, I press the Up button.

Just like the first time I used this elevator, it again moves at a fast-enough pace to make me nauseous. When it comes to a jarring halt, I have to place a steadying hand against the wall to keep from pitching out of the opening doors. But I recover quickly and scurry into the antiseptic-smelling hallway.

The bleach-like scent burns my sinuses and calls to mind memories from my short stay at the psychiatric institution. I hug the wall of the long corridor full of twists and turns and what feels like hundreds of corners. I attempt to muffle my footsteps, but it's a challenge with my heels *clickety-clacking* on the linoleum, so I'm forced to tiptoe until I reach the single doorway at the end of the path.

There is not a single part of me that wants to open the door. My heart hammers at the mere thought of finding out what waits on the other side. But I've come this far. I can't leave now — not without seeing the truth for myself. So I tuck the glasses and glove away and reach out a hand to test the door.

The moment my skin makes contact, it must act like some kind of sensor, since the locking mechanism deactivates and the door slides open with a *whoosh*. I'm left blinking at the space in front of me that no longer provides any kind of hiding place, and I keep my body frozen, attempting to draw as little attention to myself as possible.

And that's because, on the opposite side of the large room, there are three gray-uniformed guards leaning up against the wall, staring at me.

Or, on first impression, it seems as if they're staring at me, but when none of them so much as blink in the space of the whole minute where I'm experiencing a mild cardiac arrest, I realize that they might be looking at me, but they're not *seeing* me.

After risking a glance to the left and then to the right and finding no one else in the room, I edge my way inside. I continue until I'm only a few feet away from the guards.

"Can you — can any of you hear me?" I whisper, being very careful with my words, knowing that the adrenaline coursing through my body could make me more liable to slip up.

When none of them respond, I reach out to the one closest to me, a woman, and place my hand on her shoulder. She doesn't react in any way, not even when I shake her.

"Creepy," I say, feeling the need to fill the nightmarish silence.

I turn away from the three of them to take in the rest of the room, something I should have done upon entering it. As my eyes travel around what is clearly a professional medical laboratory, goose bumps cover my skin and I start to tremble. I'm used to Vanik's lab downstairs, the one I visited every day during my "initiation." I thought it had everything possible to make my life a living nightmare. But by the looks of it, that lab has nothing on this one. I don't recognize most of the equipment in here — but I'm certain none of it is used for anything good.

And it gets worse — because unlike the hallways I'd traveled to get here, the walls of the lab are a glossy black.

Karoel.

The whole lab is encased in the nullifying mineral. Any words I create in here will require much greater effort, keeping me in check. That kind of limitation is not something I need right now, given what I might be facing.

Turning back to the three zombie-like guards and not allowing myself to consider why they might be here — or what has prompted their current senseless state — I say, "If you can hear me, I'm getting you all out of here. Right now."

Before I can figure out how to do that, I hear clicking shoes and low voices approaching from the hall. My self-preservation instincts kick in, and I jump behind one of the larger medical machines — I think it's an MRI scanner — just in time to hear the door slide open and the voices become significantly louder.

"… not saying I won't figure it out eventually, just that it'll be faster if you let me —"

"I've already told you where I stand on the matter," Falon's voice interrupts Vanik, and I feel my heart sink. Clearly, Kael was wrong about him being an unwilling puppet.

"And as I keep telling you," Vanik's nasal voice responds, "you should strongly think about reconsidering. You know what her worth would be to the project's overall success."

I peek around the MRI machine in time to see him gesture toward the zombie guards as he adds, "None of them would be necessary anymore, not if you give her back to me."

Something about his words increases the trembling in my body.

"Alyssa Scott is off-limits," Falon says.

I close my eyes in resignation because they've just confirmed Kael's claim. They have known my identity all along.

So many lies.

So many secrets.

"But, Maverick," Vanik argues, "just think of how much I could achieve by working with her again. Especially if you let me carry out all the proper tests, not just the child's play you limited me to for her initiation."

Child's play? I don't want to imagine what the alternative might have been.

"You could also damage her beyond repair," Falon says, and I shudder involuntarily. "You already nearly did, if I recall. If it hadn't been for Landon —"

Vanik makes an irritated sound. "Ward coddles her. You should never have brought him into this."

"You were getting nowhere with her," Falon disagrees. "For over two and a half years, neither you nor any of her other evaluators made any kind of headway. No one heard so much as a peep out of her until Landon managed to break her down."

The betrayal stings almost as much today as it did when I first found out.

"So whether he 'coddles' her or not," Falon continues, "even you have to admit that he's getting results. And I won't have you jeopardize that, not prematurely."

"Maverick —"

"I said no, Kendall," Falon states firmly. "Perhaps things will change when she has a better handle on her control. Until then, she's just as likely to blow a hole in the middle of Lengard as she is to channel her power into something you can use for your experiments."

"The tests I'm considering don't require her to have control," Vanik responds. "I need her biologically, not psychologically."

"Enough, Kendall. You have my answer."

I hear one set of footsteps moving away, and then Falon's voice comes again, but from across the room.

"It's late, and I still have to investigate how my kids accessed a restricted area earlier tonight. If you'll excuse me?"

I remain where I am as the door slides into place behind him and almost wish he would return. With Vanik's history of going off-book, I'm not sure Falon's directive to stay away from me holds much weight. If I'm caught ...

I need to get out of this Karoel-walled lab, and I need to get out now.

But just when I decide to make a run for it, the door slides open again, and I hear footsteps. Lots of them.

"Right on time, my precious ones," Vanik says.

His affectionate tone churns my stomach.

"In, in, come in, my lovelies. Make yourselves comfortable," he continues. "Any problems, Alvin?"

"Just with Camelot, as usual. Her resistance is strengthening. But it's nothing I can't handle."

I know that voice. I know it because it belongs to Dr. Manning. But I'm more concerned by his reference to Cami.

Carefully shuffling until I can sneak a glance, I struggle to contain my reaction at the sight before me.

My friend is here, staring out at nothing just like the three zombie-like guards, seemingly oblivious to everything around her. But she's not the only one. A small group of Exodus recruits stand with her, some familiar, some not. Crew and the semitransparent Sneak are a part of the small, mindless crowd, but neither they nor any of the other Speakers appear to have any clue where they are or what's going on. It's like they're sleepwalking.

"All right, my dears," Vanik says. "Let's get started."

CHAPTER THIRTY

All I want to do is curl up in a ball and scream, but I can't risk giving my position away. Not even as I witness the Exodus recruits willingly lie down on the examination tables, one after the other.

I make myself watch as much as I can, but it's difficult. Vanik draws blood — a lot of blood. He uses two different syringes to extract other samples, as well: pinkish fluid from areas close to where their hip bones nestle into their pelvises, and water-like fluid from in between the vertebrae at the middle of their spines. I watched enough medical dramas pre-Lengard to have a good idea of what the samples are: bone marrow and cerebrospinal fluid.

Bile rises high enough in my throat that I have to keep swallowing it back down. And while what I'm witnessing is beyond disturbing, what concerns me more is that not one of the Speakers utters a sound. No pain, no distress, no struggle. These are the kinds of procedures that should be carried out under heavy anesthesia, but the recruits are wide-awake, staring blankly into nothingness while Vanik experiments on them like lab rats. Unlike me, they don't even recoil when he inserts long, *long* needles into their bodies.

I know it's because of Manning. Because of what he can do. And I know this because —

"Next one, Alvin," Vanik says after he switches out some vials in his centrifuge and starts the spin cycle again.

"You, come here," Manning says.

My heart skips when the light that flows with his command touches Sneak. Until now, none of the recruits tested have been known to me. But with the young boy being ordered forward, I struggle more than ever to remain hidden and keep from bolting out to save him.

"Lie down, don't move, don't make a sound. You won't feel anything," Manning commands.

I can sense the power of his words from where I'm crouching, even though they're not directed at me.

I don't know what the therapist's ability is, but I know it's the reason for the zombie-like lack of responses. It's the reason no one is fighting for freedom. It's the reason Vanik can do whatever he wants with their bodies.

It's horrific.

And it scares me to realize how strong Manning must be if he can wield that kind of power even with the suppressive limitations of the Karoel surrounding us. That's the only reason I haven't left my hiding place and tried to Speak a way out of here for my friends and me. There's no way I can go up against the kind of strength Manning must have, not here. Some all-powerful Creator I am.

"The samples I took during your last visit proved rather interesting," Vanik says to the semi-invisible Sneak, snapping on a new pair of latex gloves as he approaches the unresisting boy. "I think today we'll try something a little … different. A tissue sample — yes, that's what I need."

Vanik starts preparing a tray full of needles and scalpels, and I wonder if I'm going to faint.

"Alvin, pass me that drill."

My whole body seizes up at Vanik's words, at watching Manning hand over the device and Vanik line it up against Sneak's skull.

When Vanik's fingers move to activate the drill, I'm unable to keep a distressed sound from escaping my lips.

It's the worst possible timing, since my gasp is like a homing beacon to my position. I duck back behind the MRI machine, hoping they didn't hear me, but when the drill remains quiet, along with all other noise in the lab, I know something is wrong. I muster the courage to peek back out and can see neither Vanik nor Manning anywhere.

Dread wells up within me, and I know I have to get out of here. I can't stay in this Karoel-lined room for another second watching my friends fall victim to a psychopath.

Just as I find the nerve to run, to attempt to get past the Karoel and Speak us all to safety, a stirring in the air prickles my skin in warning, prompting me to spin around. But I'm too slow to react as Vanik, having snuck up behind me, crashes the drill down onto my skull.

Pain explodes from behind my eyes and I crumple into a heap at his feet, unconscious before I hit the ground.

*

Wake up, Lyss. You have to wake up.

I'm in a dream. I know I am because I'm standing on a cloud with rainbows streaming all around me, shining like glitter in the sunshine.

But that's only one reason I know I'm dreaming. The other is that Kael is here with me.

Smith projected me here, he tells me. *We don't have long.*

Part of me considers how amazing it is that Smith can project into my unconscious mind, but the other part of me doesn't have the energy to care much at the moment.

Lyss, you have to wake up, Kael says again.

I don't want to, I tell him. *I want to stay here. It's peaceful. And I'm tired.*

I know you are, princess, he says, closing the distance between our dream selves and placing his hands on my shoulders, squeezing gently. *Help is on the way, but you need to wake up, and no matter what, you have to stay awake. It's very, very important.*

I shake my head, and the rainbows blur around me. *I don't know if I can.*

You can, he tells me, his midnight eyes trapping mine. *You can, and you must. We'll get you out, but you have to help us. Just stay awake.*

Everything hurts, Kael.

I know it does, he whispers. *Just hold on a little longer, princess. But now you have to WAKE UP!*

*

I jolt awake, groaning as I come around fully. The pain I felt upon passing out seems but a shadow of the agony currently tearing through my body. I struggle to open my eyes and succeed only after a few attempts. I feel more tired than I've ever felt in my life. But that doesn't make sense. Not until I can finally lift my lashes and see the cause of my exhausted state.

Blood.

Bags and bags of blood.

All of it mine, and still more being drawn from my veins.

I gurgle in horror and try to sit up, but something holds me down. I'm shackled to the examination table at my neck, my hands and my ankles. Panic wells up within me, and adrenaline overrides exhaustion. I begin to wrestle against my constraints, but I stop almost immediately when a searing agony shoots from two points on my lower back, one in the center, one toward the side.

I break out in a cold sweat because I know — I *know* — what that means: that Vanik has already completed his nightmarish procedures on me and extracted my fluid samples. I feel so violated that I have to swallow back my dinner as it tries to make a reappearance. And then, heedless of the pain, I begin to wrestle anew.

Mindless with terror, I let minutes pass before I realize this is a useless battle — and I have other ways to fight for my escape.

With tears of fear and exhaustion in my eyes, I concentrate harder than I ever have in my life as I focus on my restraints and croak out, "Release!"

Nothing happens. No light flashes. The bindings don't loosen their hold.

"Release!" I cry again. "Release me! Let go!" I hiccup through a sob and whisper out a tremulous, "Please, let me go."

It's no use. With the Karoel surrounding me, I may as well be mute.

"I wouldn't bother if I were you," Vanik says.

I recoil as he moves into my line of sight.

"You don't have enough energy to Speak. And in attempting to prove me wrong, you'll only tire yourself out faster."

I can't imagine being more exhausted than I already am, but his words ring true as my body weakens more and more from the excess blood loss and my head injury. It's worse, so much worse than I felt after the paintball skirmish. I can barely string a single thought together, let alone concentrate enough to Speak. Even if the walls weren't limiting my power, I'd still be in a world of trouble. But just because I can't use my ability doesn't mean I'm ready to roll over.

"You sick bas —"

"Careful, now, Six-Eight-Four," Vanik interrupts, "or my hand may just … slip."

I draw in a ragged breath when I see him holding a scalpel in one hand — and a razorblade in the other.

"It's a shame to get rid of this lovely hair of yours, but it'll only be in the way," he murmurs, resting both blades on a metallic tray lined with all kinds of other instruments. "I'll need a clear point of access to extract the required tissue. A mistake could be catastrophic, at this point. But don't worry — as long as you remain still, the procedure should be minimal risk."

My entire body quakes. I don't know what "minimal risk" means, but I'm certain it's much more dangerous than Vanik is letting on.

He turns fully toward me and leans over until his rancid breath is in my face.

"You have no idea how long I've waited for this day, Alyssa Scott. Ever since you arrived at Lengard, you were kept from me. You were *protected* from me." He spits the word like it's an offense.

"You *tortured* me," I rasp out, alarmed by how weak my voice sounds.

"Electroshock therapy hardly constitutes torture," he replies dismissively. "And besides, if I couldn't study your physical samples, I was damn well going to research your brain chemistry. But then you had to go and cry to Landon Ward. He even had the audacity to threaten me. Why couldn't he see I was only trying to *help* you? That's all I've ever wanted. To help you — all of you. To help Speakers everywhere."

I don't know what's worse: the words he's saying or that he seems to believe them.

"None of that matters now," he intones. "Because with your help, I'm going to change the world as we know it."

I grimace when he reaches for the IV tapped into my vein and pauses the blood flow to swap out the collection bags. When he starts it up again, I can't suppress a quiet whimper, wondering how much more I can lose before I pass out again.

"My Speaking ability was stolen from me," he says, seemingly out of nowhere.

"Jeremiah saved you," I murmur, with no strength for anything louder. "He healed your mind. You were insane."

"Jeremiah *destroyed* me," Vanik spits into my face. "He took away the best of me and left me to my fate. And then Falon came swooping in with his regulations and edicts, saying I could only experiment on *willing* subjects. Of course, no one was willing then. Luckily, I still had some leftover samples from my initial Speaker tests."

"The people you *killed*."

"Their deaths were unfortunate." Vanik reaches for the scalpel again and holds it up to the light as if to see how sharp the blade is. Satisfied, he places it back on the metal tray. "But ultimately, they were necessary."

"Just so you can get your Speaking ability back?" I grate out. "How can you rationalize the deaths of all those people — and the rest, with the Ebola and plane crashes and other disasters — just so that you can be a mind reader again?"

Vanik raises a greasy eyebrow. "You *have* done your research, haven't you?" He lets out a dry chuckle. "You're right, but you're also wrong. I don't want my Speaking ability back."

It's an effort to focus with the pain, the fear, the exhaustion all flooding through my body. "Of course you do."

"I don't," he disagrees. Then he leans in close again — too close — and says, "It's not my Speaking ability that I want — it's *yours*. And thanks to your cooperation here today, it won't be long until I'm able to identify and locate your specific genetic anomaly. When I have that, Six-Eight-Four, I'll be but a small step away from becoming a Creator myself."

CHAPTER
THIRTY-ONE

Vanik's declaration leaves a buzzing sound in my ears. I can't handle what it might mean.

"When I'm a Creator, I'll have the authority to command my specialized army of genetically enhanced Speakers," Vanik says, oblivious to my turbulent thoughts. "Through them, I'll bring the world to its knees."

The buzzing grows louder. Enough that I understand it for what it is — I'm beginning to panic. But I can't. I can't lose it here, not now while I'm so vulnerable. I have to push it back. I have to fight it. I have to fight *myself.*

I am stronger than this.

I will not let fear control me. Not anymore.

I search for something within me, something to give me focus. All I have are the whispers of my memories, and I latch on to one and hold tight.

I need you to take a breath. We'll do it together. In and out. Come on, Chip. Listen to me breathing.

Ward's crystal-clear voice hurts my heart but clears my head. I breathe deeply, and the buzzing fades, allowing me to focus on Vanik again as he starts to move around me, slowly taping electrodes to my skull and along my pulse points.

I keep breathing.

In ...

... And out.

"Years ago, my intention was to share the gift of Speaking with everyone," Vanik tells me. "That plan has changed. Now I will share it only with a select few, my chosen ones, and I will serve out a purpose that even Charles Darwin himself would approve of. Evolution at its finest."

Although my head is now clear again, my thoughts feel like Swiss cheese, with gaping holes preventing me from keeping up with the conversation. "Darwin was all about *natural* selection," I rasp out. "If you pick and choose who you turn into Speakers, that doesn't line up with his theory."

"All that matters is that human beings evolve as a species, regardless of how I bring that about," Vanik says, finishing with the electrodes and moving away to grab some kind of scanner, which he rolls toward me. "By studying you, I'll have the means to start our race afresh, beginning with my army of Speakers, who will look to me for direction, for leadership, and who will be submissive to my will."

I keep breathing.

In ...

... And out.

I realize now what he truly seeks. Everything Manning said when he first told me about the Remnants was a lie. All along it was *Vanik* who wanted revenge against the government, right from the very beginning and still after all this time. And now that desire for vengeance has morphed into something more — he actually wants to take over the world.

"You're on a power trip." I shake my head the little I can, the whole room blurring as the motion prompts a dizzy spell. I'm so light-headed for a moment that I wonder if I'll throw up, but then I settle enough to continue. "You were stripped of power when you were captured as a teenager, and now you want to get that power back — and more. You want revenge, to make everyone feel as helpless as you felt."

He says nothing, so I know my assumption is correct.

Kael was right — about everything.

My pulse begins to *pound, pound, pound* in my ears, but I keep breathing.

In …

… And out.

I try tugging against my restraints again, but they're just as tight as before, and I'm even weaker now than when I first awoke. Alarmingly weaker. Even if I could break free of the bonds, I'm not sure I'd be able to walk out of this room without assistance. So all I can do is try to stall Vanik and hope that dream-Kael was telling the truth about help being on the way.

"You're like a case straight out of a psychology textbook," I say, my thoughts too sluggish to come up with a better stall tactic than to antagonize him deliberately. "You should book a session with Dr. Manning. He'd have a field day with you."

Vanik's face darkens, but I am beyond fear now. I won't let it control me.

I keep breathing.

In …

… And out.

Vanik's eyes change when the door to the room slides open. As if my words summoned him, Manning reenters the lab.

"Speak of the devil and the devil shall appear!" Vanik cries, sounding pleased.

Within scant seconds, Manning is beside my restrained body, his beady eyes staring down at me with not a hint of emotion on his face.

"You lied to me," I rasp. "The Remnants aren't the terrorists — *you* are."

Manning shrugs, unfazed by my accusation. "The military took our lives from us. They threw us down here and tortured us into submission. While others of my generation might not care, I'm not willing to let them find us again to finish what they started. This time, we strike first."

I only just stop from shaking my head again, not wanting a repeat of the dizzy spell that almost took me out a moment ago. "The government can't be the threat you claim they are. I've met the Speakers who live away from Lengard, and they're thriving outside these walls. And my parents, too —" I swallow but force myself to continue. "They survived away from here for years without being noticed. Until — Until —" I swallow again. "Well, it wasn't the military who got to them in the end."

"No, it was you," Vanik says heartlessly.

I feel the stab of that but manage to remain in the here and now. I've come too far to spiral deeper into my panic; it's time I faced what happened and begin to move on from it.

I keep breathing.

In …

… And out.

"Yes, it was me," I admit, my voice weak, but my words strong. "It was me who killed them. But until that happened, we were living happily — outside of Lengard. I never knew about Speakers or the military or anything else. Our lives were normal."

"And then you killed them," Vanik says, unnecessarily repeating the fact.

"Yes," I say again, also unnecessarily. And I …

Keep …

Breathing.

There's a pause, like time has stopped and the earth has halted its rotation around the sun. And then, of all things, Vanik begins to laugh.

The sound is loud and raucous, and I press deeper into the hard material supporting my spine, heedless of my injured flesh. I want to get as far away from him as possible.

"I love that you believe that," he bellows around his laughter. "I love that you believe you're even capable of that."

My forehead crinkles. "What are you talking about?"

"You're a Creator, Six-Eight-Four," Vanik tells me, his laughter waning, but his eyes still lit with glee. "By definition, Creators *create*. You bring life, not death. Your ability is only limited by your imagination, but your *imagination* is limited in this case. You are mentally and emotionally incapable of summoning the intent to kill someone, let alone the control to see it through."

I wish you were dead … You're dead to me … Both of you.

I try to shake the memory away, but it lingers.

"There's no possible way your Speaking ability could have caused your parents' deaths," Vanik states.

I hate you … I'm never talking to you again … You're dead to me …

"You're wrong," I argue, pushing back the voices in my mind. "I killed them."

He laughs again, shaking his head. I speak over him, needing to get my admission out now that I've come this far.

"I told them I wished they were dead," I say, uttering words I've never been able to speak before now. "I told them they were dead to me."

He seems to be waiting for more. "Is that all?"

"Isn't that enough?" I say. "I had no control — the words were all it took for the action to follow through. I ran upstairs after my tantrum, and when I came back down, they were lying on the floor, dead."

I close my eyes as the memory plays across my mind. My mum in her favorite Sunday dress, yellow with the white daisies. My dad in his pressed slacks and starched shirt, not a wrinkle to be found. Both staring up at the ceiling with glassy, unseeing eyes.

This time when Vanik laughs, it's a bitter-sounding breath of humor. "You really do know nothing, Six-Eight-Four."

My eyes shoot open, and I glare at him. "I know what I did. Just as I know I have to live with it for the rest of my life."

"You're wrong."

Vanik's confident declaration hits me like a nail dart to the chest.

"You're lying," I croak.

"I'm not."

His gaze is unwavering as it meets mine. It's enough to plant a seed of doubt in my mind — a seed that blossoms when he adds, "I'm curious, Six-Eight-Four. Given all that you've learned about Speakers, have you never wondered what abilities your parents had?"

My heart skips a beat.

"It's a shame you'll never leave here," he goes on, his eyes lit manically as he takes in my stunned expression. "Because I've now given you more than enough to find out what really happened to them." He pauses. "Or even, perhaps, to simply *find* them, full stop."

CHAPTER
THIRTY-TWO

I draw in a painful breath at what I think he's implying. But I can't — I *won't* — believe him. I can't allow myself to hope.

Now is not the time to wonder about this. What I need is a plan to get out of here, as I doubt I can stall for much longer. I'm not even sure I'll be able to remain *conscious* for much longer.

"Story time is over," Vanik says, checking my restraints are still firmly secured. "Alvin, start preparing the recruits to leave. All except for Camelot. We may need her ... just in case."

Just in case his hand *does* slip, I presume, and he needs someone with a healing ability to keep his precious Creator from bleeding out. Though, if he drains much more from me, not even Cami will be able to help.

I listen as Manning begins commanding the unresisting Exodus recruits to remember nothing of the night, belatedly making me realize that Vanik doesn't have a memory modifier after all — just Manning, who can convince people to do things, including forget experiences. From my limited view, it looks as if all the recruits are fully recovered from Vanik's experiments, presumably a result of Manning manipulating Cami into healing them.

"We're going to be spending a lot of time together, Six-Eight-Four," Vanik says, drawing my attention back to him. "Alvin's abilities have no effect on Landon — I have to assume the same is true for you. So to keep you from running, you'll be staying here with me. Indefinitely."

My skin feels cold and clammy, yet my forehead is dotted with sweat. I'm not sure if it's because of what he's saying or because my body is reaching the end of its limits.

Vanik's gaze narrows as it travels across my face, taking in my feverish skin and unfocused eyes. "I think you may have had enough for the moment."

I hiss when he yanks the IV needle from my arm, and I have to close my eyes against the dizziness that comes at the sight of blood welling up on my inner elbow. I know my reaction is irrational considering the bags of deep red fluid I can see, but for some reason it's different to see it *and* feel the pain of the incision point.

"I'm sorry about the blood loss," Vanik says, not sounding apologetic in the least. "Some of it will be used for testing, but mostly I had to drain you to keep you weak." He reaches forward and taps my nose with a finger. "We don't want you Speaking yourself free, do we?"

I snap my teeth at him savagely, but he pulls back with a laugh. The move costs me, with darkness flickering around my vision as I fight to remain conscious.

"I won't lie to you, Six-Eight-Four, this *is* going to hurt," Vanik says. "I'm used to my patients heeding Alvin's command to not feel anything, so I don't keep a ready supply of anesthetic handy. Instead, we'll have to improvise. Open wide."

"Wha —"

My voice is muffled when Vanik shoves a wadded-up piece of material in my mouth.

"That will stop you from biting your tongue off," he says, before reclaiming both his razorblade and scalpel. "Feel free to scream as much as you need to."

The heart monitor picks up my accelerating pulse, the beats becoming more rapid with my growing distress. My fear is a tangible thing, but I keep breathing. I remain in control.

I remind myself that I am a monster. And monsters fear no one.

Only … I'm not so sure I'm a monster anymore.

I don't know what I am.

No — that's not true.

Because I am … I am *Alyssa Scott*.

The girl who has endured Lengard for two years, eight months and seven days.

I am not a monster.

But I *am* a survivor.

And I *will* survive this.

With a renewed burst of adrenaline born from terror and desperation, I push against my bonds with all my might. I kick, I wrestle, I shove my pelvis off the table, straining against my restraints. I call forth all the physical training I've mastered with Enzo and try — *try* — to make it worth something. It's all useless. But as long as I'm moving, Vanik won't risk using the scalpel on me; he won't risk causing irreversible damage. I have to believe that. It's the only thing that keeps me moving when I have so little energy — and so much agony.

"*Will. You. Stop. That.*" Vanik enunciates every word, trying to still my fighting body. "Alvin, leave the recruits and come hold her steady. Bring Camelot to help."

No. No, no, no.

Only a handful of seconds pass before Manning presses his body weight against my lower half, restraining my legs and hips, while Cami, enforced by a Spoken command, holds my torso down. Tears well as I look up at her, so close, yet so far away. Her eyes are like those of a stranger. She doesn't even see me.

"Cami," I try to whisper, but it sounds like a strangled gurgle against the material in my mouth. She doesn't so much as blink, and I know I'm lost to her.

I renew my struggle with all I have left in me. My body is pinned, but I wiggle my head as much as my neck brace will allow. It hurts — *everything hurts* — and it makes me so light-headed that I want to throw up, but I don't stop. Not until Vanik curses at me and tightens the strap securing my neck. He takes it in so far that I can barely draw breath. I make a wheezing sound in the back of my throat, and black spots assail my vision again. I'm now unable to move, trapped and defenseless. I'm at his mercy, though I know I will receive none.

Kael, I need you! I cry out in my mind, certain he would know exactly how to get himself out of this mess.

And then I think of someone else who would know what to do. *Ward, you promised to protect me! Where are you?*

Protector and Destroyer, both so different, neither of whom I should trust, yet either of whom I would give every Spoken word in the world to have in the room with me right now. But I'm on my own.

With nothing else left, I try to take comfort in looking up at Cami, hoping to draw strength from the face of my friend, even if she's not really here right now.

But then, just as I feel Vanik press the razor up against my scalp, I hear the door slide open and the slapping sound of footsteps moving toward us, fast.

Vanik's head jerks up. "You're not allowed to be —"

"You don't want to hurt her."

I instantly recognize Keeda's voice, and at her hypnotic words, light flares, hitting Vanik in the chest.

His face blanks, and his hands drop from my head as he repeats the command in a dull monotone. "I don't want to hurt her."

"No, Kendall, *don't* —" Manning growls, releasing my lower half and rushing toward Vanik.

But before the therapist can finish his own Spoken command, Keeda intervenes.

From my restricted position, I can't see what happens next. All I know is that my rescuer doesn't bother wasting energy on words. Instead, I hear sounds of a brief struggle, followed by a *thump* and a groan, and then Manning crumbles to the ground.

The tussle allows enough time for Vanik to fight himself free of Keeda's trance, and he spits out, "What the —"

He doesn't finish before I hear the clatter of metal and a crash when the tray falls to the ground, followed by a muttered oath from Vanik, another *thump* and then ... silence.

Cami is shoved unceremoniously away, and Keeda steps into my line of vision, her face pale but her eyes determined. She swiftly unbuckles the restraints at my wrists, freeing first one, then the other. Moving to my neck, she makes short work of the brace while I tear the cloth from my mouth and inhale a large gulp of air.

"How —" I try to gasp out.

"Your ankles! Hurry!" Keeda orders.

I obediently bend forward to tug my left foot free, battling through the head spin and searing pain that come from my quick surge upward.

"Kael raised the alarm when you didn't return to your room," Keeda explains as she releases my right foot. "I told him it was a stupid idea to send you up here by yourself, but why listen to me?"

"You're the Remnants' informant?" I say, ignoring her sarcastic tone as my muddled brain puts the pieces together.

"One of them, and the best rescue option, since Manning's ability doesn't work on me." She doesn't waste time explaining why she's immune — instead, she helps me swivel until my legs are over the side of the table. "Now we have to hurry and get out of here. I didn't hit them hard — they won't be down for long."

I can see Manning and Vanik now, both slumped on the ground, unconscious. But I don't look for long, because Keeda draws me off the table and onto my feet. Or, she *tries* to. Renewed pain darts along my back, and I'm so weak that I stagger into her, nearly toppling us both to the ground.

"For someone so small, you sure are heavy," Keeda complains, trying to get a better grip on me since I'm unable to support myself. She wraps her arm around my lower back, pressing right against where Vanik operated on me, the agony causing lights to flash in my vision. I bite my cheek hard enough to draw blood, but I don't ask her to let me go. I'll put up with whatever pain it takes to escape this nightmare.

"I'm choosing to focus on remaining conscious rather than taking offense," I slur. "Just get us out of here."

I manage two steps before my thoughts catch up enough that I dig in my feet and say, "Wait — Cami, too. And the others."

"No way," Keeda says, tugging me forward. "My mission is to get you out. Only you."

Even to my foggy mind, that is unacceptable. I refuse to leave anyone behind.

Sensing my resistance, Keeda says, "You can't even walk on your own. We have no chance of helping them — not if we want to escape."

I still open my mouth, but she cuts me off before I can say anything else. "They're my friends, too."

It's the emotion in her voice that halts my argument, the realization of what she is sacrificing to get me away. I see the strain in her features, the sorrow in her eyes ... so I nod my understanding — and my agreement.

We're en route to the door, when Keeda, struggling with my weight, gasps out, "I don't get it. Kael told me you're a Creator — you could have wiped the floor with them."

I can barely raise my head right now, and I tell her as much. In case my slurred words aren't proof enough, I also point out the Karoel walls and how they're dampening my abilities and making it even more difficult for me to Speak — making it impossible, in fact, given my current state.

"No rock has that kind of power," she pants.

I trip over my own feet, again almost bringing us both to the ground.

She grunts, "Karoel's not *real*, Jane — Lyss — whatever I'm supposed to call you." She's now practically dragging me along. "Ward was meant to tell you that after the first week of training. The limitations of its so-called effects are all in your head. It's just a training tool, a way to help new Speakers learn control. It makes you think you can't do something, and like everything to do with Speaking, what you think, you imagine, and what you imagine, in your case you create."

Disbelief floods through me. Confusion, too. "I don't — I don't understand."

"The human mind is easily manipulated," she says, panting louder now. "If you believe Karoel is suppressing your power, then automatically *you're* the one suppressing your own power. Whatever you felt was imagined."

"I don't — I — Wait, if Karoel's not real, then what is *that*?" I throw my free hand toward the walls, barely able to raise it high enough for her to see where I'm pointing.

She shrugs and almost drops me in the process. "Some kind of mineral. Onyx, I think."

"So, you're saying —"

"I know you're weak and exhausted," she acknowledges, "but right now that's your only limitation, not a rock with fake magical powers."

I can't believe what she's telling me. But it makes more sense than the alternative I've never thought to question.

With another grunt of effort, Keeda continues, "You need to tap into whatever strength you've got left, because —" She looks back over our shoulders and curses quietly. Her voice is urgent as she finishes, "Because we could really use your ability right now, or else we're both screwed."

CHAPTER
THIRTY-THREE

A shout comes from behind me, harsh and guttural.

"Stop them!"

The words are Manning's, and the power behind them raises the hairs on the back of my neck.

Keeda swings us both around just in time to see the Exodus recruits leap into motion. They charge at us, and she pushes me roughly away before running fearlessly toward them. Helplessly weak, I teeter until I collapse onto the ground, where I can only watch as she attacks the other Speakers with both her body and her hypnotic words, keeping them from getting to me. But it's ten against one, twelve if Vanik and Manning are included. And since Manning is now bending over Vanik and trying to wake him, it won't be long until the two of them jump into the fray, as well.

The room is filled with a cacophony of voices and bursts of light as Speakers throw words — and fists — around like javelins. I don't know what most of them are able to do, but even just watching Crew aim his slaying words in Keeda's direction, accidentally slicing other Speakers in the process, is enough to force me to rally. I draw my feet under me, only just managing to stand.

I try to think of something I can do to help, but my thoughts are scattered and disjointed — I can hardly hold an image together, let alone attempt to create it into being. I struggle to remember anything I've learned in my training with Ward that would help in this situation. Haystacks, alpine villages, paintballs and petting zoos — none of those can help us. I could create some ferocious animal, but it would be just as likely to injure Keeda and me as anyone else, and despite the fight they're putting up, the recruits are *innocent*. I don't want anyone getting hurt — not because of me.

Useless, I stare in horror at the battle taking place. Pandora told me that if I found myself in trouble, I should be creative with my ability. Ward repeatedly tells me to use my imagination. There has to be *something* I can do.

I press a hand to my throbbing head and will my thoughts to clear enough to form a solid idea. Or *any* idea.

"Got you!" cries a voice from behind me, and two semitransparent arms wrap around my midsection.

I cry out in pain when the arms tighten, placing pressure against the wounds on my back.

"I've got her!" Sneak yells out again.

In his nearly invisible state, he must have been able to slip past Keeda's notice, and he's right — he *does* have me. But not for long. Because without the Karoel's fake suppression, *this* is something I can summon enough intent for, if little else.

"Release me!" I say, and even though my voice is but a breath of agony, I still manage to infuse my command with enough power for light to flash and his arms to let me go. I turn around as fast as I can on my wobbly legs and look in his blurry direction, following that order with another: "Leave. Now."

It's only when I see his barely visible body take off that I realize I should have asked him to send help. But before I can call after him, Cami lunges for me, having detached from the group of Speakers surrounding Keeda.

"Cam, no, don't do this," I plead with her as I sidestep. The action keeps me from her clutches, but only because my legs fail and I crash back onto the floor. She looms over me, her eyes just as listless as when she held me down on the table. I can't bear to see her like this. I know Keeda said we wouldn't escape if we tried to help the others, but right now, I'm not so sure we're *going* to escape. And after having witnessed Cami act as Vanik's mindless pawn ... I simply can't leave her under Manning's grip. Not if it's in my power to do something about it.

I dredge up every scrap of focus within me as I concentrate on the Cami I know. As I think about her pancakes and her smiles and the friendship she extended without expecting anything in return, not even my words. I call to mind her humor, her affection, her compassion. I hold on to all that she is as I stare into her eyes and imagine a tether between her and Manning; a tether I visualize severing when I say, in a croaking voice, "Be free."

Light shoots out of me and hits her in the chest. She gasps loudly and goes back on a foot, a hand flying up to her head as if she's in pain.

"Cami?"

My voice is nothing but a whisper. But it's filled with everything I feel — fear ... uncertainty ... hope.

And when Cami's eyes meet mine again, they're no longer listless — they're filled with tears.

"What — Jane, what happened?" she breathes, looking around the lab at the skirmish playing out.

Except, I can see from her paling face that she already knows, already understands. Manning didn't have the time to make her forget.

I rise on unsteady legs, but I don't have a chance to comfort her before Keeda shouts at me from across the room.

"I could use some backup over here!" Her voice is brimming with attitude as she singlehandedly keeps the Speakers back. "Feel free to jump in whenever you want!"

I just used up everything left within me to free Cami.

But then I hear Keeda cry out when Crew lands an attack that grazes along her side, and it's clear she won't be able to keep defending against them all for much longer.

"We have to do something," Cami urges. "We have to —"

"Jane!" Keeda calls, trying to dislodge the numerous arms now grasping at her.

I take a stumbling step forward with Cami right there beside me, and I realize that there's only one thing I can do in my current state. Only one thing I'm capable of. Only one thing that can help.

I need to lose control.

The monster that was once within me — I need to let it loose.

So I Speak out a single word …

… and stop the world.

Just like with Abby and the bus up on Market Street, the moment I shout the word "STOP!" everything pauses. Speakers halt mid-word and mid-grasp. Manning is still bent over Vanik, but the scientist is awake and half raised as if he's on his way up to his feet. This alarms me, but I have a more pressing concern: I'm simply too weak for my Spoken command to remain in effect. The outcome is inconsistent — and it's not holding.

One second the world is paused, and the next it's moving. Paused, moving, paused, moving. It's like I'm watching everyone in the room perform a stilted robotic dance.

"Stop!" I try again, but I just don't have the energy to keep everyone in place, which means my renewed order doesn't work at all. Realizing this, I grit my teeth and leave Cami's frozen side, staggering my way into the mess. What little strength I have left is used to pull Keeda's unresisting body back out, extricating her from the tangle of limbs as I go.

She's like a dead weight as I stumble-drag her across the room, and I only make it halfway to the door, a few feet away from Cami, when I just can't hold on anymore and my command fails entirely.

"What —" Keeda sways into me, disoriented, and by some miracle we don't go down.

"Move!" I tell her.

Fortunately, she reacts faster than I do. She yanks me close, slings my arm around her shoulders and forces me with her toward the door. Cami, quick on her feet, runs to our side without hesitation, taking half my weight from Keeda.

"Feel free to do that again," Cami tells me, the two of them struggling to hold me aloft.

"I agree," Keeda gasps, her free hand pressed to the bleeding wound in her side.

"Can't," I pant out. "Nothing left." I can't even manage a full sentence.

We're almost at the door, when the Exodus recruits notice the three of us making a run for it.

"After them!" I hear Vanik yell, confirming that he has regained consciousness. "Don't let them get away!"

Manning repeats the order, his words powered enough to make the Speakers act instantly — and rabidly. Cami remains free of his grip, however — a small mercy.

I cry out when an invisible knife slashes into the flesh of my upper arm, lacerating partway from shoulder to elbow. Blood gushes out, but slowly — too slowly — because I have so little left in me to lose.

"Hold on!" Keeda tells me as we finally reach the door.

I have no choice but to do as she says, the two girls all but carrying me now. Red is dripping from my arm onto Cami's back, but I don't dare ask her to heal me, not right now, not when she needs to concentrate on our escape.

"Come on, move!" Keeda cries out.

At first I think she's talking to me, but then I feel a jolt as she slams her free shoulder into the door, trying to get it to budge. It was touch-activated on the way in, but it must require some kind of security scan to exit. We don't have time to figure it out, so —

"Open!" I force out the word through lips that can barely move, and the door blows clean off the wall. Given how scattered my thoughts are, I'm amazed it actually worked, even if I would have preferred the option to close it — and lock it — behind us.

Keeda and Cami waste no time in hauling me into the corridor. I wonder what the plan is from here, because while the hallway is full of twists and turns, it's also narrow, which means the Speakers will be able to aim their words at us as easily as if we have targets painted on our backs. Plus, by the time we reach the elevator, I doubt I'll be able to pull my door trick again. But I decide not to tell either of them that just yet — we still have to *make* it to the elevator.

Hobbling along the maze-like corridor while ducking every few feet as the Speakers close in on us — and some like Crew continue to throw word daggers our way — I'm mildly concerned when the pain in my arm and back gives way to a numb feeling, and then that numbness quickly spreads over the rest of my body. I'm cold from head to toe, and tired — so very tired.

No matter what, you have to stay awake. It's very, very important.

Kael's not speaking to me in a dream this time, but the memory of his words echoes in my mind, and I keep my eyes open through sheer willpower.

… Only to see Ward barrel around the corner toward us.

"Landon!" Cami yelps in surprise, slamming to a halt.

Driven by momentum, my numb legs continue forward, my movements like those of a rag doll. My arm draped around Cami's neck slips, as does my grip on Keeda, and I stumble, trip and crash onto the ground — again.

"I've got you, Chip," Ward says.

His nickname fills my cold, numb body with a spark of warmth as he draws me up into his arms.

To Cami and Keeda, he asks, "Can you run?"

When they respond in the affirmative, he takes off at a sprint — much faster than we had been moving before — and with a glance over his shoulder, I can see our pursuers right on our heels.

"You called me 'Chip.'" I slur the words, my thoughts like liquid.

"Now is *not* the time, Alyssa," he says.

With his use of my real name, the spark of warmth disappears.

So.

Many.

Lies.

"Let me concentrate on protecting you from the Speakers I'm supposed to be protecting *from* you, would you?" he adds.

"You're blocking their words?" I'm amazed when I string the thought together, let alone the sentence. "Why … Why are you helping us?"

He doesn't answer, just continues sprinting around the antiseptic-smelling labyrinth. He's fast, even burdened by my weight. And despite her wound, Keeda is keeping up, as is Cami. We're pulling ahead of the other Speakers, if only slightly.

When the elevator comes into sight, Ward speaks again, but not to me.

"Kael and the others are waiting topside, so all you have to do is get Lyss up there, and he'll take you all to safety."

When we reach the wall, he slams his hand against the elevator scanner. It opens with a *ding,* and he lowers me to my feet in front of him, but his arms remain around me to keep upright.

"I've keyed your stats into the scanners, Keed, and I've made sure Falon and the guards are distracted," Ward continues. "You should have a clear run out of here, but only if you go right now. I'll hold these guys off for as long as I can."

"What? No!" Cami cries, reaching for her brother. "We're not leaving you here, Landon. No way."

In my blurry state, I almost miss the meaningful look Ward sends Keeda. I don't miss what happens next, though, because she nods once before turning to Cami and saying, as she once did to me, "You're so very tired." Light leaves her and touches Cami, likely with an added push of Ward's power to make it stronger, since Keeda has to catch my now-unconscious roommate and drag her into the corner of the elevator.

Shocked, I stutter, "You just — you just —"

"Cam's right," Keeda says to Ward, interrupting me. "They'll know you know more than you should. You have to come with us."

"You need to complete your mission and get Alyssa out of here," Ward tells her. "Cami, too, now. They're all that matter."

Even my fuzzy thoughts don't like what is happening. "Ward —"

"I'm not leaving the other recruits. They're my responsibility, and I can't abandon them." His green — so *flipping* green — eyes capture mine. "But I also won't let him hurt you any more than he already has. I made you a promise, Chip. This is me keeping that promise."

I hold his gaze as I hear the memory of his whispered words from what feels like forever ago float across my mind: *Trust me. I will protect them. I will protect you.*

"Ward —" I breathe, but that's all I manage, because he presses his hand to my cheek and leans in until his forehead rests against mine.

His movements are gentle, so gentle, like I'm made of fractured glass and he's afraid of splintering me further.

"Everything I did was to protect you," he whispers.

I suck in a startled breath, unable to deny the truth I see in his eyes.

"No matter what Falon said, no matter how I acted after you started Speaking, every second, every moment I spent with you before that was real. Don't ever doubt that, Chip."

Before my shocked but still-too-sluggish mind can think of a reply, and before Keeda or I can come up with any kind of further argument, he pulls away from me and pushes us both into the elevator beside Cami, then slams his hand on the outside panel. The doors slide shut between us just as I see the group of zombified Speakers round the bend, with Vanik and Manning leading them. The moment Vanik's eyes lock onto mine through the closing doors, I know exactly what his infuriated gaze is telling me.

This isn't over, Six-Eight-Four. We've only just begun.

CHAPTER
THIRTY-FOUR

Exhausted, terrified and drained beyond what should be humanly possible, my body must have shut down sometime between Ward shoving us into the elevator and Keeda awakening the panic-stricken Cami, since I have no memories from there on out. Instead, when I regain consciousness again, I'm in a stone-walled, dimly lit room, and I'm not alone.

"Kael?" I whisper, seeing him seated beside my bed. My voice is so raspy that it sounds like a colony of fire ants have nested in my throat. It feels like that, too.

"Here." He holds up a glass of water and presses the straw to my lips. "Drink."

I suck in the cool, fresh liquid as if it's air, only stopping when he moves the glass from my reach.

"I wasn't done," I complain, pleased when my voice comes out stronger.

"You're badly dehydrated, but you still need to take it easy," he says, placing the glass on the bedside table. "If you can keep that down, I'll give you more soon."

"I had the strangest dream about you," I tell him, still feeling half-asleep. "We were on a rainbow cloud."

Kael chuckles, and it's a deep, comforting sound. "That wasn't a dream, princess."

Memories crash into place, and I bolt upright, my head spinning as pain flares, but I push through it in my desperation to see where I am. There's another bed a few feet from me, with Cami buried deep under a pile of blankets, fast asleep. For reasons unknown, Schrödinger is also with us, curled up and dozing at my feet.

My gaze travels around the rest of the space, similar enough to Liana's room in the catacombs that I know we must be underground. As to how we arrived? I have no idea.

"How did I get here, Kael? And Dinger? I can't remember anything after Ward helped us escape." I flick through my memories, finding myself at a loss. I can't even begin to process Ward's final words to me and what they might mean. "I don't — I don't understand why he helped us."

"First answer," Kael says, leaning forward to steeple his fingers underneath his chin, "is that you passed out in the elevator, and after Keeda convinced Cami to leave Ward and escape while you all still could, the two of them carried you out of Lengard. We brought you back here, where you've been in and out of consciousness for the past three days. During one of the 'out' moments, you made Dinger appear, and he hasn't left your side."

As if knowing Kael is talking about him, my kitten opens his eyes and gives a soft *meow,* crawling up my body to nudge his head against my chest.

I pet him absentmindedly, caught up in Kael's words and thinking that's an absurd amount of time to have been sleeping, especially considering how wretched I feel. I'm struggling to keep my eyes from shutting even as we speak.

"You lost a lot of blood, Lyss, and not just from where Vanik drained you." Kael motions to the clean white bandage wrapped firmly around my arm. "Cami couldn't heal you without you being conscious for more than a few seconds at a time, so like Dinger, she hasn't left your side and has been waiting for you to awaken." Kael nods to my sleeping friend. "I can wake her now if you —"

"No, let her sleep," I tell him, knowing that it can't have been easy for her to leave her brother behind. She needs her rest; my wounds can wait.

"Because of the time that's passed ..." Kael offers me an apologetic look. "She'll be able to heal you, but you're going to have one hell of a scar, princess."

Of all the things he could have said, *that* is the least of my worries. I send him a look that says as much, and his eyes lighten in response. But then he sobers.

"To answer about Ward, he's one of ours."

Kael's declaration doesn't shock me as much as it would have had I not witnessed Ward helping us escape. I still don't *understand,* though.

"He and I grew up together at Lengard. We were close — at least, before I left with my family ten years ago," Kael goes on. "As far as I knew, he believed in what they're doing there, through and through. Or that's what I thought, until a few weeks ago when he reached out to us. There was a girl, you see. One he'd been told to get close to. A girl he'd been ordered to make trust him, by any means necessary. Turns out, he had no idea the kind of effect such a girl would have on him."

Kael eyes me shrewdly, and I hold his gaze, not giving myself over to the confusing array of emotions that surge within me.

"He did what he was asked to do," Kael continues, "but when you finally started Speaking, and he realized just how powerful you are and that you had no idea about your heritage, he knew something wasn't right. It took him a few days, but he sought us out in secret to see if we knew anything. So we told him. The truth about you. And the truth about Lengard."

I think about the night I found Ward sitting in the dark in my quarters. I'd assumed his windswept appearance meant he'd been topside searching for a new teenage Speaker, but now I wonder ... Was that when he first approached Kael?

"I bet that was an interesting conversation," I somehow manage to say.

Kael laughs. "He was rather ... resistant. But Ward has his own sources inside Lengard, and it didn't take much for him to corroborate our version of events. Ever since then, he's been working with us."

"He's also probably imprisoned now because of that," I say, and I'm unable to identify what I feel with those words. I'm still stung by what I thought was Ward's betrayal, but everything is a mess now, especially given his final declaration to me. Not to mention his desertion of Lengard — which, if Kael is to be believed, happened *because* of me.

It's too much to think about at the moment, so I deflect and ask, "Did Cami and Keeda tell you ..."

"Keeda told us everything that happened after she entered the lab," Kael says. Tentatively, he adds, "Cami hasn't spoken much to anyone, so you'll have to fill in the rest."

My heart goes out to my friend, but I know there is nothing I can do to comfort her until she awakens and we have some time to ourselves.

For now, I'm eager to get my recap over with, so I start from when I left my room, providing as much detail as I can remember. I'm grateful Kael doesn't interrupt with questions, and he only speaks again when I'm finished.

Shaking his head in wonder, he says, "I knew Vanik was crazy, but wanting a survival-of-the-fittest scenario pitting Speakers against the rest of the world? I can't believe it. I thought my dad cured his insanity."

"He's not insane," I say. "I think it would be better if he was. He's in his right mind, but he's so fixated on revenge that he doesn't realize how unreasonable his plan is. Can you believe he wants to become a Creator?"

"Worse, he now has the means to do so."

With Kael's words, I feel a phantom throbbing from two points in my back.

"Maybe not," I say, trying to remain positive while raising my uninjured arm to cover a yawn. As I do so, Dinger wobbles back down my body and curls up again at my feet. "If he can't identify the Creator gene in the samples he took from me, he'll need more before he can replicate my ability or clone my DNA. And I don't plan on providing him with any more freebies."

"Speaking of DNA," Kael says, watching me, his voice low. "You glossed over it quickly, Lyss, and I know that was deliberate, but I still heard what you said about your parents. How Vanik implied things might not have happened as clearly as we all believed."

I take a deep breath in and release it again, rolling Vanik's words over in my mind:

There's no possible way your Speaking ability could have caused your parents' deaths ... I've now given you more than enough to find out what really happened to them ... Or even, perhaps, to simply find them, full stop.

"I don't know what to believe," I whisper to Kael. "I was so sure — *so sure* I'd killed them. But Vanik said my mind isn't capable of imagining the intent needed for that kind of consequence. Is that ... possible?"

Kael remains silent for a long time, and when he speaks, he does so carefully. "We only know what happened because of Liana. She saw a vision of you yelling at your parents and running upstairs, only to run back downstairs later and find them dead. Like you, we put two and two together. But, Lyss ... I don't want you to get your hopes up, but it's *possible* we misinterpreted the events, just as you may have. Your parents had powerful abilities. If they had wanted the world to believe they were dead, it wouldn't have been difficult for them to make that happen. Just like my dad did for our family."

I swallow once and force out the words, "What abilities did they have?"

"Your mum had the most powerful ability for suggestion I've ever heard of." Seeing my puzzled look, he explains. "Manning can force people to act, but the actions are never their own — they're just puppets. But your mum — she could suggest an idea that would take root and grow, making people *believe* whatever the idea was until they carried it out with their entire conviction. Her ability was like a mixture of Manning's enforcement, Enzo's encouragement and Keeda's hypnotic captivation all rolled into one powerful package. I'm sorry to tell you this, Lyss, but if your mum suggested for you to believe them dead, or even to believe that you had killed them, then you'd have no way of knowing whether or not the thought was your own."

I don't realize my hands have balled into fists until he reaches across to pry my fingers apart.

"As for your dad," he continues, and I don't interrupt, even though I'm not sure I want to hear any more, "no one remembers what he can do. Or if they can, they won't say. Which makes me think he must have also had a strong ability. There was a reason they left Lengard in the first place and then later left Sydney entirely. No one seems to recall why — or they're simply unwilling to share."

"Let me see if I have this right," I say, my words sounding as choked as I feel. "For over two and a half years I've believed myself responsible for the murder of my parents, but it's actually possible that they're alive and — what? That they *wanted* me to believe I killed them?"

Kael's shoulders rise and fall. "Honestly, I don't know. But I promise you, we'll find out."

I slump down into the bed, exhausted beyond belief.

"I hate this," I whisper, closing my eyes. "I hate not knowing about Vanik and my parents. I hate not understanding anything. I hate that I'm out here but that the other Exodus recruits — my *friends* — are stuck back at Lengard with that psycho."

Enzo, Sneak, even Crew — they're all still there.

And then there's Ward. It's impossible to forget him. Impossible not to wonder what he's going through right now.

Needing to not feel so useless, so helpless, I draw back my blankets and drag my legs over the side of the bed. My movement rouses Schrödinger, who raises his head long enough to give me a dirty look for jostling him, then he drops his chin to his paws and closes his eyes again.

"Whoa, whoa, what do you think you're doing?" Kael demands, leaping from his seat.

Cami stirs at his raised voice, and we both glance over at her, but she doesn't awaken.

"What does it look like?" I reply, and with a heaving push, I stand, only to wobble precariously enough for Kael to swoop in and steady me.

"I don't think you're ready to be up just yet," he says.

"I have to get my strength back somehow." I attempt to push him away, my efforts making me feel even more drained. I could easily fall asleep in his arms. But I still say, "I can't just lie in bed all day while Vanik's trying to take over the world, while my parents may or may not be alive and while Ward is a prisoner in his own home. I can't just lie around and do nothing, Kael."

"And yet, right now you also can't do *anything*, Lyss," Kael tells me, leaning back enough to look into my face. "Vanik can wait. Your parents can wait. And as for Ward, he's way too important for Vanik to risk causing him any permanent damage — especially since Falon will be breathing down everyone's necks to find out where you lot have all disappeared to. So he's got *time,* Lyss. Which means you do, too."

Kael's words help soothe my turmoil. But still I say, "We need to save him, Kael. We need to save them all."

"And we will," he says. "Just as soon as you can stand on your own again."

"I'm fine." Seeing his skeptical look, I add, "Really."

Kael tightens his grip on my waist and says, "Piggybacking you around Lengard on a rescue mission doesn't seem like the wisest decision we could make right now."

Seeing his point, and vaguely realizing that the room is spinning around me, I capitulate. "Perhaps we can wait a day or two."

Spinning room or no, I still see his lips curl into a smile as he responds, "Only if you insist."

With no impending rescue mission on the cards just yet, he helps — or, rather, forces — me back into bed. Only when he's tucked me in and is moving toward the door do I whisper, "What's going to happen to them?"

His midnight eyes hold mine for a long moment, as if he's sharing his strength — and lending his comfort. "Nothing that hasn't been happening for a while," he answers quietly, truthfully. "So, rest up, Lyss. There'll still be time to save the world after you wake again."

Finally submitting to my exhaustion, my eyelids flutter shut of their own accord, but I still slur, "I'm going to hold you to that."

"I don't doubt it," he replies with a quiet chuckle. "Now, go to sleep, princess. You're safe here."

It's a whisper of promise, and it fills me with warmth all over again as I begin to drift off. But just before I succumb, one last thought crosses my mind, and I open my eyes again as I mumble, "Kael?"

"Yeah?" he answers quietly from across the room.

"You haven't been destroying my words, have you?"

A beat of silence passes before he says, "No, Lyss. I haven't needed to."

I exhale deeply at the confirmation of what that means.

"From what I hear, you've had a good grip of your control for a while now." Kael sends me a sly glance and adds, "Or so Ward told me the last time I spoke with him. He mentioned something about … glitter paint?"

I suck in a breath, startled by his admission.

When Kael sees my shock, his lips hitch up at the side. "He was still playing the role he was forced into, princess. He had to act like a hard-ass to stay close enough to watch over you without suspicion. But if there's one thing I know about Ward, he more than anyone always believed in you, right from the very beginning. Trust me on that."

My sinuses tingle, and I blink fiercely to combat my suddenly burning eyes.

Sensing my need for him to not say anything more about Ward, Kael clears his throat and continues, "You're as normal as any other Speaker now — which means, when you want to use your ability, you have to actively draw power and intent into your words if you want them to have any supernatural effect. The rest of the time, like now, nothing will happen."

I swallow thickly and whisper, "So I … Hypothetically, I can choose to *not* Speak if I … don't want to?"

Kael is silent for a moment, and then he walks slowly back until he's beside my bed. He leans down close, his eyes soft on me. "Princess, you can do whatever you want."

Then he leans in even more, presses a barely there kiss to my forehead, offers me a gentle smile and walks away, closing the door behind him as he leaves the room.

It takes me a moment before I'm able to fill my lungs again, let alone hold back the renewed tears that blur my eyes.

I'm free. The choice is now mine.

I'm no longer a slave to my words; I no longer have to fear the possibility that I may accidentally hurt — or kill — someone. But despite that, I know I'm not truly free — not yet. Because there are still things I need to do.

I have friends to save. Other Speakers. Normal humans.

And then there's Ward. I don't know where I stand with him or how I feel about everything he did, but he helped me, protected me, and I'm determined to return the favor. I *will* free him.

With everything I am, with all that is within me, I'll do whatever it takes to save them — all of them.

That is my choice. And I will see it through.

Until the very end.

EPILOGUE

My name is not "Jane Doe."

I'm not referred to as an unidentifiable, breathing corpse anymore. "Jane Doe" is gone, as is "JD," "Subject Six-Eight-Four," even "Chip." I may still be known by these names, but they are not who I am. Because who I am is who I've been all along. I've just been too afraid to accept it; too afraid to accept *me*.

My name is not "Jane Doe," and from now on, I won't be afraid of who I am, of what I can do.

I am a Creator, but I am not a monster.

I can do the unimaginable; I can Speak the impossible into being. But most important, I can now control it.

And I will be ready for what comes next.

No, I *am* ready.

Because I am Alyssa Scott.

And I am no longer afraid to be me.

I.

Am.

Free.

ACKNOWLEDGMENTS

First and foremost, my thanks go to God, for a journey beyond anything I could have imagined in my wildest dreams. Also to my incredible family and friends, for staying with me through the many ups and downs of this adventure (and respecting the magical properties of Disney and chocolate).

So, so, so much gratitude to my miracle-working agent, Victoria Wells Arms, for reminding me to breathe and for being my very own Cinderella-inspired fairy godmother. I'm forever grateful for the day you came into my life. Thanks also to your brilliant assistant, Brigette Torrise, for calling this book 'phenomenal' — I will never forget how that felt, and everything that came afterwards.

Kate Egan, editor extraordinaire ... I have no words. Working with you has been an indescribable honor and I still have to pinch myself just to make sure all of this is real. Thank you for loving this story enough to help turn it into a book. I absolutely *can't wait* to see what's next! (*Cough* Tigers! *Cough*) Thanks also to Beverley Solotov, for your sharp eye and meticulous copyediting; and to my magic-wielding proofreader — you are wonderful!

To the amazing team at KCP Loft: thank you for taking a chance on this strange Aussie author with wonder in her veins. I'm so, so thrilled to be working with you all in bringing *Whisper* to the world. Huge gratitude also to Pantera Press, for your continued friendship and support on my Great Big Publishing Adventures.

Unending hugs go to Sarah J. Maas, for holding my hand across oceans through some really challenging times, and offering wisdom and encouragement during every phase of this journey. I'm so grateful we had the chance to meet and bond over plastic frogs, stalker celebs, and our "fabulous" (ahem) dance moves.

Mountains of thanks go to my early critique readers, Frannie Panglossa, Emily Davison, Dana Summer and Krystal Gagen: thank you, thank you, *thank you* for your invaluable feedback and connecting with this story as you did. I adore you all.

Thanks also to Luke Mitchell, for inspiring the creation of Landon Ward through your character on *The Tomorrow People* (and for not being weirded out when I told you so); and to Rebecca Breeds, for reminding me that we creatives have a responsibility to share what is in our hearts in order to serve those around us. May your passion for acting never fade, nor that light that shines so strongly from within you.

Much love and gratitude goes to Maria V. Snyder, for your kind heart, your generous nature, and your sage publishing advice; to the ever-colorful Maria Lewis, my sounding board and sister in all the ways that matter (except, you know, blood); to Jenna Harper, for dropping everything to read this book in a night; to Kate Forsyth, for reminding me that writers need writer friends; to Ineke Prochazka, for the hilarious phone call catch-ups and ensuing bellyaches; to Alex Adsett, for being my wonderful and ever-helpful non-agent agent; to Alan Baxter, Justin Woolley and Marlee Jane Ward, for being remarkable authors and singularly unique humans; to Paige Belfield, for making sure I'm always where I need to be (despite frequently scaring the stuffing out of me); to Sulari Gentill, for walking a similar path and freely sharing tales of your journey (while being a good friend along the way); to Robert Dockerill, for the insightful Taronga Zoo tour and answering my gazillion questions; and to Traci Harding, for your unending patience while I asked those gazillion questions, and for being fabulous — *always*.

Lastly, to everyone reading this book — *thank you*. Words cannot describe just how grateful I am. I hope that in reading Lyss's story, you'll understand the impact words can have, and that if you feel you have no voice, you are now encouraged to *speak*.

You are brave.
You are powerful.
You are *heard*.